About th

Lulu Allison has spent most of her life as a visual artist. She attended Central Saint Martin's School of Art before spending a number of years travelling and living abroad. Among the bartending and cleaning jobs, highlights of those years included: in New Zealand, playing drums for King Loser and bass for Dimmer; in Germany, making spectacle hinges in a small factory; in Amsterdam, painting a landmark mural on a four-storey squat and nearly designing the new Smurfs; in Fiji and California, teaching scuba diving.

After a decade of wandering, she returned to the UK, where she had two children and focused on art. She completed a fine art MA and exhibited her lens-based work and site-specific installations in group and solo shows.

In 2013, what began as an art project took her into writing, and she unexpectedly discovered what she should have been doing all along.

Twice the Speed of Dark is her first book. She is currently writing a second, called *Wetlands*.

TWICE THE SPEED OF DARK

TWICE THE SPEED OF DARK

LULU ALLISON

Unbound

This edition first published in 2017

Unbound

6th Floor Mutual House, 70 Conduit Street, London W1S 2GF

www.unbound.com

ISBN (eBook): 978-1911586456
ISBN (Paperback): 978-1911586449

Design by Mecob

Cover images :
© Shutterstock.com / ArtYouAre (trees)
© Shutterstock.com / Elenamiv (sky)
© Shutterstock.com / pzAxe (newspaper)
© Shutterstock.com / peresanz (stars)
© Shutterstock.com / Katyau (writing)
Textures.com (background)

MIX
Paper from
responsible sources
FSC
www.fsc.org   FSC® C018072

This book is dedicated to the strangers, the shades – the two women a week and the nameless dead.

Dear Reader,

The book you are holding came about in a rather different way to most others. It was funded directly by readers through a new website: Unbound.

Unbound is the creation of three writers. We started the company because we believed there had to be a better deal for both writers and readers. On the Unbound website, authors share the ideas for the books they want to write directly with readers. If enough of you support the book by pledging for it in advance, we produce a beautifully bound special subscribers' edition and distribute a regular edition and e-book wherever books are sold, in shops and online.

This new way of publishing is actually a very old idea (Samuel Johnson funded his dictionary this way). We're just using the internet to build each writer a network of patrons. Here, at the back of this book, you'll find the names of all the people who made it happen.

Publishing in this way means readers are no longer just passive consumers of the books they buy, and authors are free to write the books they really want. They get a much fairer return too – half the profits their books generate, rather than a tiny percentage of the cover price.

If you're not yet a subscriber, we hope that you'll want to join our publishing revolution and have your name listed in one of our books in the future. To get you started, here is a £5 discount on your first pledge. Just visit unbound.com, make your pledge and type TWICESPEED17 in the promo code box when you check out.

Thank you for your support,

Dan, Justin and John
Founders, Unbound

Super Patrons

Suzanne Harrington
Brendan Hoffman
Jenny Hunt
Simon Jerrome
Michi Kern
Dan Kieran
Katrina Luker
Nik Maroney
Andrew McCabe
Josephine McGhie
John Mitchinson
Stephanie Monk
Lee Oliver
Tina Pepler
Donna Pillai
Justin Pollard
Suzie Poyntz
Mike & Chris Raab
Matt Redman
Jill Richter
Kathy Roper
Fay Rutherford
Mike Shreeve
Damion Silcock
Katie Simpson
Andrea Slater
Uli Springer
David Sutherland
Caroline Sutherland
Siobhan Taylor
Sally Toosey
Jane Toosey
Debbie Walsh
Matthew Ward
Fiona Winterflood
David Wolfe

With special thanks to my dear father, Philip Allison.

Sometimes I am hooked by a stray wisp of gravity and pulled back to the body of the Earth. Soft grass, hot dust, a sharp stone – for drifting moments I remember how they felt underfoot. I remember how it felt to have a place. Gravity is once more my friend, my engine. The breeze on my ghost skin brushes memories of life into shimmering being.

In this endless black emptiness, this vacuum field of bright spilled beads, I yearn for form, a body. I long for a chance to face the eternal dark of death once more.

Did I die because by chance I met a boy? Or did my destiny shape me in some way, to meet him, to become a component in his acts? No, it cannot be so. I died because he chose it. That shivers through me. The memory of it. How he could betray love so completely. He played himself so fully that he knew no boundary to his self-expression. Perhaps he didn't choose to kill me, but he chose not to prevent himself causing fatal harm. He chose not to censor himself. He chose to hurt. It is puzzling, such a choice. There is so little to gain. And it hurt so much. The thud of my heart trying to hold that hurt still echoes in the blackness. This blackness is a rich enough medium to hold such waves.

Other waves, records of love, also echo through me and the blackness. Minute, telling imprints, tiny waves. A disc, a furrowed dish. A plate of love spinning out from the warm beat of a body. The blackness holds thin echoes of those waves. So does my memory. The soft denim of my father's shirtsleeve, the solid warmth of his shoulder beneath as I leaned my head against it. The two of us in profound and mundane harmony, sitting on the sofa, watching a film. Toast and jam cut into nine small squares. My mother sitting on my bed until I slept, because I was scared. Hours and weeks and years of familial love. And sunny days of friendship – happy girls, bright with the fun of going out, high-heel–and–lip-gloss happy. I died young, but I am ancient now. The light can't find me any more to make me bright. I have no surface.

I am part of this blackness, subject to it anyway, riding the waves of its vast echo, being ridden by the jags and troughs of its monstrous silent beat. It hurls me in ferocious arcs. Sometimes, I am thrown back to the softer realms of Earth, and how I try to cling, to form within myself a holding–on. To anchor in the calm blue orb of Earth.

I often found myself, at the beginning, for long enough to gather, in the fields. I had memories of the clods of clay soil. When I lived, I was there often; it was so familiar. Many hours in these home lands. Pockets of countryside, fields and copses. Small ranges, but enough, when you look inwards for much of the time, as I did, to get lost for days. Stopping to stroke the skull dome of a chalky hunk of flint, the grey underside sheared smooth and cold as a blade. Tickling my palm with the fringed field edges – long grasses and cow parsley. A tingling memory of those sensations. I looked up at the sheltering sky for as long as I could, trying to consume, trying to become. Trying to breathe it, trying to make a new body, trying once more to become something out of nothing. But that trick belongs to a secret order. The seeds of something out of nothing are scattered liberally; it is a daily, hourly miracle. But not one we are able to perform for ourselves. I have learned for certain that you can only be given a body, not make one. You can only be gifted a place in gravity's purlieu.

To start with, when I was first dead, I was confused, caught between memory and experience, between memories from before and those since. I had pictures and knew faces, but I did not know if I had seen them through my living or my dead eyes. Because I see them still, those I loved, but they don't see me, I don't think. Sometimes I feel something, a tremor, and wonder if they do feel my presence, or think of me. But these visits, they became part of the kaleidoscope jangle of what I drag with me. I don't always know where the pictures belong – sight or memory, living or dead eyes. I hang onto each one, to sort and join together, to find its place and knit my story stronger for the telling.

Chapter 1

A winter dream. She drifts across the field towards the woods. She feels sharpness underfoot and the bite of cold air in her lungs. She watches herself move clumsily across the stubbly field. She is naked, cold, her hair fallen out, her skull fragile, exposed. She recognises her body – the dry of winter sits on her; her tall shape clings forlornly to long bones. She is mad, a scream frozen, sharpening the air around her as the frost has sharpened the ground under her feet. She is bone-pale, brittle; cold, screaming frost. If she were to die naked in these woods she would lie unseen by dog walkers and children for months, hidden perfectly in the frost-hollowed waste of winter on the forest floor. Sticks and lichen. She experiments with the idea of death in the cold leaves of winter. Cold for her, cold for her dead body, but warm and sheltering for the tiny lives of hibernating insects scurrying through pockets below the surface of the Earth. They would eventually find a home below the surface of her too, making pockets in her, making loops and channels, making her hiding place ever more complete. Though in life, this would be no hiding place; her breath would give her away. In life, she is clothed in enough of autumn's quiet pulse to be seen by others – a naked woman, bony, pale, lying stupidly on the ground in the woods. Pitifully reduced but not yet part of eternal winter. In life, she is not yet brittle enough to disappear so easily. There is a slow thrum behind her skin, the stately movement of cinnabar liquid through a time-worn muslin bag, a steady flow that will set to make jewel jars of sharp jam. Autumnal, slow, but definitely living. She turns in her bed, casts out dreams until the morning, a heavy fall into the pictureless, wordless depths of deep sleep.

Anna wakes cold, sick-feeling. Dread has leaked from her thoughts into the soft folds of her pillow. She pulls back into herself, waiting for a different voice, the trained voice of her waking mind, to assert itself. Neutralising is the first act of every dull and waking morning. And so day turns over, the usual kind of day. There is much to do, nothing to remember. Most days will not be remembered, a tick and tock of time. She complies; she holds herself steady, flattened into lustreless, manageable boredom.

She gets up from the tangled bed and goes to shower. The water streams down her body and the shower tiles, gently bashing sound into her ears, a pleasant, blocking roar. She scrapes hands down her skin, paring down, containing, shriving in the hot water. The escaped remnants of dread that cling, whimpering, in the crooks of her elbows are washed down the plughole before she has a chance to notice. But dread is not a finite resource; she has not lessened the load, rather removed it from sight. Capped off within, hosed off without.

After showering, wrapped in thick towels she sits at her dressing table, looks for the thing that will drag her from indolent torpor and, though she tries to keep it from herself, knows that there is nothing. She could sit there for days if she wished.

She turns to the window and the view across the field leading to the woods, the distant end of the nearest row of houses in the village. She has sat here so many times, noted seasons, watched small birds, caught glimpses of red jumpers and green coats in distant gardens, heard children play. She has watched each year as the hedge at the field's boundary grows and recedes, is cut, and grows once more. It is a beautiful thing, a hedge, but a thing confined, restricted, pressed into service against its natural habits. Made to contain, made by forced containment.

Content and languid becomes chilled and restless. A cape of cold drapes her shoulders between the towel wrapping her body and the one wrapping her hair. Her bones creak silently as she stands to dress. She pulls on warm clothes, runs fingers through her short hair, then goes down to the kitchen.

She lives on the edge of a village, in a large, well-appointed house on a lane that pulls away like a loose thread and trails through the woods, eventually looping back onto a busier road. Though she has not always been the only occupant, and in spite of bouts of loneliness, she has developed a protective care for her privacy and cherishes the isolation. People don't drop in.

She lives on a generous pension since retiring sooner than the university wanted her to from a successful career as an art history lecturer and specialist in mediaeval female artists. But a busy working life did more for her than secure the pension. She should not have retired, she has recently realised, whilst still relatively young, whilst her position in the university was so secure and her status there was in the ascendency, but she had known for many years that she was performing her role out of habit. She had lost the feeling that she cared whether her students did well in life and whether they understood the world they had chosen to make their own. She thought an end to the professional performance would bring relief, but the removal of the distraction of a demanding career gave her too much time for other thoughts. Cracks began to appear in the walls she had built within herself, the internal prison cell that held her grief.

Her daughter, Caitlin, has been dead for nearly ten years. Killed, apparently manslaughter – so slaughtered, then – aged nineteen years old, by her boyfriend, Ryan.

Caitlin's death caused a split, a warp that skewed Anna so she no longer fit the smooth planes of her life. She was changed by her loss. But so was everything. Grief shone a different spectrum of light; it revealed the well-formed, polished facets of normality as flawed, treacherous, deceitful. The world did not respond in a way that made sense. Her daughter had been killed, and no one beyond a small circle of family and close friends seemed to care. Where once life had run on guidelines of tolerance, understanding and certainty, now misery and hatred set the rules. She had never known such hate before. For Ryan, for the parents that raised him and stood by him, for the jury who believed his explanation of an accident. For a world that didn't find it a tale that was worth telling. Hate reshaped her.

In the long-ago months immediately after Caitlin's death and the court case that followed, Anna blasted out her sorrow with an exhausting frenzy that was at least a partial distraction from the greater pain of loss.

This early rage was further fuelled by the response of the criminal justice system. She had not been able to accept the conclusion of the court and the men and women of the jury, whom she had particularly relied upon to understand the terrible loss of her girl. They decided that Caitlin was dead by accident, that a man who violated her body with kicks and punches, demonstrably over time, hadn't meant it. This bewildering blunting of his crime almost killed Anna. Those men and women had decided that Caitlin wasn't supposed to die. She was just supposed to be cowed, controlled by the pain Ryan caused, frightened enough to do his bidding. And this somehow lessened the gravity of the offence.

Slowly, time passed and the abstract, animal efficiency of the will to survive overcame and then subdued Anna's flailing strategies. Memories of her daughter became distant, fleeting, irregular. She gradually twisted grief away. The only direction for such a motion to take was inwards. Burning anger and the parched, agonising cold of sorrow were bound together and banished to the deep dark space inside, the emptiness created by her loss. All that she felt was screwed up tight, a dense pebble of cold and heat lodged at her core, baulked and buttressed with the betraying forms of normality. For long stretches of time she felt only the pernicious and pallid warmth of the blended extremes.

Worthwhile distraction, a successful career a vital component of the mortar in these walls, allowed them to stand almost always unregarded, for many years. But now the gaps are beginning to show, and the effort of managing the constant mending, though unconscious, weighs heavy on her.

In retirement, Anna has in part achieved diversion with an endless string of domestic chores and petty errands. She shops, fusses in tetchy boredom about the house, changes cushion covers, taking weeks to decide which colour, pretending she cares. Nothing really changes; the house is much the same as it was when Caitlin died, when Anna's husband Michael still lived there, but she finds ways to string out the ordinary acts of maintenance.

She meets with a small group of friends, drinks coffee, drinks wine. She thinks about ways to fill her time. She walks almost daily in the fields and woods near her home. And she writes portraits of dead people she has never met.

Nine years before, when Ryan was convicted and jailed for causing Caitlin's death, Anna searched newspapers for a report of the crime and the court case, for signs that the world reflected her fury or had at least marked her loss. She found one short paragraph in the local paper. An explanation: he was of good character, he had snapped, he had caused death by accident; being jilted had provoked him, made him lash out. Provoked. As though it were Caitlin who was responsible, as though she had pushed violent death upon herself. Anna read this and vomited, her skin prickling with heat and cold. This disingenuous framing and the indifference of its bland retelling acted as an accelerant to her wild grief. Caitlin was mentioned only as a component in Ryan's story. No more than that.

In the ruined months after the court case, when nothing worked, Anna pored over newspapers and watched news programmes. Could it really mean so little that people died? Could it really be of such little interest? She picked over the news, online and in print, archive and day-to-day, scouring the local and national papers for references to women killed as Caitlin had been, by men who had once claimed to love them. She discovered quickly that there were many of them – the statistics were readily available. But the women were, like Caitlin, as good as invisible. Women murdered in English towns, by exes and husbands, deaths too commonplace to rouse even curiosity. Mothers, sisters, daughters. Complex, beloved lives that, if they appeared at all, were marked only as an administrative round-up of local court activity. Anna's black focus drove those around her to despair. Let it go, Anna, let it go. We know she mattered; we care.

Such cajoling tenderness, such love and frustration, such gentle holding down eventually told and Anna became compliant. She turned away from the terrible absences, the reminders of her girl. She quieted herself, externally. The turmoil inside soon could not be seen or heard. But in her quest, she had noticed others. Strangers in distant lands who died in terror attacks and checkpoint shootings. They were not even given a name. Multiple deaths from drone strikes, terrorist bombs, war, passed over as a tally of the activities of one side or the other. Death, it seemed, was only of interest if it excited the morbid thrill of the unusual, the lavish fetishising of television crime dramas. Domestic violence was certainly too drab a crime. Distant strangers were too insignificant to warrant the care of mourning as well as counting.

As grief slowed and stilled her, pulling her away from reminders of her daughter, she kept quiet attention on these other dead. It was a salve, of sorts. The news, this most ungentle showing of the world as an arena, a place of skirmishing and destroying, provided a strategy that allowed her, with unnoticed subterfuge, to tame her own grief; whilst reading, her anger came out, but as a response to news. The outrage she felt acted both as a reassurance that she remained alive to things outside of herself and as a substitute reason for her fury.

At first she noticed only that these people were not being noticed. Fifteen people, thirty-seven people, two people. She drew her private attention to their insignificance, to the careless passing over of their lives. She damned up her own anger and poured it by the ladle on their behalf. She felt a true connection, kinship, with their unknown families. Nineteen people were killed today. There has been a bus bombing; reportedly there are twenty-three dead. After a number of slowly becalming years, she went further than simply noticing them. She began to imagine what the people were like, eventually writing portraits for each. Inventing them gave weight to her care.

She calls them her invented ghosts. They have, in stealth, become a chorus, a quiet crowd, subtle sentinels of her grief and guardians of her homeless love. Over the last six years her collection of portraits has grown. Nine notebooks and journals are now filled with them. The latest one, an old green exercise book found in the attic, is nearly full.

It began on a morning much like this one, a cold and sunless day six years before and a little deeper into the winter. Christmas, itself a burden, had been passed with relative ease, though the relief of that was tarnished by the anticipation of the greater test to come. The most appalling of anniversaries was looming, a few small squares in the calendar away. Four years since Caitlin's death, aged just nineteen.

On this day, not long before the anniversary, she had not answered the phone or gone out. After cleaning already clean cupboards and shining already clear windows, she sat to read the paper. In her habitual, well-rehearsed way, she acknowledged the dead. There had been a bomb in a distant marketplace, one of several that day. A filament snagged and slowed the story down, her habitual soft focus pulled into unexpected sharpness. Somehow that detail caught her; a marketplace, perhaps the most domestic public space there is. People shopping for food, plastic buckets, scarves, aluminium pans. A place providing easy acquisition of the humbler tools of life: domestic wares, phone parts and gaudy cases, vinyl handbags, eggs, cabbages. Mothers buying an evening meal, teenagers shopping for the excitingly new and obligingly affordable. A man buying a bucket so he could clean his house. These ordinary people doing ordinary things, they would be the dead.

She thought of there being no dinner in some households, because the shopping never came back from the market. A husband whose anxiety makes him fear, as if seeming finally by prophecy rather than grinding habit, that his wife has been killed. A family who wouldn't know for long hours where their father had gone. Somewhere in a town where death might just as easily come at the hands of a checkpoint soldier, a sniper, a drone. Somewhere in a world where escape from such horror resulted in thousands of drowned bodies day by day, as boats and brutal businessmen cast people to their fate in the deceptive, seductive glint of a blue sea that pretended to show the way to safety.

Over the next days, the people behind the numbers began to materialise when she picked over stories in the news. As she was standing at a supermarket checkout she was hit by a surge of connection to the others in the queue. They were ugly and beautiful, unkempt, elegant, all mixed. Their banal ordinariness for once caught her attention, linked them to those killed by bombs in markets in Iraq or by roadsides in Afghanistan. The young man with a backpack and scraggly beard, buying four hooped-together cans of lager and some broccoli and biscuits, trousers carelessly rolled above bare brown ankles. The woman with tired eyes and pink plastic earrings, grey showing at the roots of her black hair. The old man with beige slacks and an olive cap, a small brown shopping bag ready for his bread rolls and two bananas, a small shakiness in his hands. Anna felt a tender kind of love and sadness for them, those ordinary people caught there in a tiny moment of complex lives, as those killed were caught in what became the last moment of their lives, when a crude bomb exploded near enough to kill them. Any one of them, all of them, could be one of the bodies, a life behind the numbers. She made her way through the queue and looked intently at the young cashier, haunted by a sudden picture of her, dead amidst the rubble of a faraway town, her mouth open, small teeth exposed to the heat and dust of disaster. She felt the upwell of a sob, an echo that pulsed in her chest, an inappropriate urge to shield the unknown girl from a fate that was not hers, from any fate that meant her harm.

Later, when she was walking through the woods, she thought about the nameless people killed that morning in a suicide bombing in Baghdad. What did she know about that distant place? Who were the people hidden in that neutral measuring? Her curiosity pulled them to her; she started to fill them out, describing them to herself.

She imagined first a woman in her early forties; she saw a living body, warm, plump, sensuous. She saw black hair, falling in curves like layers of raven wings. She saw her clothed in stretchy turquoise trousers, a pale-yellow top. She saw the woman asleep in bed at night, lying curled on her side, holding her husband's muscular brown forearm. Other pictures followed, describing the woman's busy life. She imagined her escaping briefly from the tumult, quietly sitting on her own, on a stool in her scruffy but beloved garden. Anna picked out these details with ease, with love almost. The woman from Baghdad seemed to appear in her mind, complete in the accumulation of random details. She has stayed within easy reach of Anna's thoughts ever since, a mute companion. Filigree ghost-patterns of love and grief crept across Anna's hollowed insides, like lichen, like salt crystals blooming on the innards of a calcified cave.

She imagined the others – a boy, men, women, a young girl. She saw in them ordinary beauty, a precious banality that at once made their deaths a terrible sadness. She saw curves of cheekbones, the sweep of a jawline, an array of clothing telling its own stories. The wonderful idiosyncrasies of ordinary people. She saw secret passions and hidden dreams, loves and pains, desires and hopes. She saw what was lost when they died. She imagined one of the men wearing corduroy trousers. It occurred to her that she didn't know if men in a hot place would wear corduroy trousers, but realising how extensive her ignorance of their life was, she accepted a broad interpretation of differences and commonalities, accepted too that her own background would tell in the details more than it should. Her experiment must be one that remained ideally universal, and perhaps pragmatically crude.

Anna was taken unawares by her experiment – her anger was replaced by tenderness. As the characters came to her she felt a bond with them, and sadness at their death, a confusing mourning of dead people who did not exist. As she walked through the woods, wintery light drifting down through the leafless branches, she saw the people standing amongst the trees, waiting and still, silent in the unexpected cold, caught inexplicably for a moment in this English woodland.

She continued paying out in words and mental pictures what the numbers alone could not. She began to write them down. It was impossible and too gruelling to be comprehensive. But she kept to a steady, dutiful acknowledgement. Some of them, especially the first woman, she thought of often, in idle moments, enriching the picture she had made, thinking of her sitting calm and content in her garden, adding details to the story that she told for her. What had grown was a hushed but powerful love, a love built from recognition, from accepted kinship. People whose heartbeats and bones matched her own, people whose lives held nothing and everything in common with hers.

So today, as on many other days, Anna makes coffee then sits at the kitchen table and reads. It is quiet; the only sound comes from the clock on the wall and a faint murmur of wind outside. Amongst today's stories, seven unnamed people have been killed in a roadside bomb. Holes left everywhere by the sudden absence of people that seconds before lived and breathed, families reaching for each other across craters of loss, a whole that has become less than a half, incomplete. Anna pictures seven people, how they look, what they care about, seven people to stand in for the ones who died in a town with a name she has already forgotten, a name she could not pronounce anyway. They materialise before her, easily and clearly; their lives run like a movie, ordinary and utterly beautiful. And she is hit anew by the terrible tragedy of their deaths.

She reaches for the latest volume, a worn exercise book, the dull green cover turning up at the corners. The book has been fattened by the dense writing covering most of the pages. She flexes the book in her hands, rolls her thumb across the edge to find the empty pages at the back. Those too will soon be filled; people die at such a rate. And though she cannot mark them all – the bombed, the drowned, the packed bodies suffocating in boat holds and locked lorries – she will keep adding to her tribe of invented ghosts. She writes quickly, stopping to think, finding in her mind's eye the details that make the person real, real enough to matter, real enough to mourn. The first one she imagines as a plump girl of eight, in a flowered dress, passing by the hidden bomb on her way home, holding onto her aunt's hand. She picks up her pen and starts to write the dead.

30 November

Seven people killed by a roadside bomb.

She is a girl of eight, warm with puppy fat and pretty dresses. She likes to eat teacakes, picking off the chocolate first with tiny nibbles. She eats all delightful treats this way so they last and last. A life so simple and so sure that a sweet and pretty cake is the greatest joy she can imagine.

Soft hair on a twelve-year-old boy's head, the nap pushed into improbable freestyle licks. He has large top teeth, showing slightly whatever he does with his mouth. He walks with a Krazy Kat lope, chattering in the still-high voice of a boy. Every so often he pauses for a small moment, head on one side, teeth on his bottom lip, then resumes his joy-filled commentary.

This man has sad eyes, dark skin, and short receding hair, still black. He has a large and untidy moustache. He plays the guitar beautifully and sings not very well but with great emotion and commitment. He is in love with a woman who lives on his street, but knows almost nothing about her. He would not wish to impinge on her by finding out. For him, emotions are to be cherished, held, explored and examined. Unrequited love is the prize in his collection.

Four of seven is a man with a dainty moustache and smart, unattractive clothes. He is plagued by a need for particular neatness in all areas of his life. He clips and tidies, sorts and saves, orders all that he can, keeps the world at bay this way. He would be beautiful if this pernickety, slightly absurd and foolish carapace did not shield him so.

A young woman, her graceful head tilted to one side like a bird, hair a long sweep, a skein, brushed with early grey at the temple. She is tired, pregnant with a second child. Occasionally, in crowds, her hands sweep gently before her growing belly as she walks, a gesture ready to become one of protection for her child.

At home, this man's children are meeting in furtive haste whilst he is out fulfilling errands, to discuss a surprise for his birthday. He has defined himself his entire adult life by the work he does to provide for his family.

A slight woman, dark and burnished by loss. She has black eyes flattened by the pain of losing her sister, her son, and her uncle to the actions of sky-borne military, another country's flag glittering on a distant tail fin. She lost her husband subsequently to anger, to revenge. And so the chain stretches out. Her loss to be handed forward to new mourners, new carriers.

Anna puts down her pen and closes the exercise book. What was the ordinary happiness or boredom that was part of them, those seven, as they walked towards the last place that anybody should have been at that perilous moment? She wonders if they knew they died, if they felt the blast, if they felt fear. She wishes she could conjure them into life, preserve them, now that they are here, from the death that she invented them to enact. She pictures the young pregnant woman, the child she has left behind and the one she will never birth. She wishes she could sit her down here at the table, make her comfortable, then send her back home to her family after tea and a couple of biscuits, intact, unspoilt by death. She imagines going to the fridge, getting two beers, one for her, one for the lovelorn man, and watching him play his guitar, sympathising with his unfulfilled but loving heart as they sipped the beer in wordless companionship.

It wrecks me. Here I am, propelled, pulled by some arcane plan, or flung, an accidental gift from those strange commanding energies that cause my shape to shift in tune with their caustic black hum. Here I am, in my old home, the home of childhood and a certainty that I bleed to know again. I bleed nothing. But I yearn. I remember the sickness of yearning. I pull myself in; it takes enormous effort to gather. My mother sits in the same chair she always sits in, the chair she sat in when I was five, when I was doing my homework at fifteen, when the two of us looked at university prospectuses in quiet excitement. When I visited, came home, perhaps hiding a bruise on my hairline. When I died, when I was gone. The same chair, the same place, the same table. She sits there, so known to me. And here I am, so unknown to her.

Before I am flung into the darkness once more, I pull myself in enough to know her, to see her, to reach out. What I can muster, it cannot be nothing, for I feel the weight of it; I feel the shriek and the pull of it. I am made of voiceless pleading, but to no avail. She is blind to me.

Her head is full of other ghosts.

Chapter 2

A new day. A new uncertain morning. Time itself holds a danger, an anniversary. Christmas a few weeks away; soon after that, the day of her daughter's death, followed by the day of her birth. Dead on the eve of her twentieth birthday. The wrapped present from Anna and Michael sat on the kitchen table, useless and powerful, until Michael flung it into the woods in a fury of grief.

A new day. The calendar squares reduce by one again, pulling her closer to a perilous destination. She would set a path that scraped as wide an arc as the radius would allow; she would choose a distant view. She would bind herself to a long, slow curve. But time ropes her to the smallest circle, the closest path, and drags her, keelhauls her round the sun.

Searching for distraction, she picks up her phone, checks emails and messages. There is a text from Sophie, her dear friend, saying Anna had left behind a cardigan after dinner the evening before. It was a happy gathering, perhaps designed by Sophie to fill these awkward days that loom before Anna. Sophie's husband, Brian, cooked a wonderful meal, though Anna wished they didn't need to talk about it quite so much. Over many such evenings, they had all made it clear they admired his prowess in the kitchen, but Brian never got tired of eliciting praise for his latest culinary adventure. Tony and Simon were there as well, full of the joys of a trip to stay with friends in Oslo. Moira, whom Anna had worked with at the university, gave the usual persuasive and enthusiastic chat about Anna writing something. She meant well, Anna knew, but she found it annoying, the way Moira made it sound as if writing a book was a sacred duty, or as if she thought it might save her. Anna had toyed with the idea of turning research into a book perhaps, because she missed working, being involved with something. But she could never find a beginning, and nothing had ever begun.

Anna replies to Sophie's message, saying, without a time or date, that she will call in for her cardigan. There are several messages and texts awaiting a response, from Michael, her ex-husband. She knows what he wants because he has been talking about it for a long time.

He talks with blunt vigour, persuasive enthusiasm. He talks so as to take up the space that might otherwise be occupied by Anna's doubt and resistance. He offers up the counterarguments before he stakes out the plans. Because he knows she will be unwilling; he has as much experience of her as she does of him, after all. What he does not know is that for her, his enthusiasm is not a warm persuasion but a bully's cudgel. His expansiveness sweeps those around him into his own plans without him noticing whether that is where they want to be. He wants to make a celebration of what for her is buried torment – twisted midnight fear and sudden, solitary afternoon panic. He wants to celebrate this impending anniversary; he wants to celebrate a life whose absence Anna has still not learned to calibrate. Her strategy, once more, is avoidance.

Michael's emotions open up, pop like crackers, corn firing in a buttery pan. He makes himself bigger, bursts with a thousand tiny breaks, confronts head-on and wails. He breaks himself to be whole again. He seems whole now, and maintains his wholeness by revisiting, re-breaking himself in small ways. He thinks Anna can do the same. She cannot. If he wins the battle to take her with him, she will not be able to skate a wide arc. She will have to get close, a footpad's gentle creep, Grandmother's Footsteps across the tarmac that has been laid down over the years. Traversed in any direction it still represents a passage to the same destination. This is no playground game. It is enough that she knows what is there – does she need to tap it on the shoulder so it turns round and once more becomes the wolf? The wolf that, granted, though it may be tamer with age, is still a dark predator loping always just off the path.

Anna sighs, turning away from the anxiety these thoughts feed. There are three empty pages in her green exercise book, room for a few more, but she will need to buy a new book when she goes shopping later in the afternoon, so she can continue with her accounting.

2 December

A boat has capsized, trying to reach Italy. Most of the people were rescued, but no one seems sure how many were not.

A woman. Her hand aches from writing; she takes a break from marking papers. A break from the words words words, repeated ideas and occasional inspiring shimmers of illuminated thought glinting in the shoals. To one degree or another, she is always tired. But whatever the tiredness of hand and eye, she puts all of her mind into building up her students, constructing them in an act of will, despite their dragging self-deprecation. She hopes to hold them up long enough to inspire, long enough for them to catch sight of themselves, so that her timid, talented girls might say 'look at me!' and in a breath, take over from her. For she knows that what she does with wearying determination, they could, by rights and with a flick of will, do with immaculate ease for themselves.

But, war began, her husband was killed, the girls have stopped coming to learn, there is no longer a school for them to learn in. She has a cousin who married and moved to Hamburg. She hoped she might be able to find her way to her.

Anna closes the book, now full. She puts on her coat and goes out to the car. The car seat is cold, the steering wheel too. She turns on a stale blast of heat. Prehistoric heat, stolen from the ancient, only source, sun. Heat that fell on different shores millions of years ago, growing bodies and shells, to be spilled from the vents as a quick, uncomfortable blast smelling of plastic. How many tiny translucent bodies grew in the tepid salty shallows, whisker limbs gently probing the tide harvest, to make her warm this cold winter morning? She reverses out onto the lane, as always empty of other traffic. There might occasionally be the odd horse with a briskly effective rider, usually Marjorie with her straight back and empire-era opinions, or one of the athletic girls from the other side of the village. John Farnsworth on his tractor, willing to exchange no more than a wave in all these years of occasional passing. A wave not accompanied by a look – he knows she is there; he doesn't need to look at her to prove it. They have spoken actual words perhaps three times, in the pub. Michael used to try quite hard to befriend John – he tries subtly to conquer everyone, she thinks, dismissively – but she is satisfied enough with a nod and a wave. She embarrasses John in some way, which does not make a basis for friendship.

She drives the slender lane down the edge of the chalk hills. At the bottom of the steep escarpment it meets a busier road. The plane stretches out, flat winter fields gradually making way for the city of Oxford. It is early enough to find a central parking space. She drives into the middle of the city, nosing the car down into a small underground car park near the shopping area. She gets out to buy her ticket, looks attentively at a man locking up his car. He is tall, taller than her, well made. She feels a longing that she thought had emigrated. Sourness that she does well to keep outside of her waking mind is there too. It has been an age since longing led anywhere. It has been a long time. She thinks she is happy with that; she thinks that this absence is what she has chosen. She turns abruptly from her thoughts. Town and people pass her by, a new briskness in her step telling her that she is busy, that she has not felt longing for a man in a blue jumper, locking the door of his car in the small car park. She accidentally imagines how his shoulders might feel under the expensive commonplace blue of the jumper, how it might feel to lean into that shoulder. Impatiently she tears up that picture, screws it into a tight ball and briskly returns to her dishonestly busy life.

In the bookshop she lingers, fingers trail and touch, flip covers to read reviews; all is pauses. Towards the till is a table covered with blank books, empty pages, journals and sketchbooks. One, covered in suede-like fabric, is the colour of bluebells. A picture of woods opens before her, the glory of April, the beautiful freedom of youth. A carpet of bluebells, the bitter sap that stays on fingers in the used-to-be time of gathering huge jars of heavenly blue. A childhood spent in chalk hills and beech woods, when late spring turns the woodland into a vessel of cathedral light. Her fingers smooth across and drop to open the cover. Bookshops invite touch quietly, the gentle ease of opening a book that you might not buy. This one has blank, off-white paper and look-at-me stitching, a book that self-consciously implies the hand that made it. She likes the heavy curve it makes in its soft covers, the petal-smoothness of the pages, the weight of it. She buys it then leaves, feeling the book banging against her hip in the large bag hanging on a long strap over her shoulder.

Wishing to find a birthday present for Sophie, she heads for a department store. The tasteful goods stand on islands between wide avenues, serene and well-tended. No racks of sale tops, jammed in and bedraggled, dangling from one end of the hanger by a now permanent bump in the cheap jersey shoulder, or garments trailing from skinny satin ribbon loops into puffballs of dust and hair under the display. Even on the busy days there is room to sweep in a direct line from the row of front doors to any department. She heads to womenswear, fingers a sea-green scarf, languid silk that slips between her fingertips, a colour she knows would suit Sophie. She takes it with her and selects some trousers and a few tops that she decides to try on. Anna likes clothes, enjoys the small tactical act of putting together an outfit that is subtle but distinctive. She has a wardrobe of tailored and stylish clothes – plums, umbers and dove greys, mohair, wool. Rich surfaces cushioning life. A statement necklace of black jet, a tactical proclamation of her individuality and status as a person with style. Something easy for which she feels she has gained much undeserved praise.

She rustles around somewhat petulantly in the changing room, glad for a solid door with an actual lock, not a too-small curtain that gets bumped open by her skinny behind as she bends to pull up trousers. She buys the trousers and one of the tops, as well as the scarf for Sophie. She leaves the store and walks down the pedestrianised street. The city is quiet. The drizzle that began the day has stopped, the clouds parted. Winter sun skims the tops of golden walls. On a whim, she makes her way up St Aldate's to the river and walks along the river path for some way. On the way back, she stops at the terrace of a pub, not yet open for the day, where many lively and enjoyable summer evenings were spent, she and Michael and the colleagues at the university who had become friends. Coots glide by in formation, losing their squadron shaping as they string out towards the bank. She sits for some time at one of the puddled empty tables, marking sad memories of happy times, slender echoes from lost summer days. She sits still long enough to catch them as they bounce off the underside of the stone bridge and skim by.

Anna is angry with herself for succumbing to the past. She turns around to head back towards the town centre and the car park.

But she is halted mid-step. There he is. All of her blood disappears; she is drained of all connection to now. The world tilts in ugly, unhelpful planes, and she is about to slide off. She sees that he has seen her. He looks startled, a moment of uncertainty, hesitation, and then he goes past her. He hurries past; panic hastens his pace. He is gone. Her blood is gone. She catches a brief glimpse of a grey coat, his back, as the world swings briefly into line. She has to sit. She sits on a bench, a town drinkers' bench, grimy and wet. Her new purchases drop amongst chewing gum and fag butts and damp. She feels sick. Her blood is replaced by gasoline, a petrol bomb churning in her belly. She feels sick. She feels vertigo, hanging off the world into the endless, endless drop of space. Gravity is skewed, no longer necessarily an ally, no longer connected to her at all perhaps. What is connected to me? What to hold onto in this unchained undoing? She holds the damp wood of the bench. Eventually, all the shards that this moment has become slowly shiver and slant back into place, slowly take a recognisable shape around her. She leans over her knees, begging gravity to hold her tight, pull her closer to the anchoring earth. She recognises the place, but she is lost, like one of the ghosts she sees, slow-blinking, unexplained, in the trees. What has happened to me? Why am I here?

Time concertinas in and out, sound wavers, sickness rises and falls. Time, squeezed or stretched, passes and soon she reckons the world with customary strategies. She notices that it is cold. She notices that she feels sick and that it is getting darker. Her body is connected once more, via this reckoning, to the world; gravity holds her, winter colds her, though her undoing hangs in the air like the ending chime of a bell, petering out into the far reaches of space. She gets up and walks, feeling the parch of her mouth, the weakness in her legs. Her bag, with keys and money, luckily already slanted across one shoulder by a long strap, accompanies her automatically, the book still bumping against her hip. The store carrier bag is left behind, soaking up the drizzle and the spilled Tennents under the bench. She fumbles for her phone. Who to call? What to say? She doesn't know what to do. She might be sick. What does she do now? She can't think of the person who would be able to answer those questions. She pauses, leaning for support on a lamp post. Her phone is dropped back into the bag around her shoulder. She wants to go home.

Back in the car she is shaky, breathless, uncertain of everything. Her hands in her lap clench the fabric of her clothes. She breathes, rusty-saw breaths that snag. Panic still flutters at the corners of her eyes. Her thoughts stumble, become uncertain, irrational. She is cold with the shock. Eventually she struggles with the car, the ludicrous pillars and turns of the car park. Miraculously she doesn't catch a cement wall, or bump another car. The car stalls in the traffic, but finally she gets home.

Home, pulled around her like a parka, like a stone wall and a moat. She sits still, though there is a demolition derby crashing under her skin. Rages skid and screech, making tight turns around her organs. She sits it out. She sits still. Night cools further on the windowpanes. She sits at the kitchen table, makes tea, opts instead for wine. The discarded tea strengthens and cools; an oily slick forms on the surface. She thinks about calling Sophie. Sophie has helped her so often with difficult times. Yet she can't bear to return to that claustrophobic care. She doesn't want to be in the middle of a web of others. She already can't move.

There is nothing she can do. Nothing at all to end what is real about this. There is no pretend, no alternative, no strategy that will change the flint-hard, flint-sharp truth. He has come back. He is here. And Caitlin is not. Her girl, her beautiful girl, is gone, and in this world there is still him. A shard of that flint shears off and starts carving her out from the inside. She is being hacked empty in small ugly chops by that savage blade.

The wine is disappearing, from bottle to glass to her. She tries to reason it out. What she wants now more than anything is to not see him. The rage she feels would make that true by securing his death, smash him out of the arena with one of the battered cars that race inside her. Run that fucker down. She grits her teeth and quells the anger, breathes hard through her nose, gritted teeth and flared nostrils. All other hates pale into a cross-stitch hobby compared to this. Every bad thing she has ever felt spins round and down onto that man, tightens around him, a winding sheet of sheer hate. Yet, his nasty surprise today aside, he is untouched, unknowing of the harm she wishes him. He will perhaps be shaken, count himself lucky that she did not manage to do more than stare; he may decide to avoid that part of town again. Then in minutes, he will probably be back to whatever life he has now, whatever brought him back here.

Maybe he is at his parents' house, somewhere on an edge of that small town, just a few miles away, that she has scrupulously avoided for years, a blank in her memory, a map of avoidance. Somewhere in that boycotted terrain, a version of family life, for them, has been restored. Perhaps their nightmare is over. Their golden boy restored to them, their darling son, burnished by what he has had to endure to even greater preciousness. His blind, adoring, stupid parents, who stood by him, who did not believe his guilt. And if he has come back for good, how long until he comes back with another girlfriend? A wife? Grandchildren? Have they forgotten Caitlin? Made her no more than an inconvenience, the cause of an awkward gap in his CV? That dim couple who would not see what their son had done.

She has dreaded seeing them, has always hoped they had moved somewhere else. Her keen eyes looked out for them, a constant low level of anxiety, even as she expected them to have slipped away in shame. But perhaps they felt no shame. Perhaps they hold him faultless still. Anna has spent so much hate on them, and counselled herself out of it, so many times, reminded herself that it was Ryan, not they, who hurt Caitlin. But, tied to him so closely, they were implicated in his acts. They can drown in the turbulence of her hatred for their son for all she cares.

Are they being supportive, helping him get back on his feet? Will he be eating a nice meal with them, cooking for them? Or praising his mother's cooking, hearty gusto acted out round the dining table? Will he tell them he has seen Anna? It does not signify, either way. What matters is that he is here; his life, his strategies, his habits be damned. He is here and her girl is dead.

The drab lumpen alloy of ordinary life is forged, beaten and stretched into a wire; the clinker falls heavy, burning her feet. The long night stretches out, painfully slow and thin, taut with misery. Endless. The wine, a second bottle, is a companion but not a help. Several times she picks up her phone, nearly calls Michael, nearly calls Sophie. Nearly calls the police, because surely it can't be right. But they have said all there is for them to say. Their part in the story is over – unless she does kill him. She thinks she hasn't the courage. Though he killed without courage, so perhaps it could be done. But no, she does not have the courage to be a murderer. Can it really be that nothing but her own death will scrape away the knowledge that sits in her now? It sits as easy as a penny on a plate. This fact has no problem with its own weight, meaning or power. It is just there. It is not damaged by its own existence. It is as bland a thing in its own terms as any other fact. The table is made of wood. It is cold outside. This ring belonged to her mother. Caitlin is dead. The man who killed her is alive. She knows because she saw him today.

She cools her forehead on the window, staring out into the dark of night. She is sour with wine, her head fat, her body hollow. Torment is exhausting. She thinks again of calling Michael, but does not. She has been told so many times that she must leave this behind, that she must stop. That it is harmful, pointless, damaging. But they are wrong. There is nothing else. How can there be another way? How could she know that in spite of best intentions, in spite of ground covered, torments ignored, endless therapeutic conversations and bitter arguments, that she is not, after all, prepared for this? That she is not, after all, able to let it go? She cannot live with the knowledge that he is free, in all likelihood a few miles from here. This life, this land, this piece of the world. She wishes with impotent storm fury that she could prevent it.

She bangs her forehead gently on the cold glass pane, rehearsing her arguments with the people she will not summon. She does not want to add anger with them to what she is struggling to negotiate now. She does not want to be shepherded and cajoled into a way of thinking that they make for her, a badly tailored coat that sits uncomfortable and restricting on her eventually passive shoulders. She does not want to be told that she is unreasonable, or that time will help, or that wishing him dead helps no one. She does not want to be told what is good for her. Move on – to what? There is no 'on'. There is no forwards or next step or smart move.

It is as if the remnants of Caitlin are being pulled from her. She has not learned a way to think of her daughter that is not framed by the disaster of her death. She is haunted to her core by that. But do not attempt to take it from her, because in that haunting is the ghost of the person she loves most in all of the world. Shreds of her beautiful, beautiful girl. She holds them tight and, though she cannot look at them, though she hides them, do not try to take them from her.

The evening spins out and on, wraps tight around her, stretches back out. She drinks more. The house is overly hot. She must have turned up the heating. She is sitting on the floor, awkward in an odd gap next to an armchair. The curve of the armrest is in the wrong place for her head, so she lies down, an unfamiliar spot in the shadow of lamplight. There are at least seven places to sit and she is on the floor in a wedged corner. She pulls a cushion down and under her head, clasps her hands loosely in front of her face, touching on the skirting board and the bridge of her nose. She wonders if she might see a mouse. She is in the mouse's territory after all, not her own. There is something comforting about being in the wrong place when all that is inside is wrong too. She feels the chair at her back, pictures her bumpy spine against the nap of rich brown fabric, the recently fashionable colour of hot chocolate, milky mauve-brown. Her thoughts are scratchy enough for pointless observations to mix in with the messy heartache. And she is quite drunk too. She imagines a mouse looking at the back of her head from around one of the fat chrome chair legs, enough animal intuition to understand she cannot possibly be a threat. But curious; if she were a mouse, she thinks she would be curious. The woman from Baghdad is there, sitting in the chair, trailing her arm over the edge and resting her hand on Anna's shoulder. She sits, Anna lies, drifts away.

'We are both lost,' the woman says. The mouse sighs, and says, 'It seems so.'

One time ago, I saw him. I couldn't understand what I was seeing. I hadn't grasped all my story, his fatal role, though I knew fear and fury; I knew all the things that face meant to me. But I didn't know what I saw, and as I pulled it behind me, my trailing tail of shredded story, I didn't know when I had seen it. I had a new memory: me, suddenly painfully full of my old self, tucked alone in the corner of a room of men, including the one who killed me. The feelings pulsed through me, iterations of new and remembered fear fanning outwards to the far reaches, to be kept forever in the waxy record of waveforms etched through the blackness. For me, the room pulsed with it, as if I had after all found myself on a sand dune and the sun's heat was making sight shimmer. I felt myself move with it; now such dances work through me always. But the men in the room, though they moved before me, were steady within themselves. Movement started inside them, did not land from afar or from the memory of harm. The old man with a hand that shook and a head that nodded as he sat before his tray, even he was subject to movement that originated, though from the betrayal of disease, from within himself.

I rode the seasick waves, the soul-sick fear, until I could accommodate them. I watched Ryan. He looked the same, though he was more contained. Moderated. It was as if he had tidied himself away and was trying to hold the cupboard door shut from the inside. He was wary, watchful. He was tidying away inside too – fear lurked squashed and hidden, forced into a small dark space as though not to see it would lessen its horrible power. Though adeptly he had created fear in me, he had learned nothing of its effect until now. Fear had flown out from his fists, released too quickly to be understood. But there he was, sitting at a table of six other men, learning the opposite of what his instincts thus far had prompted – learning not to be seen. Learning the love of the commonplace, unremarkable ordinariness. When we met, I thought he shone, but here he was, his gold transmuted in reverse, to beige, then the subtle grey of humble woodland creatures not troubled by the desire to shine.

This memory, of course, came from the time after my death, the time of his imprisonment. It took me a while to understand it. So many little fragments. But I am starting to join them up.

I have been back since. Another of those times when I sensed that my anger had pulled me in an arc back towards the Earth. I knew with a tremendous thrill that my thoughts had worked on my trajectory; I was, unaccountably at my own behest, heading towards an encounter with my past. In a delicious rush of anger I swooped towards him again.

The rush stopped abruptly. I pooled once more in a frustrating manner, as if drugged, conscious of what was around but unable to direct my gaze or order thoughts. He was there on a narrow bed. I could hear his thoughts, his memories – mutterings, anyway. How he muttered his dissatisfactions, his fears and worries, how he tried to tidy it all away, to stop thinking of how afraid he was of this or that man. Bigger, bolder men than him. Men whose violence worked its way out on other men. Men who understood violence without the certainty of weakness in another. How I tried to swim through the seas of his fear, to stir up the waves, make a storm of fear to savour as I watched him cower. But I do not know if I stirred even the cobwebs in his cell.

Anna wakes, slumped in the corner, feeling as though her bones have been turned upside down. A badly fitting skeleton. She is confused, then thinks, with the horror of fresh news, that Caitlin is dead. The thought batters her, and she panics. Slowly she realises that she has known this for ten years. She wrangles the misery back into the soles of her feet, or the points of her elbows. Back to the place to which it had been banished. All the lights in the house are still on, it is dark outside, and the curtains are open. She feels so very exposed. She eases herself awkwardly up from the floor, the house warm but no longer warm enough. She closes the curtains against the black slides of night. She pulls a warm shawl around her aching shoulders, sinks into the sofa. What is she to do?

She is to do what she always does. She is to wind down and banish, hide within her the ragged wreck of her true self. So she gets up, runs a hot bath. She forces the dullness of the regime back into command. She soaks away the physical pain with hot water and ibuprofen. She sets her jaw. It is early enough to call night-time, late enough to be a new day. The bath is refilled with hot water several times. Even in this unhappy state, she relishes the delicious curl of heat from the new water. It pacifies, aids the process of restoration. She reminds herself that the only thing new is that she has seen that man, she has seen Ryan. She knew, had known, that in theory it was possible, but she never allowed herself close enough to make prepa-rations. Knowing, incontrovertibly, that he was free was devastating. It destroyed a decade of heavily constructed strategies, rough-hewn and massy, relentlessly applied. When the strategies fell, they tore her open. And in the middle she found the thing she could not hide, the thing she thought that, against the odds, she had hidden – the absence of her girl. Still, she does not want to see that tenderness, the obscene, unviable frailty, tender as a featherless baby bird on a pavement.

If I could only stay still.

Understanding shivers, glimpsed briefly between slanted, slippery planes, then slides away. Understanding skids, finding no purchase on memories so faintly grasped. Understandings are slender and slippery, fine satin ribbons that slide through my fingerless hands. Just as part of the story seems about to shimmer into place, I am let go again. Upside downside, inside outside – it is any way round in death.

Gravity has disowned me. I had not grasped what refuge she gave. I had not understood her subtle care. I have not been able to hold on as she let go. It takes enormous will to hold back the blackness when gravity is no longer your ally. She let go her embrace, and I am pulled away to tumble, inchoate, through the eternal dark.

Gravity is the child of older powers. Those ancient parents, they have relieved their daughter of her duty to care for me. She no longer intercedes to keep me whole, to hold me. They are my guardians now. I hurtle and shift in this new vastness, an expression of direction rather than form. I see the patterns I describe without understanding the design. Sometimes, in the shimmer and the shift, I start to see the patterns of my own longed-for story, threading through the ancient blackness of my new and prehistoric path.

If I am lucky I graze the Earth, with her soft cushion of sky. Gravity holds me briefly once more, her love not after all gone.

When I can hold onto the Earth for a little while, I am full of nostalgic longing to stretch out my feeling body, to match her surfaces with my own. The ground is still a memory even as I am close enough to lie on it. I miss my body. I miss the body of the Earth. The soft moisture of grass over the muddy squelch of winter. Or to lie in the sticks and leaves of summer woodland. To have the skin that would be marked by sticks and leaves, marked with gentle indents. The ground scratchy and dry above a layer of secret damp. The runnels of bark under a pressed palm. A cool slab of porcelain at my back, still warming in a newly run bath. I remember sensations, surface memories. I try to find the memories of mind, turn the threads into something that my fingerless hands, my imaginary hands, can hold. A story that my spooling soul can reel in and tell.

I see them, now and then, my loved ones. I see that they get older; it is the only mark I have of the passing of time. I see my family. And him. I see from the marking of time on them that I spent what must have been years in a chaotic, fragmented dream, glittering here and there in the dark. For years, a dark tumbling glimmer, fine soot dust down a chimney, or harsh shards of smashed smoked glass.

As I flounder in these timeless fields, I gather chaffs of memory, try to find in the slender harvest an understanding of why Ryan did what he did. What made him able? What made his harm? I can't be sure I know why I died, but I want that story. I want to tell it. Why did he kill me? Why did I let him? How did I come to let myself be orchestrated by him so fatally? How did I come to be killed in a way that would have seemed risible, impossible, were someone to predict it? I was a girl who knew this right from that wrong, a girl who had a clear way forwards. I was not lacking in self-belief or self-determination. I was a girl who, laughing with my friend, could not believe the flip-flopping foolishness undertaken by others in the name, apparently, of love. Now I understand – there is another kind of strength in losing oneself. A different strength is required for that self-abandonment. But it is not a strength worth cultivating.

I became a girl who told lies to herself, learned them so deeply and secretly that it has taken the unravelling intrusion of the blackness to find them out. I don't share blame for my death, no I don't. But I became part of what let me die. He is the one who did that. Implicating me in my own death. That shame I put on him too.

I need to find the story, to find what brought me here. I think I have enough to start.

Chapter 3

For two days Anna stays at home, ignores the phone. Ignores the voice that, like a concerned friend, suggests she call someone. Anna dismisses this friend and does not call others. She pulls curtains across the short days of winter, exhausts herself with afternoon and late-night drinking. The clatter of television and the taut thrum of a headache distract her as she writes in the bluebell-coloured book or gazes in mute distraction out of the window. She avoids the fatal impact of her thoughts by breaking them into small pieces, a burying, weighty gravel of fragments. If only she could block out the world, achieve some form of oblivion. The seedy realm of daily drug use promises a reliable form of unconsciousness, absence from here. That strategy provides a good thick and grimy wall between all of this and all of that, no details too distinguishable. Tempting maybe – but who is she kidding? The occasional heavy hand on the whisky pour, as evidenced by the last few days' headache, is as far as she has ever ventured in that direction. She is too conventional, too afraid of death and too fearful of breaking laws, putting this reliable form of oblivion beyond her reach. Her imagination offers a retreat of sorts, a world where the sorrows of others require her notice and her compassion. She finds relief in offering them that small care, in wandering the now-familiar paths she has made, walking the woods, telling and retelling herself their lives. She retreats into the world of her shades, imagines how their lives would be if she had invented them as living people, not markers of the dead. There is at least space and calm in that sad realm. She ventures out to the woods, kept safe in their company from being haunted by her own memories.

The day is crisp and cold. The air is brittle, frozen thin, the tree trunks like metal. Victorian cast-iron pillars holding up a shelterless trellised roof. Christmas is nearly here again. Oh God, she wishes there were a hotel underground somewhere. No phone signal, no eyes to meet, no friendly enquiries about well-being and plans for the day. Just reclusive efficiency and a decent restaurant. Just a place to hide. Last year, the card from Michael's grandchildren (step-grandchildren, though he does not recognise the offset), she struggled not to burn it. What was he thinking? She doesn't think she has even met them.

She pulls away, sets her jaw again. Clenches her teeth and walks faster. There is a tart silence in the woods in this cold, broken only by small snaps of twig and freeze-dried leaves underfoot. Nothing, as she stops walking to examine her ankle, turned on a stone. There is pain but no damage. She walks on; leaves break again, small snaps under each step. She fills her thoughts with the people she will write in the new book later in the day. Twenty-nine killed by a suicide bomber. It is too many for her, too gruelling. She knows the limitations of her own accounting. But she sees some of them.

A girl, slender as willow, about twelve years old, hair that clouds around a face not yet firmed for adulthood. Now she is dressed for school, hair braided and tucked away, neat schoolwork tucked in her bag. She is a diligent worker, when unscripted dreams don't pull her away out of the classroom window to fly, storyless, with the birds.

An old man, bent and fragile, curved like the corner of old paper. He walks each day, a slow shuffle through his now-tiny world. One of his grandchildren, a boy of eleven, walking in patient companionship with the beloved old man. He had been showing him a new knife, that most prized of possessions for a young boy. His knife will be picked up and vehemently cherished by one of the men who tries and forever fails to make sense of what was left in this broken arena.

A happy man, energetic and sprightly. He chats cheerily with the various food sellers, many he knows by name. He is on his way to a bookshop to collect an order, and plans to get flowers for his wife on the way home, to celebrate the birth of another grandchild. He tells the vendors of his good fortune. A girl with her dark hair neatly held under a pearl-grey headscarf. Her young and secret heart, her loves and friendships, her talent for maths. The girl stands in the cold, silent and afraid, framed by gateposts of beech. Anna tells her not to worry, she will be all right. She wishes she knew it to be true. A man whose life spins out before him, a mosaic of impenetrable design. A colourful, senseless, perhaps beautiful pattern. Fragments and tiles arranged, it seems to him, by another, mightier hand. He too is dead, his patterns dark forever.

A young woman, nineteen. There she is; she tries to sneak in, disguised a little here and there. But she is too familiar, too close. Her long limbs, her eyes the indeterminate colour of a river. She bubbles up through the dead before Anna's eyes.

Anna stops, too close to summoning from memory rather than imagination. The shock of seeing Ryan has taken a sledgehammer to her defences. Damage has been done, walls are breached, doors cracked. Caitlin flits through the smallest chink, a wraith, a twist of pain.

Anna leans on a broad trunk, glad of its steadying girth. She focuses on the tree beneath her suddenly feeble hand. The tree has decades of practice in not losing its place, its place right there, that piece of earth and that piece of sky, roots and canopy held together by the steady trunk. She leans in, borrowing its expertise in being still, solid, placed, marshalling her evasions. She swallows, waiting until her mind is clear of trespassing memory, concentrating on the solid print of bark under her hand, pressing hard for more steadying contact. After a small while she peels her gloved palm from the kind tree and once more resumes her communion with the dead of her own reckoning.

I sift the ribbons, follow—feel along them. I try to find the one that links the beginning to the end. I imagine the change of colour, the loss of lustre, the fray and warp and pull. It started so well. Golden. I have never felt happier than during that golden summer infused with the blessing of love, overwhelmed with it. Gilded months of clarity and certainty, crystalline, languid and plentiful. I still long for that. Not for the love of Ryan. For the love of love. I could still stroke that soft, golden streamer for the beauty of it, even knowing how knotted and ugly it became. But he made it so. He was the stain and the fray. Love is not a destiny that fulfils itself; it is a gift to be born and cherished. Love was given to me and Ryan as a gift. He beat it into a curse. Perhaps it is only us, the cursed, who serve out death in this spin-

ning, chaotic reel through the blackness. Maybe death for others is a serene, wholesome arc. Sleepily adrift, they disappear in bliss. Perhaps.

I brush past another sometimes, but they spin like me. I cannot gather enough of myself in to ask them what they know. I don't even know, were I to find the mouth to speak, the lungs and throat to make the sounds, if sound is possible. Perhaps there are ways, new ways I will learn after millennia of spinning silently, new ways to make communion with another. Perhaps there will be things shared again. I sense them; we mingle, combine, rush through each other as we spin out alone to yet another far reach or dark and distant corner. Who knows if we yet have the option to communicate.

I feel my fingerless way along the knotted snags, the gnarled and stained bandage, gruesome tapes that loop round and lead backwards from my ugly death. Ribbons threaded through wooden hearts. Crime scenes. I find my way backwards so that I may tell forwards. Memories can be hard to find; stories and understandings shiver, slide into view and are lost again. I know it is all there, and I will find my tale. Though it is a labour, a stagger up black, vacuum-formed mountains, pulling hand over hand through gullies carved into the cosmos, harsh channels sharper and more lacerating than any earthbound stone. I pull against the blackness that would once more fling me out past the centurion path of comets, further than the spacebound eyes of man can reach. I don't want to disappoint, but there is nothing to tell. There is more of the same. There is still no place in which I may claim to be. I don't want to disappoint, but I have seen nothing that seems to be a heaven. Only Earth, with her kind sky and her care-giving cradle of gravity and her beautiful sun. How blessed I am when I find her again. How hard I cling.

I will try to tell it all, how it all happened. But you will have to be patient. I cannot say which bits I will be able to find, which will be torn again from my grasp before I can account for them, which I will miss altogether. We may have to wait for the giddy carousel to swoop round once more. I will try to make my remembered fingers grasp the streamer, pull it out of the blackness for you to see.

Chapter 4

Anna's occupation with the shock of seeing Ryan, the narrowing and souring of view that his reappearance initiated, excludes other concerns entirely. For a couple of days she thinks of nothing outside of her home, nothing connected to the rest of her everyday life. She completely forgets about a meeting in London until a reminder on her phone triggers a jolting return to the concerns of the present rather than the enormous abstract legacies of the past. The meeting was arranged some weeks ago, not in deference to her own empty days but to suit the busy diary of Eva. They were meeting to discuss an offer made to Anna by a former colleague, Callum. Anna and Callum worked together at the university for over a decade. He moved into another role as the director of a small public gallery some years ago. Soon after she retired last year, Callum approached her casually regarding the possibility of her working alongside Eva as a trustee of the gallery. Two months ago he called her with a concrete proposal. Anna liked Callum but found him irritating. She was flattered by the offer and felt herself to be in need of worthwhile occupation. She knew she needed purpose, and though she was ambivalent, lacking her once clear interest in the art world, a world she had occupied her whole professional life, she was prepared to go along with meeting Eva, whom she admired.

Though the weary anxiety of the last few days drove the meeting from her mind, she thinks hopefully that perhaps this is a worthwhile endeavour after all, a reinvigoration of old passions, a chance to invest in a new purpose. She tries to lift herself from the muddiness of the last week, going to bed early, with cocoa instead of whisky.

After a brisk breakfast she dresses in clothes that help her define a sense of her own clear outline and she leaves for London. She turns out of the lane and heads for the motorway. First, she will catch up with her old friend Kay, who lives in Chiswick, where Anna can park and leave the car. Kay greets her warmly. They drink weak coffee, chat about what they remember of their time as students and as fledgling professionals. They fill out some of the details of what they do with themselves since they last were together, the shapes of lives; they spin the telling out for two pale cups. Kay is affectionate and welcoming, invites Anna to stay, to come whenever she likes, have dinner later. But she is accidentally intrusive. She talks of a time when they were closer, when Anna was happy, with a young family and an exciting job in a small commercial gallery. She knows that things changed for Anna and is warm and caring, but she talks of Caitlin too easily, perhaps thinking that Anna will enjoy her recollections. The two women have become distant enough for Kay not to have understood Anna's dark reticence. It makes her seem crass and insensitive, when really compassion and kindness are in her words. Anna tells her if she has time after her meeting she will return for an evening meal, but she knows as she says this that she will invent an excuse that requires her to get back home, send a guilty text from the car, slink away without knocking on Kay's door. Anna is glad she is parked a short walk away.

Trampled wet leaves on the quiet London streets pattern the pavement like a grey-and-brown guesthouse carpet. She walks to the station and takes a train to the middle of the city. She walks across the river towards the Tate, a chimney, a box, a busy hulk. She has some time to kill so traipses dutifully through the collection. It looks tired, more tired than her, even. Twentieth-century art; it should be in a museum, she thinks. She is depressed by it. It does not bode well, she realises, for the prospect of working at a different, smaller gallery. She sees in that moment that her passion for art has gone; what remains are the habits of a working lifetime. For a long time, she has hidden this by railing angrily about the problems with art. Like a failing marriage, she has disguised her own lack of love by finding fault in the other, imagining that her criticism is a form of love, imagining that she attacks because she loves, not because she no longer does.

But she goes to the members' room for her meeting with the trustee, Eva, a woman whose passion remains vibrant and expansive. When Anna first met her, she used to make quite beautiful paintings, small and entrapping. Now she puts her considerable energy into working with Callum and concurrently running a valiant arts organisation, its many tentacles reaching out to prove that art does not belong in the elitist cul-de-sac it seems to have exerted so much effort to achieve. A good address, exclusive decor, crumbling foundations. Anna is no longer beguiled by the thick cream layer of pseudo-intellect, the slap, the greasy cover-all of invented meaning. For Eva, if you scrape that back, scrape it off, there is a vibrant, animate being, an expressive face underneath. For Anna, now, in her less forgiving years, if that greasy layer is scraped away, all she finds underneath is a plastic pot. Yet she used to love it. She used to believe. Anna feels depressed by her own indifference, feels further trapped by it. She likes Eva very much. She feels momentarily that perhaps she could follow her, let Eva's spark relight her own ashy fire. But she does not feel that she can stand next to her and match her. Let me watch, not contribute. She tries, out of a sense of duty to some kind of action in life, to keep her options open. But they are done, and she will say no. She is glad to leave.

It rains, small drops that seem to arrive rather than fall, lightly slicking the surfaces, enough to make the dark pavements shine in the street and shop lights. She travels the weary Underground, back to the car, sends her furtive text and leaves with thousands of others, clotting the huge roads out of the city. A slow procession home.

Thoughts drift to the ongoing struggle of finding a way to fill her time. There was hope in the morning that this meeting would signal the beginning of a new phase, time once again filled with worthwhile, distracting work, a mind occupied with problems to be solved and ideas to be made manifest. But she could not summon any enthusiasm. She feels herself to be emptying out, leaving infinite space for further emptiness.

The mantras of remaining occupied, finding things to be interested in, have fallen from the lips of anyone who ever tried to offer solace in the years of Anna's struggle with grief. She knows that a stoic determination to help her students at the university accomplish their goals provided her with a kind of relief. She knows it would be better for her to find something engaging, exciting even, to occupy her thoughts. At the very least achieving the compensation of feeling useful. She harasses herself half-heartedly about what the possibilities are. A question of filling up time or of being valuable. A matter of not crumbling to dust with brittle boredom. But she does not attack the problem with any vigour, accepting bleakly that useful may no longer be a thing that she will feel. She feels suddenly very lonely.

The heat of recent anger is cooled to turgid bitterness. She didn't choose this parched and wasted life. It is the subplot of another story. Small acts of authorship tumbling outwards, unfolding relentlessly and becoming historic, sweeping harms. So much havoc wreaked by such a weak, callow man. And he has paid, what, less than a quarter of the life he had already been given; the rest, the future, comes free. He paid so little it amounts to nothing. The bitterness is poison. She swallows it back down once again, a repeat dose, an endless self-administered prescription.

Traffic slowly snakes along the shiny black road. The rain persists, scattering taillights in red bursts. Wipers whining across the screen labour relentlessly to pull the lights, for brief seconds, back into shape. The traffic creaks, a heavy chain dragged through the country. It is slow but still frenetic.

Anna's thoughts turn, in a swift move of self-preservation, onto a familiar bypass. The woman from Baghdad with the turquoise trousers and yellow top might be sitting in her garden now, calm under a warm sun, enjoying a moment of quiet. Where is eternity spent otherwise? A calm garden is as good as anywhere. Anna wishes she could join her there. She pictures the house behind her, filled out in idle moments over recent months. She presumes it was most often busy with the noisy love and tumble of family, and that the pleasure of quiet in an empty house is cherished. She regrets knowing nothing about the life of an ordinary, happy, harried woman sitting in a garden in Baghdad. She doesn't know whether the dangers make ordinary life, ordinary happiness, impossible.

Imaginary friends were not one of Anna's childhood strategies. She had always been content in her own company; if real friends were not available she did not substitute an invention. A tall girl, self-contained and clever-clogs sharp, in the slipstream of schoolyard life she made durable friendships and sometimes bound less self-possessed girls to her in a way she found quite thrilling. Not a gang that had tangible status in the playground hierarchy of that bare-kneed world, but a small principality, usually ignored, occasionally strategically useful to those more involved with the statecraft games of dominance and triumph. A small principality of which she was definitely the prince. She had no swish or swagger but was forthright, and unafraid of the girls who did. And as so often is the case, these brash and needy girls, unable to manipulate her by invoking fear or envy, were enfeebled and, perhaps, privately somewhat afraid themselves.

The playground consisted of a patch of tarmac next to a Victorian red-brick school building, a patch of grass and a small, ungainly tribe of countryside children with brutal haircuts and noses red from cold. She was a child on her own at home, a child who learned her survival strategies at school. Her sense of outrage and fearlessness served her well, though it was years before she accorded her relatively unscathed school years to those qualities. She just knew that she could set her jaw, withstand people, defy them until they were no longer a threat. She liked that. Though to say she was fearless is an exaggeration. She had the will to force herself to confront wrong and was confident enough to believe she knew when wrong was being done. Where is that Anna now? Packed in the loft with the old blankets and interminable school-years diaries.

She has friends now whom she values and loves, kind people, clever, interesting and valuable people. She has more social life than she knows what to do with. But it is not enough; there is a chasm that they cannot fill. As though to compensate, she is inexorably, greedily drawn to reach for people she has invented. She reaches out as if she wishes to be friends with them. And strangely, these invented people have been accorded most of the power.

Though this woman may not be real, she stands for a real person, someone who was beloved, someone who slept, ate, stretched in the morning, someone who rubbed tired calves, or maybe rolled tired shoulders. A person whose life ended when they were shopping or walking in a market. A person whose life, in the middle of its most ordinary enactment, was taken by somebody who believed they had a right to make that choice. And what of them, the ones who did choose? The cyphers, the fools, the lost-soul assassins who walk into the midst of people like themselves and share out death.

A queasy anxiety laces these thoughts. It is a private affair, death. Not something for casual public consumption. She devoured them, these people, these deaths, for a thought experiment, then finds they have stuck in her, a sickly marzipan weight lying in her belly long after the cake has gone. She has more in common with the politicians who ripped into that country and made a hole big enough for such violence to thrive. Being from the same place, she can make a pretty good guess as to the layout of their gardens, the type of clothes they would wear. Does she have the right to disown that connection and claim affinity with a woman – dark, lovely, a mother and wife – who died in the bombing of a market place?

She feels bound to people whom she invented at the precise moment of their dying, hobbled by a tangled yarn, thickened with complicating knots. It is not, perhaps, so much wanting to become a friend, more that she is compelled to delve, to unravel, to try to understand the meaning of their death. It is uncomfortably presumptuous. She feels the guilt of her Englishness heavy on her shoulders. That young girl in the playground, now a woman, the inheritor, the beneficiary of Empire. A land that she loves and a history of which she is often ashamed.

It is curious, she thinks, the impetus to build empires. The playground games made large, the will to satiate the nag of inadequacy by demonstrating splendid power and dominion. Pared back, greed too is of course revealed. Or, more rarely, need. Need without trade, need without negotiation. Greed without care. The desire to own more than is necessary, more than you have. Does such greed come from a cold climate? Perhaps greed is a harshly rational friend in climates that set by stores for winter. Who can be cavalier about what is modestly enough when they do not know how long the cold will strangle the ground? None of us are such canny storemen that we can lay by exactly what we need. Weather soothsayer, seaweed and sixth sense, predict the winter and measure it in jars of jam and frost-cellar spuds. Excess may be canny in a land with wintertime that will not sustain more than the ounces of sparrows and robins. But the harrowing greed of conquest outstrips any demands of provisioning.

Yes, winter can last longer than you think. Longer than you

thought, Anna. What should be carefully packed in the storeroom to ride out a winter such as this? Carefully wrapped, perhaps in a bit of those old spare-room sheets, the faded easy-care remnants of her marriage acting finally as a layer of protection. Somewhere in the garage, or attic, placed on a safe shelf. What is the thing that she should retrieve to sustain her through this long winter stretch? It would need to be a generous, giving thing. A sled, pulled by sapphire-eyed huskies, glorious vitality written by their bark and breath on the cold air, ready to pull her away away away. Away to the dry heat of a Baghdad garden where cold is not numbered amongst the many perils. She would arrive in Baghdad on her husky-pulled sled, the remnants of Arctic frost burning up, giving way to the smoke and dust of fallen buildings. Find that quiet garden, where nothing will go wrong; she will insist on it being safe – the power to control the world exists after all, in the imagination. Sit quietly and ask this woman: what was your life like? What ended when you became one of my ghosts? A chance to question, to uncover the value of a life, not revel in the death of it. And perhaps to be pulled away, distracted from the thin inadequacy of her own existence.

What relief it would be to escape, by hacksaw or key, walk free of the shackles that lead back to Ryan. If she is caught by him she cannot think that he wanted to catch her. They are caught together; the irons of their shared story are not ready to give all their weight to the ground. What act or magic can break such ill-favoured bonds?

That answer must be found another day. The chain of traffic drags across the land, stretches out and eases; she gets slowly closer to home. Eventually the road leaves the street lights behind, narrows between hedges. She shares the journey with fewer and fewer cars, and turns finally onto the quiet little lane towards her house. At home, she tries to ease the journey from her shoulders, tiredly, with a few shrugs. She pulls the curtains across the black windows, a small barrier against the fathomless squares of dark. Fine rain is still softening the night. It is a gentle visitor compared to the frost.

Gathering into herself, curled up on the sofa, adrift, she resumes refuge, thinking again about the woman in Baghdad. She pictures her in the garden, still and calm, a warm hand resting on each thigh.

Anna worries that she is intruding. She wants to reach out, but she is nervous. She doesn't know if she has a right to be here. She wants to say she is sorry.

Sometimes I have felt Mum's grief pulling me, pulling me into her. I am on the end of a rope; she is the post to which I am tied. She is so firmly set, so deeply anchored in that place that however far I am, I start to circle, circle, circle, at first with a carelessness that seems to have no direction or destination, but as the circle winds in, as the rope shortens, I speed up, I feel the pull, I feel the reducing arc of my movement. I feel the dizzying rush as I am pulled and pulled until I move so fast and so tightly pulled that even without weight or body I am eviscerated by it. I become lost in a tunnel, a funnel, a wind-sucked shrinking spin that ends suddenly at my mother's feet. I look up and see that she is as still as rock. Bound tight from head to foot by a million miles of grief.

Mum – I feel it spooling out from her even here – is reshaped by sorrow. When I died it broke her heart. Her heart has stayed broken; that break has handicapped the rest of her. It is terrible to see that pain-filled vastness inside her. She has pulled tight around herself to keep it all hidden, the sorrow that marbles her bones, coats her organs, decides her fate. She is diseased with sorrow. Yet I see her smile, talk, laugh. I have seen her with the usual group of old friends, laughing and having fun. It felt as comforting to me as if I were a child going to sleep in her lap. Those adult faces that accompanied my childhood, contributed guidance and steps and gifts to my growing up. And my darling mum, loved by them and laughing happily in their company. But I could still see her disease. It glittered through her skin like the darkness waiting. Sophie knows her so well; I think she sees it too. She is such a gentle worrier, such a kind and loving friend, she would know what is plain to see. I wish I knew what to do, to pull that blackness out. The blackness is for me. Not for Mum.

There. I catch, suddenly, a thread. A time when I was younger, sullen in that ordinary way of a teenager, but not opposed to walking in the woods with Mum. As we walked through the part of the woods where the bluebells were thickest, Mum suddenly turned off the path and walked into the middle of them.

'Look, Caitlin!'

'I can't see anything.'

'No, I mean just the colour, look at it! It's wonderful.' She stood with her arms vaguely lifted outwards to encompass the yearly manifestation of colour that billowed across the woodland floor, buzzing in an ecstatic hover between purple and blue. Her face held a blissful half-smile of idiot pleasure, and for once I could see what she meant. The colour was wonderful. For the rest of the walk and when we got home, eating our pizzas and cheesecake that Dad went out to buy specially, Mum was in a happy, almost elated mood. It was easy to absorb her joyfulness, and soon Dad and I were as elevated as she. It was a very happy evening. Today's happy evening was brought to you by the colour purple.

She would do that quite often. She would stop to absorb the sight of something that she suddenly found irresistible. She would always offer up what she was seeing for us to share, but I knew that in those moments she was expressing part of herself that didn't need company. As an art history lecturer, she spent her life looking at paintings, artworks, filling her eyes with arrangements that had been created, if not inevitably to please the eye, to fill it. To be made sense-full by the cast of a human eye. She was serious about her work, absorbed, critical, excited often, irritated or angry at least as often. But it was only with scenes that happened by accident, or without the human view in mind, that she seemed to have this welling-up of wonder. She rarely articulated any thoughts about what she was looking at, certainly never subjected it to the dismantling analysis that in her work life she applied like a knife to various artworks, both to revere and revile. But she did offer the chance to share in her looking. Look, Caitlin, how beautiful it is! It might be a distant view, the accidental coincidence of building materials in an old part of a town, a decaying leaf. It might be something I couldn't spot at all.

It tears at me. To see my mum like this, to know how unhappy she still is. As weak as he is, as ineffectual in life as he is, he remade my mum. He tore her inside out and remade her. She is remade by the consequences of his acts. She is battered by my death. My death, my death, my death. Not even my absence, but my death. My death has killed something in her. As death has caused me to cede all of myself to hurtling and rushing, it has caused her to be bound in rigid stillness, held immobile under weighted coils of grief.

Chapter 5

The trip to London, though unproductive, was a useful escape from the confines of home. There was no expectation of seeing Ryan, and for that time, he was not the central black spot of her thoughts. Back at home, he once more takes up her whole view. She retraces her sighting of him so often, so minutely, desperate for clues that would tell her things are not going well for him, equally desperate for signs that he prospers. She torments herself with how young he still looked, how much life still lies before him. She thinks he can only have been out of prison a little while, though she has made a policy of ignoring any mail that may have given her concrete information. She didn't even know if she would have received any. But she had known somewhere, without deliberation, that the time for his release was due. It had been easy to think that shame would keep him away. It had been easy to hope.

She has been fending off messages and calls from Michael, from Sophie, from other friends. If only she were somewhere with no phone contact. If only she did not have to deal with it all. She listens to their messages impatiently, not liking to worry them. But it is impossible to talk about. What is there to say? They would begin their careful herding, their Anna-management. She knows it is love that orchestrates their actions; she knows herself how hopelessly far she could fall and understands her friends wishing to stop her falling again. But there he is. It takes more than common sense and self-preservation to know such a thing and understand how to live with it. He will live his life. And she is meant to believe that he has paid.

Dark thoughts chatter and scratch. Revenge is too grand a term. But retaliation, the lashing of violence sent back to its sire… Stop. She reaches, in spite of her frustration with the strategy, for the whisky bottle. The whisky soothes. She finds a calmer wish, for absence, not death. Yes, if she were in another place, she could at least guarantee she would not see him. She should just leave. She thinks briefly in terms of opportunity, of dreams from long ago – a move to mountains, a long slow drive down the northwest coast of America starting with an old friend in Seattle, a sabbatical in Barcelona. Plans that included a young Michael, a young Anna. Plans that depended, she sees quickly, on lapsed opportunities. And she doesn't want to plan a grand trip or a relocation; she just wants to be somewhere else. A holiday will do – it will provide a quick fix and a way out of the stultifying, stressful drag of the last few days. If she leaves in a couple of weeks, she can avoid Christmas too. She leaves the whisky unpoured and makes tea before settling with purpose at the kitchen table.

The small screen lights up, a gateway if not to oblivion then at least to retreat. With just a few words entered in the search bar she has a multitude of choices. For some time, she lazily paddles through the keenest advertisers, the ones who have got themselves to the tops of pages. Endless swipes of electric blue seas, water that looks potent, like toilet cleaner, beaches that are empty enough to presume human life (and all other garbage) has been Photoshopped out. Or destroyed, along with ninety-nine per cent of all germs. There is so much choice that choice seems impossible. She decides to search for breaks that include spas and retreats, the kind of holiday that a middle-aged woman can buy without qualm or attention. The kind of holiday that she could tell her friends was not a panic-driven running away, but a longed-for treat, something desired rather than necessary. Though usually cautious, she is financially comfortable on a good pension and with savings from Michael's share of the house. Sophie is always trying to get her to be reckless, spend a bit, live a bit. If she throws in the idea of luxury, they will understand her sudden change of plan in cheerful terms. It will, ludicrously, she thinks, make more sense to them than the simple wish to be elsewhere.

She sweeps through the choices. More palm trees, more massage and yoga sessions, more fat towels and cold drinks, more elaborate and enticing dishes glinting with oil in warm light. Anna has decided that she wants to be gone; having to decide where to go is tedious. Now she has given herself permission to be excessive, the choice is mind-numbing. But after all, numbness is precisely the offer. Numbness of mind and soul, a blanket of comfort to numb out the real world. She can't disapprove of a state of numbness, a state she has assiduously cultivated in herself. But this version has a richness that is unpalatable for her dry-stick appetites. Numbing down with a smile, a contented baby, drifting into milky-bliss sleep. She doesn't want comfort and luxury; she wants value-pack oblivion.

Could she leave for good? Curiously, it is also love that blocks the perfect escape. Love blocks in front; cowardice and habit, chained weights, drag behind and slow her down. Love for those dear, meddlesome friends whose goodwill sometimes proves so vexing. She does not want to say goodbye to them – she simply wants to be free of their solicitous intrusion. She blames herself, of course, her rattling, reeling and careening sometimes really did require the attention of others. She has been so steady for so long. But now and then, when a storm blew through a window it was no longer possible to fully close, she spun and teetered ever closer to the edge, and it was their steadying hands that stopped her falling. It was too often, too recent, for them to have given up the duty of care. But it was long enough ago for them all to be encouraging her into more productive ways of spending her time.

Poor Anna, they must think, she needs to fill her time with something valuable. Hence Moira's dogged pursuit of the idea that Anna write about her research into female mediaeval artists, and Sophie's transparent enthusiasm for almost anything that seemed to be even remotely an opportunity, a reason to be busy. And yet, it is the care her friends give her that creates value, that stops death or oblivion being a reasonable proposition. In seeking to fill her time, they fill her with love. She is precious enough to them for them to stop her falling. She is a thing of value to her dear friends. To herself, she is a stubborn puzzle, a confusion and a chore.

Back to the holiday search. Sunny skies and sparkling seas swish by under her languid, sweeping hand. As if she is already there, gently paddling a lilo across the flat, lurid pools. Far from assuaging wants, these perfect brochures create them, a restless unfulfillment forever ensuring return. A sleight of hand, to create a sense of want by providing something, a subtle, small trick practised on an enormous, ubiquitous scale. If what was on offer was really what we wanted, they would not need to seduce so ferociously. But want it she does. Luxury is the disguise, a cashmere coat thrown over the ragged tracksuit of her cherished isolation. She is buying off those dear friends by throwing out a bit of cash; exorbitance is the proof of her authentic desire.

The electric blue is hurting her eyes; no ikat-strewn cabin or palm-shaded bar stands out. She turns from the screen, looks instead to her thoughts. Where does she want to go? She doesn't want to go anywhere. Where would she want to go if she wanted to go somewhere? That useful, annoying trick question. Turkey, Jamaica, Zurich, Morocco, Barbados, Slough, Baghdad, the woods, home, nowhere. She flip-flops between encouraging Scout leader and recalcitrant, sarcastic teen. She is not helping herself very much. Another cup of tea, another search term. Where to go when you don't want to go anywhere, when you just want to not be here. No answers. Where to go. Away from the danger of seeing Ryan again. Away from the cardboard charade, the grime-edged enactment of unity, harmony, family. She has no family. Christmas, with its oblivious cheer and goodwill, is a curse, a slap, an outrageous reminder. So, back to the blue promise. Where are the holidays where retreat means just that? Not a retreat with massage, with oils, with hot tubs, with meditation classes, with painting, with mindfulness. No no no, just retreat. Not moving from one table of riches to another table groaning under the weight of a different cuisine. She wants to retreat under the table, with a blanket and a book.

The holidays that work often do so because they provide simplicity, narrowing life to its more basic components. The complications of regular daily life unreachable, irrelevant, blown away in an instant like a ball of dandelion seeds. A simplification of surroundings, a lessening of voices. Perhaps amongst the happiest times of her life were the two weeks spent in a cottage in East Anglia with Michael. They saw no one, did nothing, went nowhere. She remembers the mornings – his young dark head on a worn pillow, the fine planes of his shoulder under the mothy sheet. Clear, flat light held at bay by their laziness and the limp, floral curtain. The bedroom was small, unexciting, shabby, with strange angles to bump heads where the roof intruded backwards, into the house. The kitchen, mismatched and gloomy with sputtering gas rings and far too many browned china basins; how many steamed puddings can one kitchen produce? There was a fire and an uncomfortable sofa, a garden with a broken cement path and ragged borders, what might have been neglected raspberry canes draped in fallen green netting. They walked, went out to shop for food, but mostly they stayed inside, happy to be on this grown-up adventure of a holiday. Where it all began. She was very happy those gentle honeymoon weeks, the softening time, when they melted, became one, cemented themselves to each other. Impossible to imagine then how that bond would break, how it would fracture like the path from the back door of that worn, blissful little house. But not then, not for a long time. Many years for which she senses, elusively, that she could be grateful. But some things are too hard and too far away. Some things are hooped by such angry coils.

Search: self-catering holiday Christmas. Looking for a self-catering break over Christmas? Want to unite your family in one place? No, she wants to sit in a tidy, bland room on her own. Try again. Still more about meeting up with your family, organising your family get-together. Solo holidays: even worse. The first option offers carol singing and sparkling festive fun with fellow solo guests. Mature singles holidays: they insist relentlessly in presuming that she wants to mingle with like-minded travellers. Back to hotels. Search: hotels where no one talks to you. No result. So, perhaps a big, anonymous hotel, in Slough or anywhere else. Big, quiet hotel. First option is in Cambodia, could be interesting. Next possibility, Portugal, south, though in winter not a believable choice. What floats, what is she likely to do? Something she has done before and wants to repeat – she hasn't the imagination now to invent a new idea. She thinks of the places she has been. France, too close. Turkey, she was too happy with Michael when they went to Turkey, that may seem like she is creeping back to the edge, perhaps. Alarms will sound. Klaxons of concern summoning her keeper-friends. Though all who know her understand that she does not yearn for their former relationship, they might construe that she yearns nostalgically for happier days. America, so many options, too much Christmas. Fiji. Beautiful Fiji, she always wanted to go back there. One day she will. This time she doesn't want her escape to require planning; she wants an easy, quick trip. She wants to go to the airport and be gone. Tenerife, where she had taken a break with friends many years before. It is an easy flight. Hot and dry, that volcanic landscape was odd enough to love, curious enough to warrant a return. And the steady sun would warm her bones. Tenerife is the place to go. That steady sun will be her visa, her pass out of here. She searches long enough to find and then book the flight, the hotel, a taxi even. After all, she leaves in less than a fortnight.

I sift the ribbons, find the beginning, before the fray and pull. When all was beauty, all was love. The amber glow of ordinary happiness ushered in the gold of summer, the beginning. The time when the impossible end became the possible. In beautiful warm spring, I was waiting for my plans and dreams to become the same thing. I wanted to be an engineer. Working hard, studying, waiting for my world to gloriously expand. Learning, for me, was a pleasure, a self-paced adventure in new worlds. I worked hard to build a structure, ordered but readable, familiar enough to allow the free swoop of learning. For me, this was adventure. Give shape to the world then let me fly through the spaces, a swallow returned to a happy summer home. I worked hard, yes, I was steady in my body, I kept my shape, I knew my paths and my boundaries. I am learning wilder ways now, as I am propelled through unknown realms. No familiar ground below, no reference grid.

But perhaps I am learning a little of these new protocols. To begin with, all the words I could make, memory and knowing, were on elastic, slow to leave with me when I was shot forwards into another racketing ellipse, catching up when I unpredictably stalled once more. Slowly – over years, it may have been – I began to hold together better, leave less of myself behind. I travel in a more compact shape, lose less on the way. What a thrill it would be to have a body as curved as a swallow, a bird black all over, built with the same gigantic majesty as the darkness that holds the stars. The leading edge of wings the radius of a planet, calibrated to swoop through the inclines and lifts, the densities and vacuums of black space. To master these migrations and head for the burning heart of a star. Perhaps I would fly a little first.

I thought he was a beautiful swagger, a bold adventure. I thought his dreams grand. I thought them worlds that were waiting for both of us. He didn't care for his failure; he wasn't impressed too much with my own success. So I thought. These tiny glints of the goodness I first found, the pay dirt, the river siftings. I have misplaced them in the dark swell, the ravage of what followed. But I delve, rinse, sift, in the words that I can pull in to tell. I have to find the telling. The shivers and glints of gold. I did see them, treasure them. Then, my loving eyes magnified their wealth. They shone like heavy nuggets.

His own learning had not prospered. He did not have my love of it. When he returned from a politics degree in Portsmouth, his time at university ending less successfully than he had hoped, he made a new plan, teaching English in one of the numerous language colleges in Oxford. For now. Until the big plan was to start. A master's, some writing, travel. A book, of course. All these proposed in uneven rotation. Word–stories, world plans. I thought he believed them possible. My girl–understanding, my child–heart, thought he knew how to build stories into life. But he just made the shape of them with his mouth.

Hard, hard to find among the words, too, the reminder of how I was before the greyness and restriction of ugly love. The me who was not a rag in his pocket. The remembering of my very own shape. This blackness that invaded me, it was the second shifting, the second creeping–in and pulling–apart. The first intrusion was him with his fool's gold. When I first met him, I shone too, with purpose and clarity, passion. Somewhere in the words, somewhere is the me from before, the me my family made. More than all, I want to find myself in this telling.

I had some power then, I think I must have. Because he did all he could to love me. All he could. He would follow me when I moved. To London. I was going to become an engineer, and he was going to be the man who told the world its stories. From the television screen – he was going to become the bold interviewer, the wise man of important stories on the television. He would come with me to London, finding his feet somehow in the world of political journalism. The broadcast part could come later; he wasn't in a rush. Me studying engineering. Yes, I still had my shape then, I was elevated. He elevated me well.

Our two shapes seemed so whole and pure. We lay on his bed in the small flat. Intimate caress and private shared dreams.

It is a jolt, ugly for me now, to recognise that the intimacy of those days, the most open and unbound time of my life, is tainted by what followed. I stick, find myself unwilling to relate the character of it, the soft drift from lovemaking to waiting only for his return. I am horrified by my remembered willingness. My abandonment of self. It seems to presage that more malignant abandonment that followed. You do not need my words; young love evolves in the dreamlike expression of passion and the thrilling undressing of self. Not a naked body only, but one divested of all armoury and artifice. The vulnerability was not felt then, in my nakedness, my lack of self-protection. But I felt it later, and feel it now. You do not need me to spell it out. If you do, I cannot help; I am already turning away from the picture. To find it is enough. I gave him everything of myself, for in love we don't hold ourselves in safety behind barriers. And so love caused the perfect conditions for the pathogen of Ryan's harm. If I did not love him he would have been a thug, in my reckoning and in his deeds, and I would have walked away the very first time. We both betrayed me. Did we? I felt it was us both. Did I?

Anna stretches her back, relieved to have made a commitment to absence. She pours a glass of wine, calls Tony and Simon, speaks to Simon and tells him she is going away, thanks them for the kindness of their rejected invitation to spend Christmas with them. He asks if she is sure she wants to be alone. She says yes, emphatic and reassuring. She thinks she detects a little relief. Simon has always been the less sociable of the two; one of the reasons he and Anna get on so well is their slightly spiky resistance to the gossipy, collective glee of Tony and his enormous circle of friends. She calls Sophie, tells her the same. Sophie asks anxiously if she is sure she wants to be on her own. Offers the most elaborate all-areas access to their own celebration, does not detect Anna's own relief when she declines, citing that happy old fool, that unruly sun, no lover to wake, just her. She secretly triumphs that she will not be twitching with suppressed boredom whilst Brian extols his exquisite choice of wine and boasts about how clever he was to get it from x place at y time, loudhailered subtext demonstrating his own savvy taste and gourmet kudos. She will not be feigning absorption in one of her (inevitable) Christmas-gift books whilst Tony and Simon cheerily and a little drunkenly cavort on Skype with Simon's pyjamaed nephews and niece in America, for what usually seems to be hours at a time. She will not see Ryan; she will escape the gritted joviality of Christmas. Spared. All of it escaped.

The kitchen table is a steady ship, a friend, covered in gifts and bright paper. Anna has as usual been selecting gifts for her small circle of friends for some weeks. As though compensating for her lacklustre engagement with the season to be jolly, she expresses her love in generous and carefully chosen Christmas gifts. A small spill of red wine soaks into a remnant square of yellow tissue. She hums along to cheerful radio, delves into bags, feeling the pleasure of buying presents and rediscovering them a few weeks later on retrieval from posh paper bags, stiff and shapely, a drape-of-ribbon handle. A brief and furtive sourness, as she remembers the abandoned scarf for Sophie, is soaked up like the wine, with a reminder that she must get a replacement very soon. She removes elegantly printed price tags, held by ribbon or silken twine. New tape, a whole spool of ribbon and, miraculously, a pair of scissors unearthed in the kitchen drawer. Eventually a sculpted, shining pile of shapes, tagged and ribboned ready to deliver. The radio cheeps away gamely in the background; the bottle empties a further small degree. Anna is buoyed by precious drops of optimism, glad she has a plan and a reprieve.

She sits with curtains drawn, the television on for comfort. She tucks up her feet, pulling a blanket over herself, and drifts off, thoughts escaping the tedium of a television drama she doesn't really follow. She drifts dreamily to imagining the woman, still sitting in her garden. Still Anna is not talking, but watching, thinking about what she would say. Thinking too about all this woman has lost and all that has been lost with her. Anna's imagination is populated by all the people she has invented. She remembers most of them, adds details as her time with them grows. She sees them in snippets and collage, in the lives they left behind. She sees them standing sentinel-still amongst the straight beech trunks. Like a beautiful, slow and mysterious living installation. They blink in ultraslow-motion, confused and stilled by their new location – the half-life of invention, the half-life of the newly dead. What is it like to be dead? Do you feel it? The woman looks up at her and says, come down, come and sit down and I will tell you. Anna is floating in sky, hot sun on her shoulders, the heat on her head. She can smell her own hair. She can hear her own breath in the eerie stillness of sky. The sun is so hot it burns. Anna is held floating by her reluctance to talk to a ghost, an eidolon, a figment of her own need. The woman is impatient with her now. Suit yourself, she seems to say. Her gaze returns to private reverie, sweeps across the roofline, the top of the wall, the jumble of aerials, anchors thrown upside down into an invisible sea. Anna feels she is drifting away, unable yet to catch hold, to sink into that inviting, scruffy, shaded place.

The sofa is comfortable; her feet, unusually, are warm. The television burbles meaninglessly and soothingly. She pulls the rug up to her chin and closes her eyes. She feels sadness for the lost souls amongst the trees. But that sadness is not a locust swarm, stripping all nourishment before it. It is a reminder, a caution. It is a puzzle too. What does she do with it, this feeling? Throw a party for ghosts, invite them in, at least to warm themselves in her home? After all, they are here because of her. Come, come. Do you drink wine? Or sorry, is that stupid? Tea? I know, it is so very cold. Warm yourselves while you decide what to do for all eternity. Come and sit with me, tell me about your lives, tell me how you lived.

She wakes to reruns of old detective shows. A sure sign of the late hour. Her neck is stiff from sleeping on the sofa, but her feet are still warm. She switches off the television and lights, thoughtful and still in the dark room, a pause in the quiet, then goes to bed.

We pass each other sometimes. Others. I feel them gliding by me, through me. Hold me! we seem to cry out to each other; our longing thrums on a subtle, burning frequency. But they, like me, are soon gone. And all around is chaotic blackness.

Chapter 6

Michael has called seven times and left increasingly terse messages. Anna has gained fortitude from her escape plan. The confirmation emails sit in a folder on her desktop, visible signs of intention, like vitamin pills on a windowsill. You have taken steps, I am here to mark your resolve, they seem to say. She is ready, finally, to respond to Michael, and, though he no longer lives in the area, she wants to warn him that Ryan has returned. She steels herself in preparation.

As Michael is willing, pushing even, to drive the hour or more over to meet her, she agrees to meet the next day for a lunchtime drink in a pub, the opposite direction from where she might expect to see Ryan. They sit in the warmth, turned towards each other on a velour bench seat with brass studded edges in a low, black-framed window. Black beams stand sturdy between the lurid patterned carpet and the once-white textured ceiling, now coated in warm nicotine-brown, the traces of decades of convivial beer and cigarette breath. The Elizabethan vernacular architecture somehow contrives to be less faded, less time-worn, than the 1970s decor. Their glasses stand empty, on a sturdy dark table shining with polish and a pool of spilled beer soaking the edge of a cardboard brewery beer mat.

She tells him she is going away, pretends she will have a think about whether she wants to contribute anything to the anniversary event. Secretly she seethes at his enthusiastic presumption of collaboration. She has told him she does not want to be involved, rejected his suggestion, first made many months ago, that it would be good for her. But habit has made her an avoider of conflict, a mollifier. And this in turn has brewed a secret anger. Michael is solipsistic enough to miss what might be read between the lines, so he doggedly pursues his goal, believing that a shared purpose is the most desirable outcome and is within reach.

She resents his neediness and his desire for her to share his aims. She resents his seeming to need both her participation and her approval. She sees in his demanding desire for collaboration a sense of entitlement to having his world-view reflected back at him. Most of all, she resents the way he seems to wrap it all up as something he is doing for her, as if her well-being hinges on running in harmony with him. As if the long-gone unity of their newly-wed state is still the thing she wants most. He has of course changed as much as her, but he still seems to expect her to want to fall in with him. I didn't resent it when I was young, she thinks. Perhaps she should have done, then she might be free of it now. Rather than argue, she pretends unenthusiastic assent; for now it is enough to make him stop trying to convert her to his plan. In part as a way to move on, she tells him that she has seen Ryan.

'What did you do, Anna?'

'I don't know, I just froze. I sat down. It was a horrible shock. I'm sorry, I just wanted to disappear, so I haven't been very responsive these last couple of weeks.'

'How bloody awful. How awful.' There is a longish pause, then: 'Do you feel okay? I mean, you don't feel too screwed up by this? Though what else could you feel? I mean, God knows I feel it too. To think, he's... well. I just hope it hasn't hit you too hard?' It hits her too hard every day. Every day.

'I'm okay. I felt like I was going to collapse, but I'm okay now. I'm going on holiday. I'm glad to be getting away. It's time for a change, and it will do me good to be away, so at least that's good timing. I wanted to warn you, just in case. I suppose we both knew it was possible, but I just didn't think he would come back here. I'm glad I won't be here for a while. When I come back I'll have to think again. Because I can't stand the idea of seeing him every time I go to the bloody shops, or ever, actually. I'd... I dread to think what I would do. God, Michael, I really... All these bloody years avoiding, not knowing if they'd moved away. Why they hadn't got the decency to leave. I don't think I could stay here, if... I don't think I can.'

'I understand. But, Anna, you don't have to make a decision or do anything quickly. Though, for me, it was the best thing, moving away. It really helped, you know, to... well, whatever. Though, of course it was different, I... well, see how you feel when you get back.' She notes his confusion. A dull feeling, a fossilised, ancient pain; it no longer hurts but remains in the way, to be negotiated, a lifeless remnant, a bulky, pointless, unfeeling shape. Michael means that when he moved away it was different because he moved into a nest that was already built. All he needed was a suitcase and a key cut. He got a whole package. She didn't want him. She didn't want him near or around her. She didn't want him to stay, rent and howling, with her, in the wreckage of their home. But she despised him vehemently for his ability, his willingness, to make a new one.

He tells her he is glad she is going away if that's what she wants, though she senses his anxiety. She tells him she will be happier on her own, not more lost. He nods, regretfully, gets them both another drink. He tells her about his plans for Christmas, cheerfully fills her in on his busy schedule, catches himself, falters, asks if she would like to come over for one or other of their gatherings. She tells him again. She is not more lost on her own; she is happier. She tells him again, insistently, that he has no responsibility for her, that she does not wish him to have any responsibility for her. She teeters and pulls back on the brink of anger at his presumption. She is here to be friends with Michael, to help him with what he wants. If it is important for his plans that she is there, she will endeavour to be there; he should not expect more from her than that. And he understands finally that this will have to be enough.

A second drink is finished amicably enough. Michael has what he wants as, now he lets her be, does she. They part with a pedestrian kiss on the cheek. He wishes her a good holiday and tells her if she changes her mind, if she has any ideas, just email – he would love to hear from her as this is for everyone. She grits her teeth. She wishes him a happy Christmas and leaves for the car.

Back at home, Anna sits in the quiet kitchen. Memory time, memorial time. She strayed too close and finds herself trapped on a narrow shore, looking across a lake of memory, looking at the surface reflection of sky-blue happiness. There she is, her younger self, still a girl, an adult girl. Her legs are strong, her hair long and nut brown. Michael is beautiful; his hands hold her shoulders, his face rapt, angelic with fulfilment. She knows he is full of her and that she is loved.

She loved Michael, did indeed feel that his happiness was entirely bound up with her own. Or the other way around. Indistinguishable happiness. Their courtship, the first joining of their lives, is a magical and happy memory even now. She remembers the room, the warmly dim light, the happy, tired mood. She remembers her keen interest in the man across the room. After a night out, they sat with mugs of sweet tea, a slow-fried collection of friends enjoying the embers of the party heat. He, still a stranger to her, sat on the arm of a chair, Lilla's chair. Lilla with her porcelain bones, her elegance and broken front tooth, her careless charm, her careless self draped languidly at his side. Anna looked many times at the black-haired handsome man, but without expectation. People drifted off, into rooms and into sleep, Lilla too. Curled gently, folded quietly in the chair like an expensive coat, tan and beige. Anna and the handsome man left talking across the smoke-filled room, Lilla faintly snoring from the seaweed-green armchair. She can still feel the predatory excitement that filled her as that good night eased back the curtains for morning. Though she had loved others, she cannot recall ever having shared with them that rapacious, thrilling sense of elation. From that night, the night they met, they talked, they loved, they became Anna and Michael. The story unfolded; there is not much to add. It meant much; it was commonplace. They were happy, and sometimes they were sad. They learned how to be in harmony. They were happy. Blue skies and blossom drifts.

The glassy surface of the lake, the glass for scrying the shape-shift of a carefree she, beloved of the still-childish but loving he. These shadows trick-turn, perform a grotesque dance, a sickly parody of happy love, the cloying niceties of cinematographic advertising bliss. She even sees herself twirling a silk ribbon, him skipping around her as they laugh and caress and smile. She returns to herself on the shore, picks up a large stone and throws it into the water, satisfied to break that smooth, deceitful surface.

Yes, that love, in the face of a bigger test, proved to be a frail construction, one that could not last as they had promised, to the death. Another death pulled it apart. Years of ordinary trouble, ordinary boredom, ordinary difficulty, were endured. Their relationship, however stretched, had always returned to the shape of generous love and harmony, giving them both the illusion that theirs was a marriage that had weathered, had proved its mettle and would last. But in the sustained battering of a greater trial, curiously rapidly, it became confetti and matchsticks. Small leaves and tiny twigs floating aimlessly across the surface. And still she was stuck with a set of behaviours and rules that were inculcated to serve it.

The split between her and Michael was emphatic. But before the breakage was irreversible, they did try to mend. They found themselves on either side of a chasm running wild with dangerous water. Wretched as they were, they tried to build bridges towards each other, a way over the turbulence that separated them. It was much to ask. And how we find, in our massed human stories, that the times when most is asked of us is often the very time when most has been taken away. They built slowly and badly, with such impoverished materials as they could find, but they did not meet in the middle. Their bridges missed each other; their feeble stick-and-string structures were built in directions that could never join. Impossible to connect. Michael saw this, and somehow he kept building. He made a bridge strong enough to bear him across, onto a different path that carried him forwards. Anna fell into the deep middle of the river, too far from the cold comfort of the banks, and was swept away and drowned. For years she drowned. Eventually she was spilled out into a vast sea, where she has remained becalmed for many years. There are some storms; there are some sunny days. But in all these many floating years she has not found her way back home.

And yet, there is Michael now, surely in the light and warmth. He is, unfathomably, a happy man. She is all the colder for it. Not at his hand, but in the forensic light of a comparison that is always available. The end of their marriage had not meant the end of their relationship. They were tied together forever by their shared experience. So often Anna had wished to be free of that connection, but she never was. Yet she does not begrudge him his happiness. Even in her frequent rages with him, she knows Michael would bring her to that same place if it were in his power to do so; his foolishness is to believe that it is.

The same chair at her kitchen table, the place she sits, almost daily, with a newspaper, or with a book, with a pile of admin, her laptop, a large mug of tea or coffee. She sits where she always sits when she is working something out. The gas bill, a crossword puzzle, a Christmas list, a good read. She is here for calming, measuring and containing, ungrinding gears back to neutral.

There is nothing she needs to do, but knowing, on the all-knowing, blind side of mind, that calm is a pretence, she searches for distraction lest she should get wise to having once more thinly fooled herself. She picks up last Sunday's colour supplement, forages through articles about diverting, uninteresting things. She is diverted; she is uninterested. She reads the papers, repelled and held by the unbroken rampage of events. Anger that began in the most intimate, personal sphere is transformed into restless dissatisfaction with what is universal. Anna searches once more for the hidden people, tucked behind the print, unknown and unseen, faceless people piteously and impotently watching their children starve to death, or demented with anxiety because they don't know where their father has been taken. She is furious because somebody glibly gathers ever more wealth at the snapped-twig cost that others can no longer live with health and pedestrian dignity. The spillage, the messy debris of our human failing, is overwhelming, yet presently easier for Anna to confront than the twisting and leeching of emotions that belong only to her.

19 December

Today, a drone strike killed five in a village compound. I am frightened by drone strikes; the audacity is breath-taking. The hideous logic too. How angry I would be to have someone wield that advantage over my head, in my sky, onto my rooftop. How do they determine who is an enemy? A visiting uncle, trapped under the same falling roof as a military leader. A sister still living at home. A teenage daughter and her friend. How can any good come of this?

A woman with long hair with grey streaks at the front. Her hair is long enough to spill outwards, in the quiet evenings, down over narrow shoulders and broad hips. A black, glossy waterfall, curls flick turbulent at the ends, grey threads fall like foam each side of her neat face.

Her second-oldest son, as passionate and as learned as he is ever able to be. He has taught himself to speak four different languages, and dreams of a time when the babel of voices will come together once more into a world of one understanding.

His aunt, constant companion of the house. A woman bowed under the grief of having lost a daughter and grandson in an attack eight months previously. Her husband, injured in this strike, will have yet more to bear.

A proud and angry man, tall, broad-shouldered, willing to bear any discomfort or burden in his restless desire to deliver a better life, a fairer life, for those he loves. Those he does not love are barely even seen.

A girl with eyes of green or brown, not yet twenty. In reflective moods, she twists a silver bracelet round a slim wrist, an action that soothes her as she puzzles over the injustices of an unbalanced world.

Chapter 7

Sometimes the black has a thickness like wax. With a little more substance I might leave scratches on it as I pass. I bare my imaginary teeth, pull them through, make a track, a groove. The darkness of space could be played like a record. The needle of the gods, a diamond the size of a skyscraper, so clear as to be almost invisibly black, lowered gently to read the roar of our passing. Black like thick wax, scraped, I want to believe, by the tumbling speed that I do not choose but cannot resist. At least allow me to imagine I leave a mark. I remember black wax, black wax thickly and laboriously layered, coloured in by hand. Underneath, another layer of colour. A bright pattern, equally carefully laid down, a handstroke at a time, the width of a crayon–tip at a time. Filling the page like embroidery, long bright stitches made by my patient child's hand. Sitting next to my friend Toby. His hair curled up at the back, like brandy snaps. The rest of his hair had lost the curls of babyhood. I reach back in time, run my imaginary finger down the back of his round, remembered head, pull down the curl, let it spring up around my finger. Delicious softness of young heads and hair. Sitting next to him, filling the paper with carefully bordered shapes of colour, his pattern a full page of bold, diagonal stripes. I liked the order of his design compared to my freestyle shapes, but I was glad that mine was neater. I was proud of my colouring-in when I was seven years old. The satisfaction of contained edges and ordered arrangement. I am not well suited to the smoky spillage of my new form. The first coloured layer then covered with the second layer of black.

Finally, the magic part – scratch through the top layer. Beautiful drawings of Denny's car, Mark's robot with a big gun, Lizzie, Kate and Helen's princesses. Toby did an aeroplane in the sky with clouds and the sun. Remembering the arduous labour of preparation made the choice an anxious one for me. I wanted so much to make the right picture. I wanted to make it so nice that I could give it to Daddy for his birthday, which was going to be soon. I scratched the lines to show my daddy waving. It was magical to see colours appear, the lines having a special quality from being scratched, an image created by removal rather than addition. I was happy with my picture, bright lines that made a daddy in the blackness, filling the night sky, a stellar companion of Orion. The fingers on the round hand tipped with yellow as if starlit, his hand raised in greeting to me.

If only I could scrape back and find that colour now. If only I could find my daddy, heroic as in childhood, walking with the gods and me, a companion in this endless night. How I miss him.

I have been with Dad since I died. I have seen him with the woman he loves and the girls he now cares for, the grandchildren he loves with all of his generous heart. I know he still misses me; sometimes he is sad when I see him on his own. It is a vast and bleak sadness. He walks it as if it is a moor, undeterred by the scour of its emptiness. He has let himself learn its ways. He has made room for sadness, accepts its place in the geography of his heart. His heart has grown bigger in making room. I feel there is room for me in that desolate scape. Walking there affords a strange kind of comfort for both of us.

Love was never something he found hard to make room for. He will share his sadness with those he loves, I know, pull their caring around him in return. I try to share too, to hold him, to insinuate myself so he is holding me. I feel the space within him where I can curl in safety, a lair. I am often now as scared as when I was little. I am all things in one trajectory. All selves coexist within me. I am made only of memories, all of them. There is no present. I am made of the wisdom I would, given time, have come to learn. The ancient parents have seeped into me. Lent their eternal eye. As their hands pushed me off into the darkness, they gave me understanding as a parting gift. I feel I know so much; it is thrilling, tantalising. I know the taste of darkness. I have been scattered into new paths by the hissing wake of burning stars. I have touched, been touched by, been invaded by stardust other than that which made me. But the loneliness is terrible.

Each time I have found myself on the Earth, each time I have seen him, he has been happier. Now I can make sense of what I have seen, I know that he is whole, even with the break in his heart put there by my death. Soon after I died, he was as fractured as I was, inside the body that held him together. He did not believe that happiness existed for him any more.

I found myself one time, slowed and without agency, at the edge of our garden. I was passive, held in the air, like bonfire smoke at still, summer dusk. Dad came into the garden holding something in each hand. His shoulders pulled up, his back bent. He was unshaven, grey stubble and tired lines untidying his handsome face. His dark hair lank, greyer than I remembered. He moved with strange unpurposeful steps, wrongly weighted steps. He put down the two things in his hands. They were my beautiful lace-up tan leather boots, soft and tough as expensive saddlery, pinpricks of brogue styling on the neat toe. A summer's work bought that expensive treat. Dad had taken to polishing them for me when he polished his own shoes. He took hearty pleasure in lining up the neat pairs. I had not got around to taking them when I moved out; so much of my stuff was still at home. I think he must have found them in the cupboard under the stairs. He placed the boots on the edge of the terrace, a small step down to the grass. He positioned them neatly, as when he had polished them, then sat down next to them, staring past me. Past everything. He seemed to lose himself, as much lost in that bleak moment as I felt in the new rules that governed my being. I could not bear to see him so lost. Moments or hours pierced with steel stabs, a grid of sorrow. He put his hands onto his face, then slid them round to the back of his head, pulling his head down into the shelter behind his bent knees. He wept so deeply, so uncontrollably, and yet he tried to quiet it, to muffle the piteous sound. Through the window at the back of the house, I could see my mother, standing on the other side of the room. Completely still. Still enough not to have been noticed by me. The picture windows gave a broad view into the house. She did not move. I did not know how long she had already been there, immobile. My father sat on the step, his hands grasping at the nothing of his thoughts, sifting through his hair, searching his skull. Shoulders trembling and shaking from the sobs he tried to contain. My mother stood as still as the furniture in the empty house.

I remember happier times too. I witnessed them.

I remember worse.

Dad went back to one of my favourite places recently. A picture of a place, a memory, by a river. I was there with him; he was walking along the small road that bends round a corner and over a bridge. I know it. Yes, I have two memories, one from before and one from after death. The bridge is built of stone and is curved, a twist in two directions. Across the bridge is a small path that leads down to the bank of the little river. I had made a drawing of the bridge from this bank before I died, some years before, for a school project. Dad framed my drawing later; it hangs now in his new house, in the room where he has a desk. It used to be in the kitchen of our house, tacked to the wall above the telephone. But Dad took it with him when he left. Both of us left the house. My death made new homes for us both.

The sky, in my memory–picture, in this place, was that hushed grey, the neutralising flatness that holds England so steady. The land, too, was steady, held here in an ancient balance between the using of man and the shaping of nature, an ancient compact, one edging into the other until the blend is seamless. The river bent away, the arced curved across it, and magically, in the solid stone of that bridge, the two intersecting curves were held in perpetual and unmoveable solidity. Time had been caught in those two slow-moving curves. Shapes made by walkers and water, a path and a stream. Shapes that make and remake themselves, shifting over decades like the slowest snakes. These shifts had been corralled by the hands of a stonemason and a builder so that their meeting point became fixed. Though still a young girl, I was seduced by that magic. And though my death was not far beyond the time of that drawing, I am older, so much older now.

Along the bank is a bench, a gift from someone, I think, with a memory attached, a small brass plaque with the name of a lost beloved. It was where Dad and I sat so I could do my drawing of the bridge. Dad sat down there, on my dead visit, alone. He traced a finger over the letters on the plaque, and I felt the shudder of his heart contracting as he thought of me. It squeezed me, unhappily. We both felt squeezed by sadness once more. But soon placid calm reasserted hold, and Dad sat quietly. I heard snatches of his memory mingle with my own. The day together, helping at home to mount the picture on card to take into school, the easy happiness of the passing of time when you have no notion of endings.

I think that drawing made a choice; it became a choice for me. I discovered an abstract, sculptural passion for form, and my curiosity wished to understand its emergence into being. Which decisions had been made first?

Which part of the bridge was built first? What were the limits and how were they combined? What other bridges could those men, with different limits, have built? An exercise of imagination became a purpose for me. It became a dream the future held.

Sometimes in the longer stretches, my old dreams comfort me. I feel wonder at what is around me. I imagine I have the power to intervene, to create on an epic scale what I did not have the time to make on Earth. Space is all direction, span and arc. I imagine glittering black highways curving beautifully, forever. A ring road for paradise. A motorway slicing like the deft sweep of a scythe through Stygian fields. Satan promised that his gate to hell would be easily found. A regeneration road of the most epic, dastardly intent. Imagine the thrilling cambers and seductive speeds on that road. Imagine the bridges, cantilevered off unnamed, unseen distant planets. Gateposts that would rise beyond the view of a mill-pond lens, a lens the size of an arena. It is pointless, I can tell you, to attempt a lens to see to the ends of the blackness. Pointless too, to fashion a tool that would let us see the limits of Satan's ambitions for hell – forgive me if I disappoint, but I have not seen hell, nor have I seen heaven. Though the tar-richness of the black, the sonic boom of dark emptiness bisected, scratched eternally by unalloyed speed, do make hell easy to imagine. But this place, it is not punishment. It is too unfathomable to be punishment. It is frightening. Unresolved. Lonely. But I do not believe it is punishment.

I hope that it is not eternal.

And the love that brought me here, I once hoped that might be eternal. I did not know what a perilous wish that was. I did not understand the unkind way it would come true.

I did not understand eternal, and he did not understand love.

Chapter 8

The remaining days before Anna leaves are wiled away doing ordinary things. She makes herself busy with lacklustre chores. Time is spent in a trickle. She is suspended somehow, so determined to hang onto this leaving-behind, still resolute that the shock of seeing Ryan need not be healed, or even absorbed properly, until she gets away. In that getting-away she has invested all the possibilities and likelihoods of a remedy. When she is on holiday the chance of a further meeting is impossible, and thus she can contemplate repair. For now, aside from the first night's drunken stumble through the wreck, and the occasional irrepressible burst of anger, she simply hasn't looked.

She fills her thoughts instead with her legion, her tailor-made ghosts. They sadden her, yet she is beholden to them, her dead, her ghosts, her numbered souls. Stuck between invented life and real death, a no-man's land of water and wood and dusty city. She dreads the news but scours it for further numbers to be added to her book. She looks up points of information: life in Baghdad, life in Syria, life in Somalia. She looks up whether women have businesses there, whether houses have glass in the windows. How does an ordinary man live in Northern Pakistan? The first results for that question give information on drone strikes. So her guess is an ordinary man in Northern Pakistan lives at least some of the time in fear. It tells her too that his life is of interest only in certain narrow, elliptical ways that relate to her own.

How much does the structure of life inform the person? A frightened man is a frightened man in any corner of the world. A disappointed woman, a shy child, a beautiful youth. A hungry soul, a beaten wretch, a pompous fool – they live in every corner. A loving heart, a soothing hand, a graceful arm. An aching back, thinning hair, a generous smile, the beauty of a child's profile. These things are not changed by whether church is on Sunday or prayers are on Friday or if God has no claim on any day of the week. It makes no difference if houses are wooden or built of stone, if skies are cloudy or the ground too hot for bare feet. These things would exist if the body were clothed in floor-length gowns or denim shorts. These things existed in the times of powdered wigs and of mammoth hides. They will exist forever. We and the dead are the same, she thinks. She would know them. She does know them.

But Anna also knows that she knows nothing. She doesn't know anyone who has even been to a city such as Mogadishu. If she has met anyone from there she did not ask them what it was like, more interested in what they are like here, in her context, more interested in that which was before her own eyes, contributing to her own world. She doesn't know if the men in Iraq wear cord trousers, or if all the women wear scarves, if the children play roaming on their own or stay close to home. She doesn't know if the food is shared at one table or eaten hurriedly between work and other duties, or, like here, a mixture of all those things. How different would the fundamental acts of living have to be to make the lives of others unrecognisable to her? We all eat. How different a way of eating does it need to be to make it a different thing? We live in families or alone across the whole world. How is life for women like her in Aleppo? How does a single woman like her, sometimes sharp and sour, live in Homs? Even without the rigours of war to contend with, she doesn't know for sure whether she would be herself in other places. She may not live alone in a big house, but there is still room to rattle in a small one. She would perhaps love the languid stretch of a range of brown, shrubby hills as much as she loves the ancient curve of chalk. She might love a dense jungle crept through with furtive paths like she loves the spacious tank of a beech wood. How much of love, then, is habit?

She wonders what the legions risking their lives in rickety boats and suffocating lorries think about home and habit. She wonders what they, or the woman from Baghdad, would make of Anna's home, her bored prosperity and secret hate. This well-appointed country house with its spic and span furniture, its stuffy heating and comfortable abundance meant for one sole inhabitant. The quiet woods that Anna herself has populated with ghosts, where she creeps in fear of elusive, loping wolves. How would it compare to the havoc-worn city of their home? A city rudely disjointed by checkpoints and acts of destruction. The wolves and the witches still roam, though in hordes; they roam in town squares, in car parks, in market places. No need to go down to the woods today.

Three people were killed this morning at a road checkpoint. Civilians. Twelve killed in a bus crash. Anna wonders how it came to be them. What chose that awful fate, what accident, what design? When the woman from the Baghdad garden died, when any of them died, the bomb was there to cause as much death as possible. It was designed to kill passers-by, shoppers, people going to work or strolling for pleasure. It was a deliberate act causing death by accident. If the woman had spent five minutes longer than she did before leaving for the marketplace, perhaps in her garden, the accident of it being her might not have happened. Anna pictures the scene: the house is empty; her children and husband are busy with their days. She has cleared her house a little, enjoyed a moment of quiet in a recently busy kitchen. She gets ready to go, her bag and purse waiting on the table, scarf hanging on the back of a chair. While she is running through what she needs to buy, she gazes out of the window. She tuts as she sees a plant that irritates her with petty regularity, its weedy efforts an annoyance, its ungainly shape, the way that even in its feebleness it interferes with a prettier neighbour. It irritates too that she has been noticing it for weeks and has not done anything about it. She decides to go and pull it out now, instead of being annoyed by it again later. She goes outside, picks up a small trowel kept on the outside kitchen windowsill, digs enough to disturb the roots, then easily pulls the plant out of the light soil. She looks at the new gap with satisfaction, thinking about what might grow well, something compact and pretty, in its place. Then she washes and dries her hands, picks up her jacket and scarf and goes to the market as planned. And is frightened, because she can't shop; there has been a bomb and several people have died.

The man who was buying flowers, for his beloved wife, for a beloved new grandchild. He didn't stop to talk to his old friend from the bag stall because when he passed his friend was busy behind the wall of bags hanging at the back of the stall, trying to find some stock he wanted to put on display, a buried box of green tartan and patent black bags, a gold clasp that could be Chanel. So the man went straight past to the bookshop, picked up the book he had ordered and returned home to his wife, smiling behind the flowers he bought to celebrate their joy. Later he would hear of the deaths, and worry for his friend working in the market.

The old man walking with his grandson. He lost his spectacles as they were about to leave and their walk to the boy's house, back to his dimpled, smiling mother, was delayed long enough to miss being in that horrid circle, delayed even longer because they were caught up in the frightening chaos of the aftermath. The mother stops smiling when she hears of their walk. That evening the boy and his two brothers are clutched in a tight embrace by their father, tears hidden in their sleek heads; they are confused by his burst of emotion. The old man spends the night with his daughter and grandchildren, suddenly immeasurably frailer, too upset to return home.

All of these accidents were possible.

When she walks through the woods, along familiar paths, she is swirling amongst the imagined dead. Every time she walks in these woods she sees them standing, confused and slowed as if all is under-water, clear up to the heavens. What can she do for them? There seems to be nothing. She can barely do for herself, after all. She holds onto them, makes an alliance. She has brought them into her world and must have some obligation towards them. Perhaps she is to tell what she sees, stop the wedding guest, interrupt the stranger, bring the dead before them. Do you hear me? Do you see these dead, these unhappy legions, these lost beloveds? No? Then let me tell you of them.

Later, in her kitchen, rage strikes and she breaks a mug, thrown hard against the wall. That fucker, how dare he be here, barely even looking older, still with that stupid blond fringe? Still with his shabby, easy charm, no doubt. Still, she bets, with that stupid, glib swagger some pretty men have. Not beautiful, but pretty enough to feel a little easy power in the world. Not handsome. He used that charm so heavy-handedly that she didn't even like him at his most likeable. He auditioned for them all, convinced he was going to get the part. All undimmed, his stupid light. Undimmed and uncontaminated by the darkness that he wrought. His aim was small; he wanted small harm, small but brutal harm. Yet he caused a vast circle of destruction. That man, that feeble coward with his floppy blond hair and his easy charm and his politics degree and his pretentious books and his fucking good manners. You would have thought she'd be done with being haunted by such a nothing, such a pretty-boy wastrel as him. You would have thought she might have wrung that haunting dry.

But she amplified it, added her own destruction, battered herself again and again. The storm she made nearly destroyed her, yet he was untouched. Not a bruise. She sees, with glorious spite, a bruise billowing across his face. It could be true; she could make it true. She clings to that.

It is not easy, finding these memories of the love that started my decline. Not just because of the betrayal of it, but because I cringe to think of how I was at that time. Bold as brass I was, abandoned; impervious to any sense of danger. Love is like that. I was unaware of the need to protect myself. I no more considered his harming me than I considered myself harming him. Even as mistrust, then spite, crept into our vocabulary, violence seemed as unlikely as hate. Love was a miasma that prevented understanding, clouded truth. For those first months of summer, happiness and good fortune and love all combined. Alloys in a chain of strength and durability, linking me to all I thought I could want.

We did argue – how could we not? Love is like that too. I learned he could be jealous, and sometimes that jealousy became mistrust. But love explained that. He loved me so much he was afraid to lose me. What could be more logical than that, when he could later chide himself and exalt me once more as blameless? But piece by piece, in those arguments and insecurities, the story changed; there was always something to prove. Moving to London to study became a thing I was doing to him, not for me. He talked about travelling in the new year, saving up some money and taking off. He talked about me moving in with him. He talked, in short, about me giving up my dreams and joining him in his. There's another thread that makes my story. I gather it in. I wind the threads together.

He was so full of possibilities, an infinite variety of possibilities; day by day they changed. He made the shapes of them, spoke them. I thought his carelessness was bravery. But it was avoidance of the troublesome need to do as well as to say. He seemed so confident that I came to see my own care-filled progress as weakly predictable and boringly anxious. In the light of Ryan's grand pronouncements, my wish to create bridges from steel and cement became a dull plod to safety, an easy option. He said I was not adventurous like him, that I wanted an ordinary life. In that casual, self-serving criticism, I lost sight of the path that led into my dream. It had been the best adventure I could imagine – to defy gravity, to know how to create magnificent grace in defiance of crude materials. He made it seem dowdy, predictable.

He persuaded me into a new shape. He said in so many words that I didn't need me. I had we. We could do anything together; it didn't matter what. Planning was for the unlucky, the ones who didn't have our freedom, our potential. I put my plans aside, still cherished but seen only at the edge of my eye. Here I see so much, though I have no more eyes than I have fingers. Oh, how I would love my body, a repository for all this new knowing. A place to hold it, to unravel, to make sense of what I grasp at. Wrapped in gravity's cloak, to look down at my hands and feet and remember in a continuous line. I could write the words down then, pin them one at a time onto paper. There they are, I'd say, those words that tell my story. Being alive, it is so neat.

But it is coming back to me. Piece by piece I see how it happened. I recall now my rapt, upturned face, unwelcome enough but such a part of my story that I won't turn away. The face of love, spilling first its own light. But soon, lit only from without. Soon enough, lit not at all.

My eyes were fatally primed to see in him a glorious spectrum, a nimbus, a halo. So bright a light shone before me that older flames were consumed and became invisible. But that was carefully crafted by him. By design, not fate. I was dimmed. Slowly, a new plan emerged. A 'we' plan. Slowly, almost without me noticing. A plan not for me but for us. London, learning, it's just, do you really? Can't we, instead? If you loved me as much as I love you. Of course, of course I do! Disgust, almost, is what I find with that remembering. I don't want to dwell. But so strong, in this place of such primitive strength is the telling wish, the story–finding wish. Perhaps my story trails behind, around me, and I remake myself by pulling it in. Perhaps I find my mass, my surfaces, as I reel in the tumbled, tangled skeins, bundle them up into me. Ravel a new self. Knit myself up from threads of remembering.

Chapter 9

The flight is busy and cramped, but Anna is content. Sitting in a window seat, she takes pleasure in watching wintery England recede. She has always enjoyed flying and travelling on her own. She stares restfully out of the oval window, the pattern of fields below becoming smaller and more intricate as the plane rises into the cold blue sky. She feels anxiety recede too, feels it reduce, become granular, like the fields below. A background pattern rather than a set of obstacles. She is finally elevated enough not to be overwhelmed.

But like the fields of England, her anxieties are not removed, they are deferred for another time. They are still waiting for her. During the short flight, she relaxes, allows herself the feeling that she has temporarily escaped. Ryan will not be seen, Michael has been mollified, Christmas will be ignored. She may this year evade the stealthy slide show of nineteen Christmases with her girl, tricked into life by every glint of decorations, every gaudy gift, every Christmas carol. Pictures she doesn't want to see projected suddenly onto a special-occasion damask tablecloth or reflected in a shiny bauble. Pictures that mean Christmas is a time of choking back and endurance. Surely these pictures will be at least muted, sun-bleached in the heat of an unfamiliar place. She stares restfully into the cold blue of the sky as the plane heads south.

On arrival at Tenerife airport, the sky is no longer cold; the sun burns high. She is glad she chose a destination that so quickly marked its difference to home. The airport is busy with happy and slightly frayed travellers, dark, warm clothes draped over suitcases, mostly pale skins glowing vulnerably in the warmth. It is not overwhelmingly hot, but the contrast magnifies the heat. She collects her case and takes a taxi to the hotel.

Her room is on the first floor. It has two neatly prim single beds, a small dressing table or desk, windows with both shutters and gauzy curtains, and a balcony overlooking a wide sweep of bay. The sea is a little choppy, the expanse of dark turquoise dotted with curls of sail and kite in lurid, factory colours. Anna opens the balcony doors and lies on the bed. Little of the day remains. She reads, dozes a little, eats from the room service menu, then reads some more until she falls asleep.

Even at the beginning, during those happy times, I was subtly moulding myself, and he was even more subtly moulding me. It seemed easy to wait for the future I had imagined, easy to let him persuade me that after all there was no rush. He played, I see now (and did, in some secret, well-hidden eye, see then) with a swagger to his hand. I knew even then that there was an element of lavish bluff to disguise the value of the cards he held, but I chose to believe him. I chose to invest him with the careless mastery he claimed was his. The bluff, the buff and shine of the thinnest foils of gold.

As the months passed, I saw that the kind of waiting Ryan favoured was the lifetime variety. He didn't want me to leave him. To better him. To be successful. To fly. In short, he didn't want me to fulfil my own dreams; he wanted me to augment his own. It took a long time to understand this. Who can accept immediately, whilst tightly held within its embrace, that love may contain such severe reprisals? Secretly then and clearly now, I have learned to stop seeing Ryan's actions towards me as love and recognise them instead as husbandry. For to understand him fully, I was a beast, of greatest value when broken entirely into the obedient servitude of a passive dairy cow or farrowing sow.

From this distant view, I can see the details that I wish now had been more apparent, less ignored at the time. I had feelings I did not wish to acknowledge, an unwelcome draught at my back. Even then they caused a shiver of something I would have called alarm if I had been able to slander my love with such harsh terms. The colour changed from gentle love to bitter accusation by one chromatic drop of pigment a day, a seamless blend that, being unable to track, I also could not master. It is only now that I fully see the deliberate smoothness, the entrapping, determined guile of that progression. He taught me how to mollify him. He taught me how to undermine my own understanding of events. He taught me how to say to myself 'it's because he loves me'.

So, if he played his hand with an empty bluff, I played mine with my own sleight. Ryan would have been gratified if only he could have seen how close our aims were. I too wanted to elevate him. Our future together had come to exclude my long-cherished dreams of grand buildings. So, like the bridges I had dreamed of, I wanted to see the strength and grace in the base material. I wanted him to be as grand as my dreams had been. Perhaps he led me to the table, perhaps love seduced me into taking the first bite, but once seated, I heartily ate of my own accord.

Young love is mightily powerful. Self-fuelling, its biggest sustenance is its own wonderful grandeur. It is often destined, if a new, more enduring source of energy cannot be found, to burn out. But in that glorious moment of the stars aligning, gilded by the combined light of all those billion stars, such a prospect is too ghastly to contemplate. We may find precious parts of ourselves willingly sacrificed as fuel to keep the fire burning.

Those stars, I have a different view of their light and their power now. Their might is scalding without the softening protection of the sky. Still, I hope one arc, one mighty ellipse, will fire me into the heart of one of them, ending this vagabond journey. But let it not be just yet.

I deferred the start of university for a year and moved into the flat in Oxford with Ryan. It seemed a small step. Just a step through a doorway, almost. But one step can be as great a distance as any.

Dad drove me over one evening, several boxes of books on the back seat of the car, a case with a few important objects and most of my clothes, spilling over into laundry bags. I took a small desk from my room to put in the corner of the living room. A mirror, a bag of shoes, some bright new kitchen things that Mum had bought for me. When we got there, Ryan was happy, nervous in his willingness to get it right. He had put flowers in a glass vase on the table. It was welcoming and orderly. There was music playing quietly. He had emptied more than half the drawers for my things. He'd bought a laundry basket because I had jokingly complained about his smelly socks lying on the bedroom floor like dead rats. There was a new light next to the bed so I could read before sleeping. Dad was cheerful and helpful, offering to go back for some things I had forgotten, but when he left – leaving us to it, as he heartily said – he and I were both sad.

After the brief sadness of goodbye, that was a very happy evening for

Ryan and me. And so was the next one. I spent my days as I had done for much of that summer, lazily waiting, strolling the city, being at our new home when Ryan arrived back from work.

Chapter 10

She wakes feeling groggy, a heavy weariness, a hangover from the tension of the last weeks. A hangover that, in being built over a number of weeks, is likely to take more than a morning to dispel. Now, in the refreshing newness of her surroundings, Anna feels even more grimy than she did in the rumpled anxiety of home.

Empty out her head, the baggy old bag. Tip it all out into a handy bin, a turquoise plastic basket under the hotel room desk. Let it overflow. Kick it into a neat pile and go out until it has been taken away by the nice young woman who cleans the rooms. Yesterday, Anna slept. Today, her second day here, she starts early. She wants to run along the beach, let the sea wind blow her clean. Shake her head like a galloping horse, shake out staleness and confusion as epic music soars, thrilling at her freedom. Speed along the beach with the top down, throwing out the rubbish, a litter lout in a fast car. Instead, she walks. She walks down paths, along roads, round the curves of the bay, onto the uncivilised part of the shore. For the odd second, the wind lets her feel as if she is running, that its movement is actually her own.

She has got to the edge of the small town, away from the beach. She walks past low buildings along a new-looking road that is empty except for the occasional passing car or airport taxi. There are not many trees, as the town thins out not much shelter at all. The edge of town has an unresolved quality, petering out rather than ending at a clear boundary. There are odd piles of building material, destroyed buildings, unfinished buildings, a trailing-off of endeavour, an uncertainty. Near the road, advertising hoardings stand sentinel on the hill, clocking the visitors in and out and reminding them to spend some money while they are here. Signs for restaurants, resorts and night-time entertainments. After about half a mile and with the town now gone, she walks away from the pavement-less road, sits to rest on a concrete block with rusted metal tendons poking out from one end. Her head aches a little; her feet hurt. She rests forwards, leaning on her bent knees, gazing across the uninhabited land, with a three-quarters view of a gaudy billboard for a supermarket, a smiling woman, her mouth big enough to eat Anna whole. Perhaps not a nutritious meal. She feels empty. She is full of garbage, yet empty. A small interior voice asks, 'What is at the core of me?' She is a collection of feelings and strategies so habitual, so well worn, that she does not know if there is anything authentic left underneath. She doesn't know what she is. She is not even a grieving mother any more, the last role she fulfilled with any certainty, so long ago that the meaning is petrified within her somewhere. She is built on the fossil bones of her grief and the carved-out, meagre understanding of a state she didn't choose and never mastered. An empty structure built around that grieving mother. Is she still in there? Is she still her? She feels exposed, if only under her own gaze. The sun warms her, the wind strokes. There is a self that feels these sensations, these gentle strokes and rays, but where has she really gone? She recognises that for many years, her only certainty has been that she does not want to disrupt the fragile architecture she has built with those fossil bones.

She built a refuge and populated it with ghosts, a throng to fill the empty halls and grim hollows. A sea of souls, a procession, an endless crowd of many to hide the one. So many that she is bound relentlessly in her duty of care for them. She wants only that which will strengthen the building. She wants only to augment her own binding.

Yet so ineffectual has it been that one glimpse of Ryan threw her off the safe plane of the world. Michael's desire to celebrate what would have been her daughter's thirtieth birthday as well as the anniversary of her death has sent her running in fear. Nothing is protected, yet huge effort is exerted to keep everything static, held tight, held just as it now is. She realises too that she has always known this, and has allowed herself to stay blind to it. Like walking around for years with a china teacup balanced on her head in the wildly exotic belief that it will protect her from harm. Carrying it at great cost, incorporating all the necessary compromises of her behaviour to stop it from falling, and refusing to weaken the charm by asking herself whether she actually needs to keep it there. Faith is all with magic. She will not or has not tested the reason for this awkward situation; instead she has remorselessly served it. And whilst she has skirted around this knowledge for years, caught the absurdity in her corner eye, as it cramps her form, her movement, limits her action, she has never openly admitted to herself how bloody ineffectual a strategy it is. She is angry, thinking of all that wasted stupid effort. To do something so deliberately without ever noticing whether it works or not. To keep it up for so long for fear of rocking an unhappy equilibrium.

On the thin edge of anxiety, unnerved by such self-scrutiny, her gaze flicks around without settling, breath flitting against her sternum, not filling her lungs. She doesn't want to peel back the layers any more. Time for a focus switch – a fast and purposeful walk; the accomplice body willingly supplies unexpected energy for tired legs, willing to aid in retreat. Appreciation of the landscape and a brisk walk. She's not ready to knock over the teacup just yet.

There is beauty in Tenerife's stony land, the arid scree, the spat-out insides of the earth frozen in stone, sliding slowly down to the sea that in turn slides all the way to the Sahara. It would not take much of a curve through that sea, an easy tack, to miss Africa and go from dry heat to frozen Antarctic cold. Equator to sun, pole to sun – so small a difference between the two. It is ninety-three million miles to the sun; this equator-to-pole difference is a tiny fraction of that great distance, only that of Earth's radius, a minuscule percentage marking the possible extremes of the land's temperature. What other extremes exist on a scale we cannot really understand? That which we currently experience as outer limits in reality denoting only an insignificant, tightly angled section in the middle of the spectrum? Good and evil bounded by our human imagination of heaven and hell. Heavy and light, weight and mass have expressions that expand or crush into oblivion, not measurable with our bodily reckoning. The calibrations made in space dwarf our arm-spans and thumbs of measurement. Perhaps it is this intuited, groping recognition of the limited span of our experience that means our stories to explain the inexplicably crazy chance of our being here at all often start with the limitless sky and its perpetrator gods.

The red-brown and tan land stretches away behind her, back to the blue sea. Off the road there is a patchy covering across the pebbly ground, a sparse drift of knee-high shrubs. Small thin clouds, insubstantial like sifted icing sugar, move across the sky, barely enough, when they intersect, to dim the sun's light. She is on a road that tips upward a little, away from the sea. Minutely nearer the sun in height, minutely further in distance. She decides to walk as far as the next curve in the road. The tarmac is smooth and new, an unlikely integrity to the black surface; it looks silky in comparison to the dusty expanse of the landscape. The tar surface bears a language of dashes and stripes in white, a sharp, geometric contrast with the stone and shrub. The whole road could be peeled away from the crumbly surface, taking a thin layer of stone but otherwise without damage. Like Sellotape on an old brick wall. At home, a road would come away like an old scab, leaving a patch of soil or chalk, fresh, moist and raw.

Once she gets to the corner, she keeps going. The road bends further inland to a lunar expanse of dusty stone. The sun has lost its overhead glare, dropping subtly richer colouring onto the undulating rock and shrub. It is late afternoon. She decides to cross further into that field of stone, loosen her connection with the road and town a little further. She turns off the road and heads for the middle of what appears to be nowhere, nothing, no-man's land. Though there must be few places on this small island that could be truly deemed so. There are no fences, no buildings – it appears there are no prohibitions to her walking here. The ground is uneven, and in places the footholds between oddly shaped low shrubs are difficult to find. She would fare better with long giraffe legs, though then the droopy wires of the low telegraph poles would have seemed to be a fence excluding her entry. What animal life might have roamed here before the services of the airport brought the sneaker-wearing sun-seeker? Before liquorice roads and bright hoardings and jet planes? Her imagination populates this shallow, sea-bound slope with machine beasts from a sci-fi film. Perhaps small mammals would inhabit the cooler, greener region on the higher slopes looping out from the hub of the island's central volcano, mingling with lush songbirds cruising the hot and humid air of the northern side. Here, it seems to be a land for insects, rodents and robots.

Progress is deliberate, steady; she has flimsy lace-up shoes and doesn't want to turn an ankle. The ground, though stony and prickly with low plants, is at least flat, and she enjoys looking around her feet as she picks her way, taking in the plants, their subtle shades and patterned shapes. With a higher, wider view there would be an infinitely varying order of plants, a subtle shift of an almost-repeating pattern: circles, ovals and stars in varied combinations, as alike as snowflakes but never exactly the same. A pattern by familiarity of impression rather than by direct repetition.

Just ahead, there is the curve of a dirt track heading to the tarmac road she had recently left. She walks through a relatively clear area, stopping at a small patch of low grass that doesn't look too scratchy. She sits down on the ground, glad once more to rest her legs, thinks fleetingly of scorpions as she pulls her feet onto her spread-out jacket. The energy bought at the expense of her uncomfortable insights some way back on the road is ebbing, and the sun feels relentless. She angles her hat to keep the late-afternoon sun from her eyes and looks across to the sea. Before she left this morning, she checked the news via the Wi-Fi in her room. A small scandal in London – someone claims that another lied, a heat that will die quickly unless more fuel can be added. Mock outrage is a good fire-starter but often does not have enough fuel for a witch-burning, particularly if the witch happens to be a powerful man of government. The news companies will move on, but for now the feeds are crammed with this little story, stretching it over pages, through video links, via comment pieces. Meanwhile, four or five pages along, in twenty lines of bald prose, six people have been killed by a roadside bomb. Where? Elsewhere. A different road. She starts to acknowledge them, staring across the dirt track to the road beyond. The view is not spectacular, but it is beautiful. She can see the people beginning to appear, like ghost images on an old photographic plate. Not wanting to forget them, she digs out a notebook and pen from her bag and starts to write on the small, thin pages. She makes notes, scratches quick words that describe them. She does not give them names. A concession to their unreal reality. She writes and scribbles, looking ahead, seeing them quiet and slow, called into being to experience the moments after death, standing on the dirt track etched on the remains of the volcano, as curious and uncertain as the others were in the soft cold hush of the beech wood. Quickly and easily, she sees them all, six new lost standing in the aspic of confusion, trying to make sense of their own deaths. When finished, she gets up stiffly and turns back to the town, stopping at the supermarket for bread and large tomatoes, olive oil and black pepper, olives, paper hankies and a bottle of water. They bump against her leg in a thin plastic bag as she walks through the welcome shade of quiet streets back to her hotel.

Back in her room she showers and eats, a tasty and simple meal. She sits at the desk and, looking at her scratchy notes, begins to write them all down in her purple-covered book. As evening settles, she writes, stopping occasionally for more tomato and more bread, more water. Stopping to gaze across the small balcony to the sea, refreshing her mind's eye with a wash of steadily darkening blue sky.

23 December

She is striking, with a face that is powerful rather than beautiful. Her features are strong and dark, a sheen of expensive face cream smoothed over rugged bone structure. She is quick to see the worst in people but has depths of compassion that spring up occasionally, lava-like, hot, undeniable and impulsive. She has been responsible for unexpected acts of great kindness. She is never able to accept gratitude and avoids the people she has helped ever after.

He carries a large cotton bag over his shoulder, filled with notebooks, stones, scraps of paper that momentarily seemed to be poignant ephemera or important clues. He is visiting, part of a longer journey. He feels at home in this human hubbub of trading and tattling. In his bag, he has a picture postcard, unwritten, stamped. Ready to fill with cramped writing and expansive love for his sister.

Thirteen years old, whip-thin and pretty, springy dark hair assembled into order with bright clips. She has an older brother, chased home on the tail end of some undisclosed hangdog failure. She is cross with his sullen presence, annoyed by the heavy, unsaid tide held at bay by her parents' sour silence. She tries to cheer her brother, tries not to nag or question him, tries not to spill the words dammed behind her mother's tightly fixed mouth.

An old man, shaped like the walking stick he uses or the pipe he occasionally smokes. Tall and thin, bent over from the shoulders and neck. He walks with small steps, barely lifting his large brown shoes. His hands are large, wreathed with garlands of age. The one not holding the stick flutters gently at his side as if tenderly encouraging the rest of him to keep going, keep going.

A man in his twenties, he has a vividly animated face but speaks little. He lives alone, since his mother died, in a dowdy two-room apartment with newspaper taped over the windows. He keeps one of his mother's old jumpers in his pillowcase and one of her geranium lipsticks (there were only ever three) in his trouser pocket. Sometimes he lies on the woven rug and imagines a procession of invented, wiry creatures that compel and frighten him in equal measure, marching in multi-legged time along a crack in the ceiling.

A nineteen-year-old girl, prone to dreaminess yet possessing quiet determination. A girl whose long arms and legs move with grace and deliberation, a slowness as if underwater. A girl who wanted to build bridges and viaducts.

She finishes abruptly, once again pulling away from a description that is too haunting, too familiar, and turns to the open doors that lead out to the balcony. The sky holds only a faint trace of blue; it is nearly black. The light from the mighty sun left behind, dropped around the corner by the industrious, busybody little Earth. She is tired, but exalted almost, glad to have caught the six people, secured them to the page. Now she will not forget them.

She wants to stretch legs that are tired and cramped from sitting sideways at an uncomfortable piece of furniture, halfway between desk and dressing table. She changes a loose gown for light trousers and a top, puts on a silver necklace set with a resin circle, a hard colour to name – greenish, light, pearl, yellow, all translucently combined. A sour moon set on a thin, curved shoulder-blade of silver. She takes the chains that hold it, locks the fiddly clasp behind her neck. She runs a hand through her hair. She has filled time well, it turns out, and she is pleased with herself for a change. She picks up her room key and bag and goes out to find late food and a glass of beer in one of the bright cafes that populate the plaza.

It is a pleasure to be out in the mild evening. The breeze strokes softly, a wisp of sun-warm remaining on its fingertips. A sense of freedom in walking out of the door without a plan. Occasionally, at home, usually with visiting friends, she ventures out on foot to the local pub, once convivial, good for beer and listless wine, now selling fancy dishes served inexplicably on squares of slate. The cutlery lands against it with a teeth-jarring jolt; portions are kept tiny so they don't fall off the flat edges. They do go and eat there sometimes, but she misses the old pub. She reminds herself that tomorrow she will call England to reassure and wish well.

There is enough holiday trade for the square to be busy still, cafe tables occupied, candles flickering gently inside bars and cafes, interiors glowing invitingly. Some, surprisingly, have Christmas trees or other decorations that seem to belong in more northerly cold. She smells a summer smell, at odds with the Christmas twinkle, enticing garlic on a passing plate of seafood, and decides to stop at the small bar from which the plate emerged, carried by a casually dressed waiter to a table of smoking diners who are sitting outside. Inside, the tables are small, and there are a few empty. She sits down at one of them with her back to the wall, looks around the half-full bar, waits to catch the attention of one of the good-looking young men that wait at table. She guesses they might be some of the daytime kitesurfers sheering thrillingly across the bay or lugging things onto the beach, legs in sealskin wetsuits, the upper half brown and bare, the suit hanging empty around the waist. The kinds of young men and women that have necklaces of twine and leather, tied permanently, a charm, a spell set at the gentle waves of collarbone, until seawater and sunlight wear the material to weakness and the charm drops, perhaps to be found by another beautiful creature. Perhaps swallowed by a fish. She feels a fondness for the possibilities of youth. A time when summer is made longer, not just wished longer; summer as the reason for living. Though by the calendar it is still winter, intentions speak of a summer mood. She smiles at the waiter, orders a beer and a plate of garlic prawns; she is hungry, thirsty, glad to refuel.

She catches sight of a blond head, a long fringe, and flinches as she is reminded of Ryan. Ugly feelings stir, wriggle malevolently, even at this slight acknowledgement. She grits her teeth, bites down before the feelings can either escape or be swallowed, she is not certain which. Unprepared to spoil the gentle calm of the evening, she rejects these thoughts, looks instead at the other diners, mostly couples or small groups. The place is not busy. There is a man sitting on his own at the bar, the seasoned look of a regular, though he doesn't look local. He is chatting amicably with the man working behind the bar, who cleans and serves as they talk. The customer wears old jeans, a T-shirt and a faded open shirt. He looks roughened by sea and sun. For the waiters, the young men and women of the beach, wind and sun smooths and burnishes; when one gets to our age, thinks Anna, the age of the man at the bar perhaps, the effect is to roughen, as if the sand too has begun to work on the form. His hair is scruffy, rather long. He has a handsome profile, grey stubble. His right arm ends without a hand, about four inches below the elbow. He looks interesting, has a rangy grace in his large frame. He and the barman are smiling and laughing.

Her beer arrives. It is cold and tasty. The prawns come in a heavy clay dish, orange oil still sizzling enticingly. A basket of bread, thick, round white cuts on a red paper napkin, a neat pat of butter in its folded square of blue-and-silver foil paper. The prawns are delicious. The bread soaks up the chilli and garlic oil when the prawns are finished. When she is finished eating, she gets out her notebook, reads again the six from today. She thinks of the traveller with the cotton bag. He would stop in a place like this, would roll into a town with a beach like this, with his tan, his crumpled clothes; he too would have a charm, a stone or a shell on a leather cord round his neck, several round his wrist too. He would probably strike up a conversation with the men at the bar, three crossed paths meeting at this small turnpike, sharing a beer in a little bar in Tenerife. They would talk of where they came from, speculate about where they may be going next. She wonders if the man in the faded shirt is an unexpected resident, someone who arrived, then, without meaning to stay, never left. Perhaps he met a woman who did not want to leave. Perhaps he is Spanish, born here after all, though he looks northern European somehow. Perhaps he owns the bar, stepping in to keep an eye, enjoy the upside of his business. Or perhaps he is on holiday, investing in the experience to the full, an outgoing man who finds it easy to meet new people, has a gift for connecting with them as if they are old friends.

Holidays are like fairground mirrors, backed with cunning silver that lets us see ourselves in a new light, a new place, a role that changes us, a geography that defines new intentions. That, perhaps, is their greatest value. She pictures a life that would make her a regular visitor for garlic prawns and a familiar face, a smile and wave, a chat with the young men and women lucky enough to score a job that keeps them in rent and bread and time on a surfboard in the wind. Or she might make longer-term connections, friendships even, with locals who stay to make their living from the healthy flow of sun-hungry Europeans. She would speak Spanish, sit in the shade, write portraits of all who die. As Charon gets his coin, she would watch and write. Then, for consolation, come here for a beer, or a stemless glass of rough red wine, chat to friends whose lives pass in mysterious ways. She is alone and in company. She is new, unchained from the boulder of her past. She will never see that hated man outside a department store, or anywhere else, again. She catches the waiter's eye and orders another beer.

The next hour passes in easy thought, in observing the workings of this small part of the world – as laid out, at least, for the curious visitor – and making space in it for future her. The great game of travel, the pictures we conjure worth as much as the ones we bring home on our cameras or send to friends' screens. She drinks her second beer then heads back to the hotel, walking briefly down to the small waves that spill onto the wet sand as the tide recedes. She is bound for a safe bed, to wake up on Christmas Eve, to write or walk, to explore safely. She wonders: if she were to make herself the centre of a star, how many points it would have, if each tip were a town where that certainty is not possible? More destinations than are served by all the planes that leave from the nearby airport. She reminds herself that she is after all a lucky woman.

Chapter 11

Even now, it is hard to track the changes that turned a happy start into such misery. I cooked meals in the evenings, read books, played at a kind of romantic idleness that could never be sustained. A pitter–patter life. However much it gratified Ryan in a manner that, at that time, fed my own happiness too, perhaps it was not a state that would have lasted, even without the darker turn the tale would take. I started to get bored; we started to get short of money. I got a job. It was boring. I drifted through a work day. Boredom and tiredness took the shine off cooking elaborate evening meals. Boredom thins the joy of a relationship like tepid water weakens a drink. Maybe it was the onset of boredom that caused such anxiety in Ryan that he feared the way things were changing. Maybe he really did believe I secretly admired the nice but unremarkable Josh, who worked with me and whom we met one evening by chance in town. Maybe he did believe I spent all hours regretting not going to London without him. I did spend minutes, guilty minutes, wondering what I would be doing if I were not wearing my brown uniform dress, tidying the magazine rack, hoping that the evening would be a happy one. But I had not yet come to regret my choice. Love was all. Love was not to be betrayed by regret. Love had not failed me yet.

But tension became the mark of that love. It was difficult, I thought, to make things work. It was difficult, I thought, for Ryan to be trusting and happy, because, by his own defining, he loved me so much he was afraid he would lose me. I wished I could find a way to make him see that he needn't fear that. I tried. I shrank and moulded, I mollified and flattered his insecurity. I bent and bowed under it. Look! Look at my contortions and take them for proof. I stopped talking about university as a possibility at any time in the future. I stopped talking about people at work. I did go home and see Mum and Dad, but became cautious about expressing too much of a desire to do even that.

Other people were dropping away, firstly because other people caused bad moods that implicitly demanded I question my need for others in my life. After a while, he made those demands explicit. Why did I need anyone else?

Didn't I love him enough to be fulfilled? The one exception was going as a couple to visit our families. For some months, the only people I had meaningful interactions with were Ryan's and my parents. Secretly, after a few months, I attended to the admin necessary to starting my university course once the year had elapsed, should I decide to go, but I kept it to myself, utterly fearful of broaching the subject but unable to let it disappear for good.

Aside from this one nervy subterfuge, I built a fence around my own activities, delineated my boundaries to reveal myself to him as knowable, quantifiable. I extend this far; you can see all of me. Is that not something you can trust? But it wasn't enough. Ryan began to draw those fences ever further in, to reduce the scale of me. He became slowly more demanding and more angry. But, you must understand, even though I find it hard myself to understand, this was still sweetened by love. Between bouts of angry misunderstanding he rebuilt the beautiful tent-palace of our love, brought me back to a time when the little flat was a precious refuge, a quiet hub of passion amongst the discord of our dulling daily lives.

It helped me believe that once Ryan could understand he need have no fear, we would return to an open and joyful existence. Of course, I see now that would never happen. Ryan didn't want reassurance. He wanted ownership, control. He didn't want me elevated by his love but reduced to something he could hold in his pocket, a shape worn down inexorably to fit, smothered in his hand.

I could fit inside his ribs now, through the holes in his shoes. I could thread through his marrow and let it taste the darkness that awaits. I could make him shudder with the sudden intrusion of my presence. I could, I am sure, if I knew how to command myself.

Next morning Anna goes down to the breakfast room, taking a book. The day is overcast, but the beach is still bright with activity. Glad to be alone, she enjoys the visual company of the other diners – the rangy youths on the beach, the swift and hushed solicitations of waiters and waitresses who revert to ebullient clatter once back through the swing doors to the busy kitchen. There is a couple at another table, a pair of solitary diners, held in mutual silence, in a smaller space than that which she is allowed to occupy, being truly alone. They have no space for a book. Their yawning silence overspills by a lifetime the precise boundaries long settled inside the confined space of coupledom. There are other pairs who seem to enjoy each other. A family who thread the airspace of their table with constant incursions – hands and arms steal and tend and share with each other, young children have faces wiped, glasses held, parents are fed morsels of croissant or unwanted crust by little, clutching hands. She enjoys their gentle drama as she consumes breakfast at a leisurely pace, reading, drinking coffee slowly until it is cold, spinning out the sips, dabbing crumbs one at a time from the plate.

She makes her way back to her room. It is time to call home. She will text Michael too, to avoid him calling her later. She calls Sophie, who is wrapping presents. Anna tells her about her walk, the beach, about the hotel. She still doesn't talk about the colossal, ugly thing, the enormous presence, the return of Ryan. Shortly before Anna left for Tenerife, Sophie had, with her gentle care, let Anna know that she had heard Ryan was back. But Sophie knew her friend well and let the words brush past them. Anna said enough to confirm that she knew already, and Sophie said if Anna needed to talk about Ryan she should, she could.

She might well need to talk about him. But she doesn't. She can't. Not yet. She trusts Sophie to understand her reticence, but there have been weeks of dread that other, less careful, people would bring up the news, angle for the illicit, vicarious thrill of her feelings. Having seen so few people, she thankfully avoided such a conversation. That awful encounter has remained horribly private, intimate. It is wrapped round Anna, thin threads tied around her waist, around each thigh above her knee, around her arms, around her thumbs and her toes. There it is, difficult to forget, but secret, discreet. Sophie talks over the tug of the thread, tells her about some disaster involving the turkey and a necessary trip to the other side of town to an unknown butcher. Doubtless Christmas dinner would've involved the director's cut of this story from Brian; indeed, it is possible it will crop up further in the future. She braces herself impatiently in advance. She tells Sophie that she is happy, enjoying her time away. They promise they will talk again soon. Her dear friend – Anna pictures her with an exuberant pile of paper and bags of slightly odd gifts that accumulate as during the weeks leading up to Christmas she adds extras and finds things she likes better. She has a gentle face, eyebrows that express concern however serene her mood. She is one of the nicest people Anna knows.

Next Anna calls Tony and Simon, leaves a message on their answerphone. She gets a text from Tony a few minutes later with the message 'Sounds great. Aunty L on the way, can we swap?' She had forgotten that Simon's Aunt Laura would also have been a Christmas guest, and once more is glad she is out of the way. She likes Laura, but she is a sour and difficult woman. Tony and Simon are afflicted with a need to challenge her moodiness, resulting in constant attempts to make her happy. Entrenched, lopsided buffoonery ensues, with Laura retreating further and becoming harder to please, forcing them into ever-greater clowning servility. It is the one time Simon ditches his arch hauteur. It is exhausting. She wonders briefly if she is an unsuspecting understudy for the future role of Aunt Laura. Perhaps she is already there, an apprentice, a milkier version.

She showers and lies on the bed in the hotel towels, generous in both size and thickness. The wind blows; the taut curl of a kite pulls a surfer over a wave, into the air briefly and back onto the slopes of the sea. The sun warms the air from behind the cover of cloud. It's Christmas Eve. A sigh forms, expanding outwards through her skin. In that stillness, a distant cloud advances, the rumble of unwelcome thought growls nearer. With it, anger rises. She gets up, paces a little round the beds, looks from the balcony over the sea. She pulls the towel off her head angrily. She shakes it out, but it drops, falls, reshaping and opening, to the edge of the sea below. Waves push and pull slowly. It furls and stretches in the water, catching now and then on the wet sand. A secret wish embellishes what she sees, and the black satisfaction of a drowned man flits furtively through Anna's thoughts.

She dresses hastily and leaves, snatching up her bag, her purple book and a green fountain pen she bought passing time in the airport. She walks back along the beach, glimpses the white of the towel, looking fat and heavy in the small tug of the waves. She leaves it, enjoying the spite of profligacy, allowing an expensive towel to turn into waste. More miles of thread. The towel, with no purpose, goes softly nowhere in the shallows; the surfers, taut with purpose, zigzag nowhere in the bay.

The cafe from last night is open. She sits facing towards the sea at one of the tables outside. Fortified with a coffee, in the double shade of cloud and umbrella, with an empty page before her, she chews the end of the green pen. It is smooth, with a tang to the taste, like spectacles. Her teeth skid satisfyingly off the hard plastic. She drinks her coffee. The small handle is irritating, a round hole inside a squarish stub of clay, too small for her fingers to go through; the thick white china of the shallow cup needs better leverage. But the coffee is good. Staring out to sea, focus drifts away so easily. The sensations of now, let them curtain for a moment the restlessness she feels. The warm air, the gentle breeze, the two colours of sea and sky. The rich taste of coffee, the heavy clay weight of the cup. Let them take up all attention.

She unhooks her gaze from the horizon. Turns back to the tabletop, the page and the pen – helpmeets, decision-making machines. So she hopes. A page is dedicated to rough notes, words, ideas, disordered thoughts, in the hope that in their accidental arrangement, their scuffle on the page will form an answer. The page becomes two, with looping links and twig-piles of scribbled underlines. But order does not arise from the inky melee. She does not know what to do. There is so little path and so much woodland; what paths exist are so rarely used that they lose their footing before she does. She would need a machete to pass.

There is a little of Christmas's ubiquitous cheer in the hotel, but Anna spends the days quietly, restfully. She sometimes seems to elicit curiosity, but nobody troubles her. There is a formality, a reserve, about the place that allows her solitude. She is glad she ended up here. In the mornings she goes for a long swim, along the shore these days rather than out far from the reach of land as she used to when younger, when less concerned with monitoring how much energy she had and when it might desert her. The sea is usually warm and steady, though the winds that attract the kitesurfers can kick up a bit of choppiness in the waves. As she changes into dry clothes back in the hotel room, she likes to look from the balcony down the long beach, to work out how far she swam. This morning was longer than usual, further than the smartly kept beachside buildings that host various tourist activities. As far along as a salmon-pink building she manages to pick out from behind a group of large, spiky-leaved plants. The exercise has been restorative. Walking at home kept Anna fit, but the sea swimming is more demanding, bringing a pleasing ache to her shoulders. She feels the hangover-like residue of stress and care being loosened and slowly flushed out by the quiet passage of time spent on her own and by the exercise, the cold of seawater being dissolved by very long hot showers once back in her room.

Yesterday was warm, the air too calm, too steady, for surfers. After showering, she went out to the same bar for an afternoon coffee and some cake. The place filled quickly, the seasonal party mood drawing people out. She sat alone at her small table until she was asked, first in Spanish, then, as she struggled to respond, in English, if she minded a young couple joining her. As they settled down with a beer each, they chatted with Anna. She learned that they were Karl from Germany and Estela from Spain, and they were there for the kitesurfing, spinning out as many months of all-year summer as they could. She was gratified to hear their stories, glad they showed no interest in her own.

From her balcony, she can see Karl and Estela now, lugging gear onto the beach. They exchange a cheery wave when they spot Anna. She watches as they lay out and clip and unfold and unpack. Then they are flying across the water. Estela's brown-and-blond hair flies out behind her. She uses her weight and balance to counteract the pull of the wind. Anna thought that Karl, being larger and stronger, would seem to have the advantage, but watching them, she feels that Estela looks to be more supremely flying with the wind. Her slight frame does not seem to be a disadvantage and adds a beautiful sense of coop-eration with the natural forces. Their exciting freedom spills around them, and the gentle outer edges are shared with Anna, watching them contentedly from the balcony.

After some time, she goes inside and lies on her single bed, with the windows and balcony door wide open. A fierce blade of sun races in, laying a decisive track across a corner of the room. The wind follows gently, stirring the half-open curtains. She lies with her book on her chest, the moustache-shaped end profile curling out from the creased spine. The book is boring. She turns to her tablet and skims the news pages. The heat of scandal caused by the dishonesty of a wealthy and powerful man is fading out. She wonders how to map the consequences of those lies, wonders whether the anxiety of discovery and the temporary fading of power can be deemed fair recompense. But these stories are commonplace; after a few short weeks of prissy public chastity, this same red face will be filling screens once more, self-serving and bombastic as ever.

She looks for a story about death, death by numbers. It makes her feel anxious, but she looks. Reliably, there has been a bus bomb in a small town. Nine people have been killed. Seven more in a small town whose name she recognises, whose name has appeared on this screen several times, the place of other bombings and other deaths. A small town where raging certainties and howling furies scale the walls and steal into homes. She closes the novel, hefts it towards her suitcase, and reaches for her writing book.

27 December

Roadside bomb, seven killed.

His skin is tanned to the neck and sleeve by long hours of work outdoors. He has thick black hair and eyes fanned by lines, a face crinkled from laughter. Recently he has repaired his relationship with a beloved grown son, become perilously distant with the misunderstandings of a care that became oppressive.

A man in his thirties with thin hair, long from neglect rather than design. He lives in a small flat, found serviceable and utilitarian, remaining baldly so even after many years

of his habitation. He works as a labourer building roads –
recently, a viaduct strung taut and agile between distant
hills. He feels a beautiful, angelic calm, a deepening of
breath, standing on that ribbon of slender grey, beguiled
by the enormity of the space that falls away around his feet.

Carefully made-up and brightly decorated, she is a lively,
successful woman of thirty-two, slim and muscular, with
curly black hair and colourful clothes. She talks quickly
and with animation. She is a jeweller. She stores things
for later; she has a small collection of material leftovers –
shards of gemstones, scrap-like nuggets of gold, remainders
of commissioned pieces – in a small metal box. She calls it
her tinderbox.

A bumbling, fat young man, clumsy, large waist, disastrous
jeans. The only time he feels himself not forced into
fettered retreat is when confronted by frailty in another.
It creates a vacuum before him that pulls him inexorably,
almost ecstatically, towards them, where he shares his
compassion for them, for himself and for all the lost and sad
people in the world.

An exuberant man, wind-and-sun-battered, pell-mell
chasing his freedom in the outdoor world. Whenever
possible he is outside, blown by wind, caught by rain and
sun, quantifying himself joyfully in the geography of the
unmade world.

A gentle old man, a great-grandfather, his white hair as
thistledown-soft as the kind air around him. He would
define himself as happy, the kind of happiness that exists
as a deep and satisfying contentment. He is haunted by
the memory of one betrayal, his own, of a fragile woman
whom he learned he could never love and abandoned for
another.

A woman, or still a girl, skeins of bark-brown hair, still-

river eyes. She still has, at the age of nineteen, her childhood toy, a ragged dog, tucked away safely in her room. A
woman or a girl who never had a child herself. A girl, gone
from life before she had held life in her arms.

It is evening. She looks across the tawny beach. She imagines the
people standing on the sand in the smoke-blue evening air, dragged
out of their own lives by a deadly articulation of someone else's
certainty and rage, dragged here by her counting of them. Who
knows what transformations they have undergone on the journey?
She sees the elderly gentleman; he has his back to her. He looks along
the bay, as if searching the gauzy sky above the distant mountains for
an explanation of his current circumstance. The fat young man sits
on the sand, staring at his hands, turning them over, staring. All these
dear and varied hearts. All these thrown-away souls. She wishes them
goodbye. She says how sorry she is to call them into this terrible fate.
She tells them that she cares about their death, that it pains her. Then
she turns back to her room, returns to the present need for food, some
movement in her legs, some faces that will smile at her.

She heads for the same small bar, grateful for a sense of connection that may only come from her own routine but still accords a
welcome sense of being part of something, belonging somewhere.
She has been here often enough to smile and raise a hand in greeting
to the young man behind the bar and a waiter or two. In a small way,
it is her place, but she has a new book in her bag as the company she
keeps is most likely to be her own. She orders food and beer, pulls the
new book from her bag and puts it on the table. She will visit her new
waifs again. Not now, but soon.

She eats, orders a second beer. She reads some more, then turns
to her writing book, open to today's passengers, her alternative ferry
across the Styx. As she reads, she feels sadness expand into her chest
and seep down her arms. She feels trapped by the absurdity of
mourning the loss of people who don't exist, mourning a proxy, a
stand-in. She knows that if she could learn who the real people were,
their loss would be as tangible and terrible. But she is confounded by
her sadness at mourning the death of a person she has invented.

She is snapped from this strange private enigma by the unexpected and cheery arrival of Estela and Karl. They sit themselves down comfortably, then rather unnecessarily ask her if it is okay, do you mind if…? She can be a prickly woman, but she smiles inwardly at the notion that she would say no by this stage of the proceedings. She shuts her book hurriedly, brushes past Estela's curiosity, her charming way, on seeing the handwriting, of asking if she writes a book. Karl is using his clunky-sounding Spanish on the waiter, ordering for them both, asking whether Anna would like another beer, to which she might as well say yes. Luckily, they are both willing to speak English and do so with easy competence and attractive variation. They talk about their day. She tells them she watched them surf, how impressed she was. They of course pretend to think she should try, that she would love it, that no, of course she is not too old. She fears that anything more than a moderate gust would be likely to pull her arms clean out of the sockets, so soft, so weak does she feel compared to them. Compared to a younger self, glowing sun-browned limbs backdropped by faded cyan, a polaroid memory of a young woman who revelled in the strength of her body, who crashed through waves, flung herself headlong across asphalt after tennis balls, who laughing, jumped off rocks into swirling river pools, confident of avoiding the treachery of boulders hidden just below the racing, cold, peat-brown water. Whose arms learned a powerful strength carrying a restless and frightened child for night-hours at a time, her hot wet cheek only cooling when laid against her mother's collarbone. She flicks that memory away, closes the lid, turns to her young companions.

Estela tells her about how she learned to surf, why she loves it. Anna is touched by her enthusiasm. There are light freckles on the younger woman's cheeks called out by the sun, tentative as the speckling of blackbirds' eggs. Her eyes too have a blue that belongs to the same family as those delicate eggs. A slightly brown aquatic-blue, a striking lightness against her brown and gold skin and bleach-streaked dark-brown hair. She has a wide, crooked smile and wonky teeth. Karl watches her as she speaks, smiling, his strong, long back straight. He leans forward towards Estela, folded brown arms resting on the table before him. He is a tall man, quite good-looking and, Anna presumes from his rapt and slightly gormless look, very much in love. They are both charming company, and she starts to squeeze up inside to make room for them.

Karl leans forwards even more, to emphasise his words. 'You see, Anna, we did not make the world like it is. We don't want it like it is, but there's nothing we can make, so we don't be lazy, we just try to be outside of it. Not all of us can be the fighters.'

'What else can we do?' says Estela. 'Nothing makes it different, nothing makes better, is better just to enjoy, to be happy, to be good in the world, to make other people happy. I was at school, I learned all these things, all what is needed, only I find it is not needed, it is not help for me. I just must join this big machinery that I don't want to join. It is not a life I love. So Karl and me, we make money, a little bit, then we surf and live cheap a little bit.'

'Will you always be able to live this way though?' says Anna. She looks at the couple and envies them their carefree certainty, regrets her anticipation of it inevitably ending.

'Sure, what will make difference? We don't need a massive TV, a sport car. We just need here, what we have.'

'But you are both so young. There are so many choices ahead. Perhaps one day you will need other things.'

'Yes, so my father says!' replies Karl. They laugh good-naturedly. Anna suspects she is not far from being old enough to talk to Karl's father as if he were a wayward child too.

'So, what about you, Anna? What do you write about in your book?'

Of course, Anna won't speak about it. Not now. Maybe another time. So she says, oh, this and that, a journal, odd thoughts. She wonders briefly why they talk to her at all, wonder if they are curious because she is alone. Perhaps her Aunt-Laura-in-waiting status is apparent and already conferring value; perhaps she is becoming a character. She pictures herself in Vivienne Westwood tartan and a jaunty bobble hat, clutching a bin bag of possessions and shouting at the letterbox in the village. She could live with that.

Anna notices that her hand is resting protectively on the cover of her book; she feels the suede-like nap under her fingers. She flatters herself if she thinks that their curiosity is enough to make them snatch and pry. They are too nice to pursue her reluctant explanation, and the conversation moves on. The three of them chat easily and inconsequentially, enjoy the warm atmosphere, cheerfully enlivened by the mellow yet vibrant acoustic guitar being played over the small speakers, happily not too loud.

The man Anna had seen previously, with the faded shirt and one hand missing, walks into the bar. He smiles in their direction then comes and chats with Karl and Estela in Spanish. They introduce her, switching briefly to English. His name is Stefan. He greets her with friendliness and a light, unplaceable accent. He perches on the corner of the table and resumes chatting in Spanish. She understands enough to hear the friendliness of their talk, sit content in the warm eddies of their chat. Karl turns and says they are talking about a plan he and Estela have to rent an apartment from Stefan, some things they need to work out, that they could speak in English, but she is happy to be on the outside. She manages to convey that convincingly enough for this polite young man to continue with his Spanish conversation.

She leans back, relaxing in the quiet suburbs of their busy social city. Over in the far corner is a table with a well-dressed couple, around her age. He is still and formal, she glamorous, tanned. Anna guesses she would smell perfume if she sat next to her. She wears a jersey wrap dress, the only ripples caused by the fabric. She is either too spare or too toned or too undergarmented to show the small undulations that age brings to all and clingy jersey ruthlessly displays. With age, Anna thinks, even if we do not gain weight, we seem to gain surface area; bumps and furrows appear fractally across the geography of our skin as we lose the oneness, the wholeness of youth. But the woman across the bar has kept this growing disintegration, this complication, at bay. She is handsome, dark-skinned, hair a rich brown, if dyed, done well enough to look natural. Anna thinks of one of the women in her book, from a few days ago, the woman whose acts of generosity embarrassed her, straining at the meeting of compassion and selfishness, perhaps believing that to be selfish is a powerful expression of self-belief, that compassion is a weakness.

Anna wonders, presuming on their intimacy, how the man sitting across the table from her would cope with a life in which she had been killed by a bomb. Where would he be now if she had not returned from a trip to buy a bunch of fresh coriander and some king prawns for an easy evening meal? The white wine cooling in the fridge, the shallots sitting unchopped on the wooden board, her cookery book open on the kitchen table, next to some rings and a large bracelet made of heavy amber resin, a deep-space swirl of clouded light. Would he remember having seen it on her slim wrist? Would he notice, perhaps for the first conscious time, her habit of removing jewellery before she cooks? But then she sees the woman, elbows resting on the table, one hand gesturing gently as she tells her smiling companion something, and she feels terrible, guilty that, momentarily, she made her dead. She wants to rush over and gush her apology, I'm sorry, please don't die. If she saw that through, she wouldn't have to wait until she could shout at the village letterbox to earn her crazy stripes. Instead of apologising to a woman she has never spoken to, for a fault she will never know, Anna compares her in greater detail to the woman in her book. She thinks she has the same kind of polished glamour, a buffed combination of time and money more influential than any style element. Anna's ghost had a more sculpted face, a more crudely hewn and handsome bone structure. She can't remember exactly without looking in her book, but she thinks that the woman in the bar is taller, more willowy. The woman in her book, she thinks, would be wearing a headscarf if she were here, and she would not have a glass of wine before her. Or she doesn't think so. That woman was at home when Anna saw her, sitting in an armchair, thinking about something that baffled her, unwinding the puzzle of complicating events brought about by others.

Stefan interrupts her remembering. 'Would you like another beer, uh, Anna?' He looks questioningly to see if he has her name right. She says yes, then wonders with slight agitation whether she should go to the bar to help him carry the drinks or not. But she is sitting with her back to the wall, chairs and people to disrupt if she were to get up. She dithers in a confusion of politeness and embarrassment. Meanwhile Stefan has placed his orders and returned to the table, this time pulling up a chair from another table and sitting oppo-

site her, and there is no dilemma – the waiter brings the drinks over
on a round tray.

With the drinks, her table companions switch back to English.
Stefan has a place here, so is indeed a resident, though he tells her that
he too is German, but he and Karl speak Spanish when they are with
Estela. She asks if Karl and Stefan know each other from Germany,
but they met when Karl and Estela were here last year. He has been
staying here to be near a daughter and her two children. He says that
he has found such joy in being the grandfather of these two that he
no longer wants to leave the island. She wonders about the daughter
and how she came to be here, if the story contains a husband, a local
man, a departed lover, an unexpectedly extended holiday romance.
The four spend an enjoyable evening together, and Anna is gratified
to be asked if she would like to meet them there the next evening,
when there will be live music in the bar.

Chapter 12

Out of the spin and tumble, I have found enough of what I need to tell, how it happened. Not willingly, but with determination. It has to be. I have to find myself in the story.

There was a period of ordinary decline in the mood of love, and then it changed for good. After a row one evening – me talking to one of his friends in the pub, so small a thing – we spent the evening in tight silence pretending to engage with other things: he on his computer; I reading. But the tension hummed like tinnitus in the room. We went to bed separately; he, when he joined me, lay angrily with his back turned. I curved softly towards him, showing only that I wished to erase the pain he was feeling, the pain I must have caused. A geography of night–time I already understood, an uncomfortable yet familiar place. I did feel anger and resentment somewhere, but I ignored it. I felt I had not done anything to deserve blame. But I understood only that this was not apparent, that I had misrepresented myself in a way he perceived as harmful. If only I could learn to express myself better, I thought. I can remember the slow, long ache of those night–times. Often repeated, they merged over the weeks into a familiar feeling that even now is clear in memory.

So many mornings too, after these baffling nights, played out in a predictable way; terse, uncommunicative, cold. Too many occasions like this to tell them apart. But this one morning has details that I find all too easily. Daytime came and both of us prepared to go to work. I resolved, as I usually did, to make amends, putting myself aside in the hope of finally showing that he had no cause to doubt me. I was careful and pacifying, in a way I had learned well. I was not yet completely abject but, having put myself to one side, was ready to become so. Look, Ryan, I don't even need myself at the moment, does that not show you that my love is a thing to trust? Though I was quiet and serious by nature, this meekness was new. I tailored it for myself over the months we had been living together. It had quickly become so engrained that I no longer noticed.

I made us both coffee, brought toast over to him sitting still and sullen at the small table in the bay window. I moved back quietly to the sink, cleaned the little kitchen, trying to think of how I could put the sweet balance back, re-establish the love that had been my moving-in gift, my precious dower, surely rich enough to assuage these difficulties. Not a word passed between us. He ate toast, I washed and wiped a little, then, resolving to try once more, I walked over to stand before him, yearning for him to realise I loved him, to reject the mistaken belief that I was rejecting him. I thought that to appeal to his memory of a time when we planned our future together might show how little I needed other people, that our plans were enough for me.

'I know things have been difficult, but it needn't stay like this. We could still do what we planned. Do you remember how we thought we would be able to manage it? Going to London together, it would be so great, and you could maybe start doing more exciting work. I know it wouldn't be easy for you, but I don't know if I can miss another year. I would lose my place. It might be difficult to start with, but I know we could make it work, just the two of us.'

He looked up at me, chewing the last of his toast.

'Ryan, I know it would be a big move when you have everything set up here, but maybe it would be better for both of us if we had more exciting things to do, rather than being stuck in work we don't like. I want so much for us to be happy together, and we were so excited about it, weren't we?'

He looked at me, still, silent, a stillness that turned imperceptibly to contempt. In one movement, he stood and punched upwards, hitting me on the underside of the jaw. Then, picking up his bag, he left for work.

I stood still for some minutes, short breaths and shallow heartbeats dancing a jerky quickstep in my chest. After a while, I stopped fearing his return, and the chemistry of panic subsided. I sank to the ground, still clutching the edge of the small table. I cried until I ached, until my knees hurt from my position on the ground. Over and over I asked myself one question. How could he? In those three words lay subtle designs, patterns of trust, value and worth. These threads, so complexly interwoven, combine into a utilitarian, vital fabric; a material, often beautiful, sometimes threadbare, on which we build our lives.

Before this, there had been arguments during which he gripped my shoulders and shouted, inches from my face, shouted into me, violence smothering me as a wave, without the percussion of a blow. But they were arguments, not assaults. They were arguments that people have, weren't they? New arguments with myself flew around me in harpy fury, a cacophonous confusion. He loved me, didn't he? He said he did. But does love allow such things? Was it a mistake? What was I supposed to do? Should I go home? What would I say? I lay in our bed, surrounded by a Sleeping Beauty thicket of thorns. Unreachable. Exhausted and overwhelmed. My hand went up often to the tender underside of my jaw, gently soothing the remnant pain. Trying to make sense of it. I became hollowed by the shock.

I feel myself now, mixing in with the dark misery of that time; it seems part of the blackness, or part of me. It engorges, floods me where my blood once ran. Yes, it is part of me. I have brought it with me to this place. The journey to here started there. A little prying, loosening away from gravity's hold, a little opening of the way that joined me up with this dark medium.

The text message read 'So so sorry. Love you so much. Don't know why I snapped xxx'. Did it help that he was sorry? I couldn't tell. But slowly, the explanation that he, by his own calculation, had snapped began to clear a way through. A direct route that was broad enough for both of us. He had snapped. It was inexplicable, appalling, but perhaps it was not unforgivable. Anyone can make a mistake once.

I battered myself with this idea of a resolution. It seemed a long time but must have been only a few hours. My phone beeped again. This time the message said 'Please please forgive me, Cait. Couldn't live without you. Will bring curry and wine? Please forgive me xxxxxx'.

I awaited his return with anxiety, unresolved but looking for a way out. When he came back, after a brief and fervent flurry of tenderness and shame, Ryan operated as though to forget was the best medicine. He was implacable, evasive, robust with good humour. He barged back into our shared life with brassy cheer. He reacted to my first clumsy attempts to talk about the morning as if I were recklessly exhibiting a will to sabotage the harmony he had gifted me.

I am furious with that now, his easy sidestep, his table–turning. I was angry then, but frightened too of a slide back into anger. He asked, hurt, why I had to spoil things, as he gestured to his valiant efforts, the brown paper bag with the foil containers, the bottle he had just opened. I had thought the food and wine might be the opening gambit of a peace offering, a trust–gift before healing negotiations. I had hoped that reconciliation after a difficult conversation would follow. But they were a lure, a bribe to turn me in the opposite direction. The harms he made so weightless, so easy to toss aside like litter, they were anvil weights to me, awkward burdens that I didn't know how to put down. Under their weight, silence consolidated its hold on me. That is how it happened. I see it now. I let fear and hope bind me.

I am undoing that binding. As tight and inescapable as it felt then, it is no match for me now. I redeem hope and discard fear. I pull it off me as I unravel. And I make a choice, I think, about the ravelling. I remake myself with the tale told true. In the harsh cost of this undoing, there is at least that gift.

We were lifted, yes, back into the realms of promise and light, by Ryan's determination and my hope. Until some weeks later when he hit me again. Anyone can make a mistake, and be sorry, oh so very, very sorry. Pleadingly sorry, and in such misery that, to spare him, I let rational, systematic thoughts overtake instinctive ones. I quietly led my fear out of the back door then sat, measured, in the front room and heard his confession, his reparation, bent to the floor beside me so that he looked up into my darkened eye.

Was it necessary to accept that anyone can do it twice? I hadn't yet found the reasoning to make such a choice.

But I did find it. My heart sinks at a memory of a profound and subtle shame that rings through this blackness, rings through the substance of me now. I feel the shame of her, the girl I was then. Now, I feel only compassion for that girl. I am not ashamed of the choices I made. I made them for love and hope. There is a mistake in that, but there is no shame. The malevolent cocoon of our relationship had taken me away from those that could help me; confusion and the chaos of a terrible new uncertainty had taken me away from myself. How I longed for Mel, my oldest and best friend. I longed for Mum, longed to lean into that spare frame and be pulled in by her protective arms. How I longed to call my dad to come and pick me up. But I did not know how I could subject Ryan, for whom my love had not yet vanished, to their disgust and approbation. I did not know how I could bear their faces, the concern, anger, sorrow, when I told them what had happened.

I know that Mel and Dad have seen each other since I died. Both of them have moved away, but they are able to live with the past, unlike Mum, who is held captive. Shut in and shutting out. I have been with Mel and Dad sometimes. They became caring friends to each other in their shared love for me, after I died. They warm each other, tell each other well—worn memories. I hear them and remake myself in their telling. I wish only that Mum would be with them too. I wish for her she could be. I wish I had not been the cause of breaking her. I wish with all my resounding fury that I could make Ryan pay for all that he killed, for it wasn't only me.

But I must find the rest and tell the whole. For it did not end with a bruise, else I would not be here. How did I manage to believe in a future after this? How did I come to accept that the love, the bountiful backwash of his violence, would not be once more stamped out?

This is how. Grazed hope was soothed by precious reserves of healing care, the emptying bottle tipped onto cotton wool and wiped gently to ease the pain. Shattered hope was bandaged with dreams already made. Hope, that great self-healer, bandaged and strengthened, for a while at least, itself. Because once more, he pleaded, he worshipped and cherished. I had learned well how to believe in that, had learned how to turn it into hope. I was given an enormous power, the power to end all hope of his happiness, all meaning in his life. And subtly, within the bestowal of that power, I was made culpable for my own harm. Only because he loved me so much did he lose his self-control, a result of the terrible fear he had of losing me. I was still so young; I had not learned how much a human heart can weather. I had not yet learned the ways we make ourselves robust.

I understand now how that undid me. He took me away from myself; he laid the burden of harm at my feet. I was weakened enough to take its weight in my own tired arms, on my own aching shoulders. For peace.

So we made a new pattern for our lives. He was loving, attentive and cheerful, but he was also watchful and wary, alert for the slightest betrayal of this newly decreed harmony. A harmony in which he played the role of *perfect boyfriend. He was flawless if allowed to be blameless, admirable. I became aware that to do other than embrace this act was a betrayal. He sensed a betrayal in me if I did not appear content with his display. In my disheartened state, I didn't have the strength to insist, to demand we do things my way. And, being far from knowing what my way was, I was unable to resist the passivity that, truthfully, was the only thing Ryan's bullying required. I was tired out by my shock and sorrow. More than anything, I wanted some peace, to regain myself, return to myself after the shocking battery of his unexpected violence. At least precious peace was abundantly available in the cocooning embrace of passive compliance. It took a long time for me to understand how consuming and exhausting my constant and minute reading of the conditions had become.*

I was young enough to believe in part that I made him this way, that he loved me so much and I disappointed him so profoundly, communicated so badly, loved him so inadequately, that his rage was inevitable. Oh, I was young. How I long to meet that young woman, see her in the mirror, reflected in a pool, passing in a dream. Reach across and take that self-blame away from her.

In this tangled blackness, though I am whiskered out like a stain in the dark, I start to see all, know all. I just can't hold myself together enough to be. Though knowledge is a comfort; at least I know I have myself as ally, I did all along. I did not love myself so poorly as I had thought, but I lost sight of self-love. If only I had known it then. How I wish I could go back and tell her that she did none of it. He did it all. How I wish I could go back and say that there was no way for her to put him right, no way for her to make their love whole and harmless again. No door to unlock that she would ever reach, no key to find that she would ever uncover. No secret she would ever divine, no trick she would ever learn or language she would understand. These were all things for him to find. Not her. Poor child made to feel the weight of her own undoing. That is perhaps the most damaging assault of all. For it is the blow that knocks the self away, out of reach.

Longer fragments of my story catch hold and eventually coalesce. The threads plait or weave in sections, begin to make a fabric. I take more of my story with me, and hope that it grows into a cloak to wrap around myself for protection in the limitless unknown. For now, it is company at least. I understood much of it in the last few weeks on Earth. I began to find myself. I began to untangle myself. I believe I would have found the way to make myself safe. And to end the humiliation that only I would feel.

It is a strange force, humiliation, undermining in such a destructive manner. I felt diminished by Ryan in a way that imprisoned me. Shame was an alloy in the metal bands binding the strong box that Ryan locked around me. Shame, humiliation, pity. These subjective injuries have such insinuating craft, and such brute strength. So many ways to attack, to inhabit, to compromise. Like wily viruses that can find a hook-hold in any host. These subtle hurts work tirelessly, conditioning for the material blows of flesh, of fists and boots.

Yet they are powerless in the face of self-worked magic. If I am not ashamed, Ryan cannot shame me. It is I who decides if I am humiliated. That is what I began to learn. This learning worked like crumbs on the forest floor, leading me back to myself. A thread, played out, catching myself back again with a soft hook, pulling myself in.

I had found enough of myself to make good on a second kind of self-admonishment – first I felt shame he had hurt me at all, then I felt it that I had let him. I had allowed it to become a part of my life. The extraordinary became the commonplace. We are primed to accept the catastrophic single failing, the first act of a redemptive tragedy. How much more difficult it is, I found, to deal with once grubby from overuse.

So he shamed me, and I, in response, shamed myself. He put a taint, a blush, a rash on me. I looked in a mirror and burned it into my bones. For only I could take it below the skin. Once there, it became a disease for both of us. We were both diseased, but only my body was marked by the pathogen.

Ryan veered between contemptuous aggression and contrite adoration. After an episode of violence, he worked so hard to restore my precious elevation. He claimed his extravagant love for me in the rage he said I drove him to. He claimed only love so great could inspire him to such fury. He claimed, in short, my responsibility for the harm he did me. As I sickened under his violence, he looked on me and saw the symptoms of his own disease. He stopped asking me to forgive him, because he did not wish to feel responsi-

bility for his rage. For Ryan, all could be repaired by the easy steps of time, the distance measured in the mere minutes that followed his dark anger.

The phases of his violence did not end because he chose to restrain himself or to love me better. It ended because a few punches and the odd kick satisfied the need he had to hurt me. He let himself be free to do what would be done. I should have had, any person should have, more fear of someone who allows no limitation to their own desires. But we find ourselves playing strange games. We rationalise the parts, make a sense of them as best we can. We say to ourselves that this game of chess will continue to function; this hunk of dry bread, this old tin of paint, they are much like the pieces. I will move them as if they are, we will proceed. And we do proceed, moving strange pieces and mastering difficult new rules that are only discernible in actions we must somehow learn by trial and error. So bent are we on trying to apply what was once rational to what no longer is, we do not give ourselves enough space, enough clean air in our lungs to say that we will no longer play.

What a waste. All of it a stupid, terrible waste. My father weeping in the company of tan brogue boots, as lonely as my mother, silent and cold as stone a few feet away. Ryan learning new ways of being, suffering from the fear of violence he found so easy to ignore just a few months before. Me, exiled to the darkness, ridden by all the waves that curse and course, spinning along channels of endless night.

Chapter 13

Anna's phone pings, a message from Sophie, checking she is having a good time. Anna, having just returned from breakfast, is sitting in the morning shade of her balcony, reading. She replies to Sophie's message saying it is warm, quiet, the sun is shining and she is very content. Sophie asks for a picture. Somewhat self-consciously, Anna struggles to take a picture of herself with the clear sky and sea in the background. The best effort catches most of her face, with a photo smile for her friend. She sends it off, then hastily deletes all of the pictures. A few minutes later, she chuckles at the response, a picture of Sophie grimacing in the rain with her hood up, pointing at her windscreen to show the parking ticket. Anna feels a surge of gratitude that she decided to leave. The steady warmth, the peace, all help to soothe. She checks herself, cautions against too much blinkered contentment, for she knows that nothing has changed. But sitting calmly in warm shade is preferable to the curtained winter retreat of skulking indoors at home. She thought that simply not being at home, away from any possible contact with Ryan, would be enough, but the benefits are more positive than that.

She thinks about the evening ahead. She is flattered to have been asked to meet Stefan, Karl and Estela again, to tag onto their group of friends. They are an interesting trio. She hadn't expected new connections to be part of her stay. She wonders why they have been so friendly, thinking that perhaps, being alone, she is an oddity, or they pity her. She doesn't mind if either is true as the result was a happy evening, and she is looking forward to seeing them again.

As the evening slides in, Anna goes down to the hotel bar. She finds a chair, a deep square of black leather, orders a gin and tonic and a toasted sandwich. There is the usual standard jazz playing, heavy on the inoffensive piano, sticky and sweet like the cocktails lavishly described on the elegant, embossed menu cards standing in a slotted chunk of polished steel on each table. She watches the lights down the bay switching on as the sky darkens. A sparkling chain of brightness lapping at the sea's edge. She orders a second gin and tonic as she eats her sandwich. The evening has a formal quality, couples dressed up and gleaming. Solicitous elegance performed as dues to the location. Except for the couple who don't speak to each other over breakfast – they apparently don't speak to each other over aperitifs and olives either. At least they're consistent. The piano tinkles away, irritating and inoffensive. She finishes her quick meal and leaves for more interesting company.

The bar is busier than usual; people stand, filling the floor. She spots her new friends sitting at one of the tables, makes her way over and is offered a chair and a beer by Karl, who heads to the bar. There are two new people, an Australian couple who have been staying, friends of Stefan's. She is glad she is not the only reason for dragging the conversation into English. They tell her it is their last night before they leave tomorrow for London. Karl comes back with drinks; the atmosphere is happy and lively. The band set up and begin to play acoustic guitar, gentle enough to work as background music so they are able to stay at the table and chat. The evening spins on happily. Soon Stefan's friends leave – early flight, time for bed. She hugs them goodbye, the warmth of the evening forging acts of friendship; they talk of future days in London where they will be for some weeks, but it is mainly for form. Stefan gets up and walks them to the door for more sincere goodbyes.

The tempo and energy of the music builds, luring some dancers onto the floor. Stefan comes back followed by a waiter with fresh bottles for all. Karl laughs and points out a friend of theirs who is dancing against the wall, looking perilously like it is only the wall that is stopping him from falling over. The conversation continues more gaily, more laughter, she is giving them a cruel description of the unspeaking couple, they all laugh. She is thoroughly enjoying herself, free of her own story, untainted.

But she is hit by an unwelcome intrusion, sensing that if elsewhere joy is tainted, then here too a polluted seam must course or creep through somewhere, somewhere. And on cue, bitterness rises from her stomach, passes her heart which shudders at the contact, coats her breath with an oily film. The strings round her limbs and her fingers and toes shrink, pull their reminding into her flesh. She sits back, holding onto her bag, then, to disguise her embarrassment at being so taken in such tenderly new company, gets up, rather roughly pushing past Estela, and gaudily offers another drink all round. She spins out the recovery by going to the loo, sits as long as she can without declaring some kind of difficulty, dabs her face with cold water and goes to the bar, clutching her purse, clenching her jaw.

When she returns to the table, she is briskly cheerful, and if this strikes a false note they are unfamiliar enough with each other that it passes unremarked. Conversations carry on gaily; she joins in, working hard at maintaining her showroom smile. Round the edge of her thoughts flits Ryan, Ryan in a new life, maybe with a wife and baby. She thinks of Stefan with his grandchildren. She is jealous of him. She feels a spike, a hit in the bloodstream. The bitter dose provided by intrusive thoughts of Ryan has leaked outward, contaminated everything. She wrestles her thoughts, exerting ungainly, aggressive control, then forces herself to smile, to brightly face the world as defined by this table, this bar, this fresh beer. She is getting drunk.

And drunker still. Some brandy. They are having fun, they are doing joy. In a real way, in a false way that disguises its counter. Two weighted ends of an iron bar that spins, fast enough and blurred enough by the beer to blend unclear. Look, she is laughing, she is doing joy. Weights shift inside of her, and balance becomes something that demands attention, something that she can get right or wrong in that moment. She is partially failing, almost succeeding. Heat slides across her; perception slows, lags behind movement. She feels ghastly. She's lost the thread, the knack of being part of this group, and she longs to be alone, cooled and weighted down. She gets up abruptly and heads for the door. She doesn't think she stumbles but can't be sure. The dark of the sea beckons her, the cool oblivion of darkness. Not death – or maybe death? The iron bar still spins, though now there is misery at one end and despair at the other. She presses across to the wet sand, not in a straight line but in a purposeful, determined one, sinks to the cool ground, sits still, sits still. The darkness before her provides a welcome simplification. Cold flat sand underneath her, dark water and sky before. There is momentary relief in this simplification of sensation, the heaving of drunkenness stilled somewhat. And then, there, on that broad stage, spacious, wide and open, she cannot hold on any longer, and like horses, thoughts gallop out of her. She cannot halt them, bridles slide through her feeble hands and they are free. She weeps, she cries. There is too much space. She has lost control. She is unable to stand, to reign in, to capture. So she sits still and she feels it all.

A hand touches her shoulder. It is Estela, gentle and concerned. She explains that she came to find Anna because she left her bag in the bar. Estela tries to talk to Anna, tries to get Anna to talk to her. She wants to know what is wrong, but Anna does not speak. She can't. Estela has sunk down next to her on the sand, gently placing an arm across Anna's shoulders. That slim arm is so tender, and hurts Anna so much. She turns to her and cries, loudly and extremely, into Estela's shoulder, shakes her head to all of her words. She cannot assuage Estela's alarm, can't even find the beginning of her own. Sobs squeeze her ribs, stamp down on her sternum, mug her breath. The bones of her hands twist over themselves like small animals in acid torment.

For a long time they sit like this. She thinks at one point Karl is standing behind them; he talks to Estela then leaves again. Eventually, she becomes calm. Estela says nothing but sits calmly too, one arm still around Anna's bent shoulders, her other hand, tanned, slim fingers wearing slender silver rings, resting lightly on the sleeve of Anna's forearm.

Her head thrums, her mind still fogged, poisoned by alcohol. She feels sabotaged, uncertain, confused. She knows she has watched through dark and light again, at least that long. She is in her room. She has eaten some bread that was dry as a loofah, dipped in the oil that tasted of supermarkets, left in the bottom of a flimsy plastic pot once the olives had been eaten on a more lustrous day. She drinks water from the tap. She moves to the balcony, to peer and scowl, scans the beach, the edge of town, the sea. It is an unquiet day. Harried. Palm branches flick, shooing away a troublesome approach. A pesterer. Begone! She frowns in the cloudy brightness and cavorting wind. It teases her; she flicks at it like the palms. She goes back to the room, shuts the wind

114

out on the balcony, plaintive Cathy, wheedling for entry. Bugger off, Cathy, Heathcliff must have thought sometimes. She gets into bed, pulls up the sheet and the thin blanket, tugs it over her eyes, over her whole head, and sleeps.

Her room is crammed with the dead, her dead, not the fictional ghost banished to the balcony. Mine may be made up, but they are not fiction, she says. They rise from the pages of her book, slip out between the leaves and shift around each other, over, under and clean through. The room is a swimming pool made of the dead, a volume of liquid movement. From above, the surface might shimmer, glare in the light like the hotel pool, small waves bouncing into each other off the square sides, kicking back the sunlight in a charming web of brightness. But down here, it is tank-like, light softened by depth and algae; the movement is gentle, lulling. Soft shadow and pale light stirred in together. She has to concentrate to see them as individuals, her sleeping eye discerning only the movement and the pattern. Subtle motes eddying in the thick liquid air. Sometimes one stops its slow swirl long enough for her eye to locate it. See him or her, through the thin blanket and the sheet and the pylon thrum in her head. It is a little nauseating to be surrounded by such translucent paisley shifting. She pulls tighter under the covers, the fabric clenched in her hands. The tight pull of material around her head seems to steady her as she bobs around the bottom of this gloomy tank, noticing the odd recognisable feature, a known body, a limb that shows itself as whole in the viscous mass.

At the bottom of her bed there is a stillness. A figure has sat on the end – it is the woman with turquoise trousers and a yellow top. She is her first. Anna tries to visit her in her garden and isn't able to, floating around pathetically like an insecure deb at a cocktail party waiting for the hostess to come and talk to her. This time she has come to visit Anna, sitting with the same garden calm, not looking at anything, or perhaps gazing through the window to the beach and sky. Anna observes, not the woman exactly, but the sensation of her presence. It soothes her, and she drifts further into sleep. Later, in the full dark of night, the tank has emptied, the dead are gone, but the woman still sits on her bed. The fat darkness lies heavy upon Anna, a drug of sleep, a swoon into night-mind. The sound of the sea snakes through the balcony door, now open. By me, she wonders, or by the ghosts as they left? The curtain-ghost blows in the night-time breeze. She settles comfortably in the bed, curled on her side, exhales, slowly and without tension. After a while resting in thoughtless companionship, slightly adrift of the shore, Anna speaks.

I'm sorry for all that you have lost. I wish I could have known you before.

Yes, I am sorry too.

...

Did you know you were in danger?

Life has been full of danger for many years, so yes, I did know. I didn't know I was to die on this day at this time. This bomb. I feared it many times, and fear can feel like a rehearsal.

...

It had been a lively morning. My younger children are often fighting, and the noise of it fills our home. There is a moment of quiet each morning and, as you know, I like to sit in the backyard and feel the sun on my face. It is as if I collect the turmoil on myself, and to remove it, I have these breaths in the sun. Don't get the picture from this that my family is difficult or that I am burdened by unusual demands. It is the ordinary way of a lively family living in a small, too small, space. Living too in a place that causes fear and uncertainty. My boys want only certainty, and being young, believe they have been able to find it. It is beautiful, the clear purpose of the young, isn't it? But you can't help wishing for them that they would not miss the often equally beautiful, less defined bits in between. Well, so I think about my sons anyway. They are clever enough, they will find it, I hope. And I understand the anger that fills their hearts.

...

Did it hurt you? Were you afraid?

...

I felt my life pulling out of me, fast, like a train leaving a tunnel. My body lived on long enough to feel the vacuum. To feel the blank emptiness, the eternal connection to emptiness. It didn't hurt. But I was filled with ancient grief.

When Anna wakes up next it is in the pewter light of dawn. The sky, though grey, glints with small lustre, the promise of brightness. The woman from Baghdad is gone from the end of her bed. She can't expect a night-long vigil after all. The loofah bread is gone, the plastic pot is scraped clean and on the floor. There is still water in the tap. She takes a long drink from the tap, then fills the bathroom glass. She sips from it as she shuffles through the tumble that has formed in her room over these last scattered few days, pokes her feet around in clothes and bedding on the floor, moves curtains this way and that. She's got to think, or at least find order, pull it from the tatty muddle that has been her hiding place. She's got to think. She's got to grasp.

She bounces off whenever she tries. That is the difficulty. Her fear is a bauxite sphere; gritty, unwieldy, squashingly large. Nothing to grasp; the girth is too wide. It hovers, an Earth-born planet, next to her at chest height, in the way; scratchy, rough, blocking. Not a thing she can hold or move or order. She puts her hands over her face, pressing in, willing to give up at the slightest difficulty, frustrated by her inability to proceed.

She feels a keen sense of embarrassment at her unravelling, at her need for Estela to take care of her, at her drunkenness. But Estela's gentle kindness assuages some of the pain – it seems ungracious to feel embarrassment as a result of such generosity. Estela stayed with her for a long time and would probably have stayed longer if Anna had not insisted that she was better now and in need of sleep. She feels a precious gratitude for the young woman's generosity, but with that comes a poignant thread; a crystalline reminder rings through her of all that she has lost. She sees in Estela the beautiful blossoming of opportunities, a young woman poised on the threshold of making her mark in life, making the choices of adulthood with the carefree winds of youth still filling her sails. There is a terrible emptiness, a longing for the time when she looked on her own daughter with the same admiring wonder. She chokes back a sob. Holds onto the expression of sadness, fearing once more the power that might surge behind it. She is not ready for it.

There must be, eventually, a right time. There must be a reckoning, an unpicking. A harassing, a harrying, a hunt and a chase. A death and a dissection, a bloody inquest. A hanging, a tale-telling, a laying down of the truth from which the myth was born. A slaying of the beast, a naming of the enemy. This pageant will need a great field, a heraldry of secrets, a change of horses. And once the pageant moves on, she will weave her way across the dewy field barefoot, collecting the clues, tucking fragments into muslin pockets, muttering words to make a web, piece together the story that she needs to tell of herself.

Now is not the right time. She stays in her room to sit out a chunk of this wrong time. She hunkers down to wait it out, as the wrong minutes and hours tick by. Be in this as-good-as-any place, filling up the wrong time.

I wait in the darkness. This soft inky darkness surrounds me like a cloak. The soft darkness of night-time on Earth is a refuge. It meets my boundaries with courtesy; it does not steal in and thread itself through my bones.

She will find me here, soon.

Remote-controlled bomb, four killed.

A barrel-shaped woman with piled-up grey hair in an old-fashioned coif. She wears shiny black shoes on tiny feet, a flowing and colourful scarf. In fear of robbery, she clutches a black handbag, old and flat, under her arm, held tight by pudgy fingers brightened with gold rings. She feeds stray cats in her back garden, taking out pretty, cheap ceramic bowls of leftovers and cat food. She won't have animals in her expensive silent house.

The working day as a scaffolder is punctuated by songs sung in loops and snatches. He loves his son and wife with a fervour that is so animating he sometimes feels the need to walk it off. Amongst competing financial claims, he has secretly saved enough for a holiday at a place where his wife made happy childhood memories. He has been trying to decide whether to keep it a surprise.

She takes a hurried trip across town to meet an old friend; she wants just briefly to see a part of the world that is distant and different, carefree. All told, a break of under two hours. Then anxious return to the hospital and her precious child, born in translucent frailty, all the feebleness of her innermost body somehow visible through her pale skin and huge, tarmac-dark eyes.

A quiet, serious girl, absorbed by a determination to understand the underlying way of things. She has eyes the unresolved colour of a river. Her gaze is steady, her look intent, concentrated as she pieces together the workings of the world. Those steady eyes with their unresolved colour, they see nothing now. They will never be seen. All that they took in, understood, learned, studied, all that they beheld. All gone.

She counts these four, just four of how many? So many died today, so many killed. Drowned, suffocated, tortured. The countless dead amongst the numbered that appear on her news screen. There are always more dead, so many different dead. Likely none of them unmourned or unaccounted for in their homeland. Her accounting for them is not because she is an only eye, a stupid god. They don't need her to do this. But she still feels she must. There is no shortage of stories. Nine people were killed on the same page, another bomb in another town, the other end of the same country. There are so many different ways of being ignored.

Shut the book, drop it into the sluicing bottom of the boat, throw the mooring line onto the rickety quay and step onto the land. She has waved them all off on the other side. Goodbye, dear ones. I am sorry for your loss. I am sorry you have become lost. Goodbye. She lies on the bed still. She is still. What a grimy day. But nearly done. They will find their way as all others have before them. There's no rush. She cannot say that all left here will find their way; after all, she does not seem to have found her own. She is wayless. She may as well wait until some other soul in a boat with a purple book tells her they have come to drop her off at the other side.

She decides to leave the hotel, find a cafe or a shop somewhere, take a walk out into the morning. She guesses, at this hour, for breakfast. She realises that it is the start of a new year. The celebrations of New Year's Eve had passed her by. In any case, she was indifferent to it. There is no refreshment in the prospect, no happy renewal, just a flat grey river-stone dropping into the pool of her belly. Another anniversary coming up. Breakfast first.

Passing the reception desk, the woman working there hails her, calls her over – she has a note. It is from Estela, enquiring whether she is feeling better, giving her a phone number and an email address, saying Anna should get in touch with her if she wants to. Anna is very touched by this. She tucks the paper safely into her bag as she leaves to find breakfast. She walks the promenade next to the beach. It is still quiet this morning. Still early. She walks past shops and cafes opening. Racks of hats, sarongs and gaudy towels, beach balls in laundry baskets brought out from the inside. Ashtrays and salt cellars placed on outdoor tables, umbrellas hoisted. A woman hoses down the terrace in front of a small restaurant; a little tide of fag butts and sugar packets sluices into the gutter. Anna remembers a place she saw on an earlier walk, further along the bay, which advertised croissants and pastries. On the beach, she walks on the tide sand, firm and cool, rimed with a delicate, uneven scallop of small shells and dark seaweed threads. The high-tide mark holds more pungent charms, knots of old rope and mermaid's hair. Sailor's souls and mysterious hanks of sea-death. She keeps on the magic side, the Atlantis road that appears twice a day.

The cafe is open and invitingly empty; there are baskets of bakery goods to choose from. She orders coffee, bread rolls and butter, and a pastry. As clouds still drape the sky, she sits outside on the terrace at the beach edge. She is still thirsty and asks for water. She is shaken by the last few days. But also grateful that she is unobserved and away from home. There should be nothing to explain. Estela may wonder what went so wrong. But she doesn't carry a well-worn version of Anna's bedraggled tale with which to explain recent events – we are all allowed a crisis in the present. It is only problematic if it hangs around, Anna thinks. Her problematic, dog-eared crisis; how it lowers her. The slow grinding of gears stuck always in the same glitch, caught always on the same burred and broken tooth. How it makes her head ache. She stretches her shoulders back, drops her head to stretch her neck, rub her eyes. She watches some of the local boys playing football on the sand. Spills the rest of the day quietly existing between the sea and the hotel.

Chapter 14

The days bled into one another. I felt implicated, imprisoned first by Ryan's violence and then, after the third or fourth time it had erupted, by my lack of resolution in the face of it. It became, remarkably quickly, a matter of endurance, avoidance, secret pain and secret shame. I couldn't bear the exposure of telling my friends or family, couldn't summon the courage to confront Ryan on my own account. Hope, like a sturdy torch that had become heavy in my hand, had taken me so far into the woods that when its light finally died, I no longer knew the way out again.

How did I make that escape? For I did go to London. I remember such joy at being there, beginning again with bridges and highways, building my own roads that would take me to wonderful freedom. How did I get there?

It was the weekend of Dad's birthday. We were spending the night at home with Mum and Dad, Uncle Paul and Aunt Marie. I dreaded it, but longed for the secret escape of being safe at home, in company. Ryan knew enough of his wrongdoing to understand he could not show it before others. He knew that, if he would not accept it from me, the blame from them would be inescapable. We went home to celebrate with Mum and Dad, Ryan genially handing over a bottle of wine and the gift I had chosen, playing out the charm of which he felt so certain. I eased off my jacket, explaining that I had slipped in the bathroom and hurt my wrist. My face was pale from lack of sleep, from dread of this evening's demands. In the kitchen, Mum asked me if I was okay. Stolidly, without invitation to further questions, I fobbed her off – my job was stressful and dull, I didn't have much aptitude for it. It's fine, I'm just run down, I offered. Mum looked at me ruefully, but she didn't get anywhere near the truth. I knew she had been disappointed by my university deferment. She believed, I think, knowing that something was a bad fit, that Ryan was resisting my moving eventually to London. She thought, with maternal, pragmatic tenderness, that it was inevitable I was finding the prospect of moving away hard, but I would get over it. I was in a difficult, but regular, part of growing up. But in that moment, set fair for enjoying the evening ahead, she didn't want reasons to take my side;

she wanted to welcome both of us, her daughter and her daughter's chosen partner.

Ryan did not consider that he would change my mother and father's life. Though the final manifestation was an accident, he did mean to hurt me. Even to the secret point of considering my death – there were moments in his rage, I see them now, when that illicit desire screamed piercing, distant inside him; he could imagine, with an ugly thrill, my death arriving at his hand. But he didn't ever mean to destroy my father's life. Such matey bonhomie, such a keen desire for approval. Almost to the point of obsequiousness, or flirting. Dad didn't really notice, but I knew that Mum was pushed further away by his efforts, put off perhaps by the sense that he wanted to be liked and was willing to play a part to achieve that end. At the beginning, as he got to know them, I shrank, wishing somehow to pull Ryan back with me. Don't, I thought. Just relax. Let her get to know you and you'll be fine. Ryan, don't show off. I loved him at that point without intrusion, and so wanted Mum and Dad to love him too. Dad was impervious to mistrust of those who try too hard. He enjoys good times and is willing to warm to anyone who seems prepared to invest in the same outcome; trust didn't come into it for him. But eventually, betrayal did. My poor father felt so bleakly the times he had welcomed Ryan, helped him, drank friendly beers with him. He had let him slip through his fingers. By the time my father knew what he owed him, Ryan was safely shielded behind the protection of the law.

Dad never felt he had been betrayed by Ryan; he heard betrayal only in the screaming trumpet blast of accusation that he levelled at himself. He felt he had betrayed me by not knowing, he had betrayed me with his friendliness to the man who had hurt me. He had betrayed me by not coming to our flat and insisting that I leave with him. Every pint, every smile, every back-walloping hug. But whatever my darling dad holds against himself, he was doing these things for me, not Ryan. He has learned to negotiate the blame. He has understood them as the workings of grief. He has understood that he feels guilt not because he is guilty, but because I died.

Not so Mum – she still hears that clarion-call of blame. You didn't hear your daughter's need; you didn't see her peril. And though I would do anything to unthink it now, I remember so well the disgusting sense of *furtive betrayal I did indeed feel. They didn't know; they didn't know, and I almost hated them for it.*

I mustered a happy enough performance through that evening. I was truly glad to be at home and relieved not to be at the flat. I would have chosen for myself a small room far away, a retreat of my own, distance from all. Distance, peace, space. Above all, distance. But I didn't know how to avoid this terrible proximity. I wanted to keep intrusive concern at bay. Worse still, sympathy, that deadly destroyer of strategy. With effort, I managed to keep control, wrapped up enough to be quiet but seem happy. Wrapped up enough to deflect unbearable, loving intrusion.

We stayed the night. The large bed of the spare room was occupied by Uncle Paul and Aunt Marie. We had already agreed we would be fine in my old single bed. By bedtime, Ryan was drunk, had forgotten that his bonhomie was faked, had forgotten the tension we arrived with, had forgotten, probably, his violence of the previous evening. I lay in the small familiar bed in my old room, along the edge. My back turned to Ryan, who drunkenly, with recent memory hazily deleted, nuzzled and fumbled at my back. I lay stiff and straight, a coffin, a cell block, my teeth and jaw clamped shut on words of disgust for his greedy, inelegant hands and wine breath. Luckily the wine told on Ryan before either memory or conscience could. He snored behind me. I cried without sound or movement; my bones howled like prisoners through the night.

In the morning I woke early, unrested. The scrabbling of rodent thoughts had kept me awake through the darkness. Only as light began to appear did I snatch at sleep. As soon as I was awake, I eased stealthily from the bed. I dressed with creeping caution, careful of the pain in my wrist and fearful of waking Ryan, of bringing his presence into the precious emptiness of the early day. The kitchen was quiet, somehow the sleep of others in the house tangible, contributing to its peaceful ambience. An idling engine, not yet fired up for the activities of the day ahead. I remember a sad nostalgia, feeling so right in the familiar warmth of home and simultaneously so wrong in my own skin. I remember the wish to grasp for familiarity, retreat into my family. I made, as I always had done, a large cup of tea in my old mug, leaned back against the cupboards and gazed through the window.

Being at home caused such internal friction. It made me feel so deceitful; it made everything feel so wrong. I often avoided home because it upset me so much. I avoided upsetting myself in the same way I avoided anything that would upset Ryan. Any kind of balance felt safer.

I tried to make sense of it all as I stood in the kitchen but, as usual, could see no recipe for harmony. I turned from these thoughts in frustration, resting my forehead on the cupboard, scrunching the fingers of my pain-free hand into an unsatisfied fist. What to do, what to do. How to see. How to understand this hideous tangle. I turned, sighing, as I heard the door open and my mother coming in, her old towelling robe and fat slippers a soothing familiarity. Mum's short hair, tufty from sleep, tickled my cheek as we gave each other a quick greeting hug. I felt a new protectiveness for Mum, felt implicated in a wrong done to her of which she was not yet aware. How devastated she would be to learn of the harm to her daughter. She would feel such terrible sadness if she learned all that she had not been told. We two women stood next to each other as Mum waited for the kettle to boil. I leaned over, shorter by a few inches, resting my head on my mother's shoulder. I remembered these unfastened embraces from smaller days, leaning against my mother's leg, a stillness, contact and balance. How much I would love to revisit that stillness, how much. As usual, Mum reached an arm around me, pulling me in.

I was swayed in that moment by my responsibility to the welfare of others. Not wanting to bear any longer the disgusting betrayal of the people who loved me, I understood that, for them, I had to change things. For them I could find the means to act. I closed my eyes. In the calm familiarity of home, the balance of innate and thoughtless understanding, I felt an unexpected lifting of my mood as a possible future was glimpsed and a solution became evident.

'I'm going to go to uni, Mum. I know it will be for the best. I'll just have to work out a few things, but I'll definitely be there to start in September.'

I remember that little bubble of hope that rose. It lifts me even now.

'Yes, good, definitely the right choice, darling.' Mum leaned over and kissed the top of my bent head. 'You'll see when you get there that it's the right thing. So much will open up for you. And if you want to keep part

of your life the same, or you know, stay together with Ryan, that's fine, you can do that.'

The mention of Ryan caught the gossamer drift of my mood. My escape snagged, and I was slowed.

'Mum, don't say anything to him yet. I mean, I guess he's expecting it, because I haven't said I definitely wouldn't go, but we haven't talked about it for a while, so I just need to tell him myself first.' I had seen freedom in a jump, a skip to a new time, had seen the result and floated serenely, briefly, towards it, but had not yet imagined the strategy to bring about its achievement. But though I felt my heart sink a little, it was in a new, more buoyant medium, not the empty well of night-time. I knew it could be done. Relief swelled within me that if I did ever reveal what had happened to me, I would also be able to say that it had ended. With new optimism, I sat at the kitchen table, chatting about arrangements for the day ahead as Mum brewed fresh coffee.

It is a point in my story that matters, a point when the weights swung, changing the pendulum arc. How near that change came to saving me. So I try to pull it all to me. To remember how it happened. I find lots of it, knowing perhaps how much I want to tell you that I nearly saved myself. I will tell you all I can.

Aunt Marie came down from upstairs, dressed in pyjamas and a jumper. The long plaits still in her hair from last night were fuzzy and her face pale. She complained good-naturedly about a headache, held her coffee in both hands. Mum told her I would be moving up to London after all. Marie leaned over and gave me a delicate, cheery hug, her voice croaky with hangover.

'Remember, love, I said you would be welcome to start off in our spare room. We can see how it goes, but definitely come and stay for the first few months while you work things out. It's small, but there's plenty of room about the house if you want to keep away from us!'

'Thanks, Aunty Mar, that's really kind of you. Don't mention it to Ryan yet though, will you?' Mar mimed a zip across her mouth and smiled at me. How precious that shared complicity, for reasons that at that moment she did not understand. With it, I felt greater certainty in the prospect of a

safe future. I pictured myself, without Ryan, living in my aunt and uncle's house, free of this present painful anguish. Expediency gave me the excuses that my heart and self-interest lacked. Too much to expect them to take two lodgers, after all. Space, distance, autonomy. I saw that it was possible, it was possible just to leave this horrible difficulty behind. I thought perhaps with that separation, I need not go through the trauma of saying goodbye. Perhaps all we needed was a little distance.

Distance, direction, motion. Terms that can be understood on Earth. I don't think I can tell one from the other here. I can't tell a distance because I don't have the edges from which to measure. Distance. A mighty curve. A flat line forever. A sickening rush. But back then, it meant those meagre miles between home and London, the narrowed measure from one edge to the other of a bed for one instead of two. My courage and resolution, sitting in the beautiful, ordinary harmony of family women, grew big enough to count on. Though I wasn't bold enough to test my resolution on Ryan, so I left to visit my oldest friend, Mel, who still lived at home on the other edge of the village, before he emerged from his hungover sleep.

There had been so many times I had nearly revealed to Mel the dark secret of my relationship with Ryan. But like with Mum, I let her believe that my lustreless moods were the ordinary boredom and weariness of badly paid work and uncertain times. She had never fallen for Ryan, seeing in him then what I can see now. His weakness, his dangerous vanity. So she was not sad when I told her, even in my face-saving, tentative way, that we were probably moving apart.

We had seen so little of each other that she had had few opportunities to see behind my clumsy evasions. But I knew that her sharpness, her smartness, her fierce care would not have left my secret hidden for long. So both Ryan and I had put distance between us. Our beautiful friendship, so undeserving of that neglect. I am sorry, Mel, I am so sorry that I didn't come to you, that I didn't let you pull me from this stupid fate. I am sorry that your wonderful love, your strength, all that you would have given me, was not called upon to save me.

I felt embarrassed by my unwillingness to hurt Ryan, and though it takes this backwards view to recognise it, I felt shame because of it. I have already said I will not feel that now. There is no blame I hold against myself now. Shame came with me, like luggage. But I understand the girl whose story I am telling, and I won't keep what she does not deserve.

Leaving him because of what had passed between us would hurt him, perhaps less in the loss of me than by the revelation that his own failings were to blame. The exposure of his own failure, in the glaring scrutiny of blame, seemed so heavy a retribution and potentially a danger to me. Though I understood it was not as damaging an assault as his own, I felt compelled to protect him, and thus myself, from the knowledge of how badly he had failed. Quietly, without being entirely aware of this knowledge, I understood, I think I always had, that failure was Ryan's great fear. He was afraid of being inconsequential, afraid of not living up to what he imagined for himself. There was no true self-love mixed up in his high self-regard.

What I wanted was to leave an unhappy (and, though I did not truly admit to it, frightening) situation, with Ryan's illusions still intact. I wanted to be absolved of a role in the story. Who would not wish to creep quietly away, without a sound, from something that had already caused them such harm? And to hurt back, to accuse, that is not a silent action.

I played down the increasingly commonplace occurrence of his violent outbursts. Unprotected by experience, unarmoured, I had absorbed enough of Ryan's needling, his slow poison disguised as remedy, to feel responsible for his actions to a small but significant degree. I was lacking indignation and self-righteousness. I was trusting, believing. And he had carefully unpicked me. When Ryan told me that he loved me so much it drove him to extremes, I felt hurt by the unfairness but longed to help him, to prove to him that if I caused him pain, it was a mistake on my part. I baulked, in spite of everything, at causing him to feel a failure, to be hurt by his own mistakes.

It would make too, for an easier exit, played as a slow extrication, a slipping away, but it wasn't only because there was danger for me in blaming him, in making him angry.

Collusion is such an ugly accusation. Black-and-white news reels showing the shaved heads of French women, the shearing making them distinguishable for all to gleefully join a crowd that pulls and pokes at them. Hanged, sackcloth bodies on ramparts that now protect new tenants. Collu-

sion ends with shame. There it is again, glinting strongly, woven into the fabric of my tale. This terrible darkness did me at least that one service. As a result of this complete unravelling I saw and caught that glinting, ugly thread and pulled it, pulled it out to straggle shapelessly behind me, burned off finally like my own comet tail. It wasn't part of me. I carried it for another.

But then, at that uncertain, difficult time, in my propaganda–handling I felt the shame of collusion. I was only trying to make my story more manageable, but in so doing, I lessened the damage, I reduced the harm. I excused, to a certain, confusing extent, his actions. I wanted to be free of the intrusions of all and so minimised the truth of what was a part of my life. I didn't know how to account for it. How to answer the questions it prompted. Why, Caitlin? Why didn't you call me? Why didn't you come home? Why didn't you leave? I don't know I don't know I don't know.

This grand and terrible darkness, when I can stop the words from sliding from my fingerless grasp, has given me a chance to make right with myself again. The strange effect is that though I no longer have a vessel in which to hold what I gather, I am finding all the self that Ryan caused me to lose. I find myself in the undoing. But at that time, I shrank. I skipped from under the responsibility of responding to what he had done to me by pretending that he had done little. I colluded with him.

I shudder at all the intimacies that enveloped us. I don't know. Do I shudder? It is hard to say. Perhaps I am bobbing in the memorialised waves of shame, still seeking me out even at this distance, a billion widths of a bed.

I feel the sickness, the fear I had when, later that day, on our own but still in the safety of Mum and Dad's house, I told him of my decision. I was scared. I dreaded his reaction. But I longed, in quiet, secret excitement, for that narrow bed in Paul and Marie's little spare room. Later they offered to swap it for a double, but I claimed I wanted the floor space for yoga. I was excited too by the distant prospect of returning to my dreams. I was filled once again with blessed, if tentative, optimism. Bit by bit, it strengthened me, lifted my sights, made me resolute. My wrist stopped its nagging pain as if his hold was loosening.

He had never said he didn't want me to take my place, only implied that in doing so I would leave him behind. He pretended to understand from *this that leaving him behind was the very thing I had wished for all along. And finally, he was right.*

How meagre his view, when all sights must loop back onto him, when all acts have him as their reason. How compromised his understanding when the only sense he could make of anything was in relation to himself. And yet, in insisting on that pattern, he had created truth. Where once I longed to go to university because of what it would give me, now I longed to go, as he had ever thought, as a way of leaving him behind. He had tailor-made his truth. He had been so maliciously set on predicting my departure that he had brought it about. I would have travelled penniless with him. I would perhaps have given up dreams of highways for good. I would have done so much to coddle the love I had felt for him. But now, hurt and confused by the way the story had changed, I wanted to leave him behind.

I haven't, even now, left him behind. Comet paths, planetary orbits, the unmeasurable distance between life and death, and I still have not left him behind. When I began to try to gather up my story, to take with me a form that would tell me who I am, I had not wanted to make him a part of me. He is there, bound inside a knot of fury that stretches and screeches, elastic, scorching, through my core. But I will find the glinting, ugly end of that knot too and, like shame, will pull it out, the sickly exit of a parasitic worm. A horror-pull, disgusting and necessary. I do not want him part of me. I have seen him, lost at his own hand; the violence done to me has worked equally hard on him. What waste. What a terrible waste.

Sometimes movement is a bouncing skim; a flat stone I am, skipping over the black mirror depths of a still lake. Sometimes I drag like a crippled anchor through knotted rope and kelp on a deep-sea bed. The knowledge of what little shifts were needed to save me weighs me down. How close I came to knowing nothing of this dark world.

If he had been angry when I told him I was going to London, then my story would be of the kind that takes place with new friends, over a drink. I was going out with this guy called Ryan, but it was difficult. He didn't like the idea of me going to university, so I broke up with him, I would say. Perhaps in the intimacy of a new relationship, I would have eventually been able to put aside such bold insouciance and tell of the disembowelling effect of his violence. But he wasn't angry. He was pitifully sad, humble even. He blamed himself for his failure and once more cherished me. He turned back the clock to the summer of gold, became gentle, caring and loving over the next weeks. He invested once more in my happiness, I see now only for the purpose of impressing me..

I have seen now, too, that in the middle of his bones, it plagues him, the knowledge that he did wrong. Perhaps not for any nobler reason than knowing he will be tainted with that in the eyes of others. He didn't mean it, he thinks, pathetically. My fury howls with me as I speed towards him. I lose my thought as the directions and speeds of space make holding on impossible.

And, inexplicably, here I find myself. Inarticulate, my fury spent in the stomach-turning telescopic rush that brought me to Earth to sit, stagnant, surfaceless, unable to touch, move, react. I sit here as if in a further penance, in the air around him, slowed to a pace when fury acts like a sickening deep bass thud, making me nauseous and static at one and the same time. I can do nothing but feel this ghastly stillness of being around him. I can meditate forever on my rage.

It becomes harder to tell. The memories are elusive. Perhaps having had less time to be held, they were not as strongly kept. Memories get stronger with use, like muscles. I have to work harder to find the ones that didn't have time to become strong. When I died, all that had recently happened had not been rightly processed, had not been assigned its place. Like leaving home in a rush with belongings thrown together into a large bag. Though I notice, as I grow used to my new form, sometimes I have made directions out of my wishes. Taken towards what I am thinking of, not by an articulation of desire exactly, but in some way influencing the direction of my own black odyssey.

I know that I hoped for an easy end. Entropy, not destruction. But at least I made steps. I moved to Paul and Mar's to begin my studies and to escape my harms. Dad drove me. Oh, how happy I felt as he drove me out of Oxford, away from the flat, to a new start in London. How instantly uplifting safety is. Ryan was so carefully repentant and so embodied the act of loving me that it was easier than I had anticipated. But yes, I strategised a little. I left some things – clothes, some books, belongings I didn't mind losing – making a show of things being unresolved. Enough of my possessions to seem lightly hostage to the future. Nothing was officially ended, so no fight was needed. He was sad, obsequious, accepting. For weeks this went on, weeks enough in the mayfly life of a teenage girl to seem that all was now certain, the world had changed. I had made it to London, started the course, settled with great, quiet joy into the little spare room at Paul and Mar's. I began to see those sweeping roads, to think in cambers and spans. I began to think of myself as an originator of new possibilities, not a component of someone else's dreams.

But I was afraid, more afraid than I had expected to be. Not as afraid as I had been of violence, not the gut-clenching fear of imminent danger, but the steady, low-grade fear of uncertainty. I had learned that I could forget myself, and that knowledge meant I was slow to find myself again. Having been undone once, so unexpectedly, became a cautionary tale that kept me prisoner in uncertainty and anxiety. I was cautious, and though not vehement in opposition to Ryan's renewed love, a tentative player. I took once more the path of least resistance, reasoning that time and distance would more safely achieve separation.

It is hard to remember why I let him have any role in my life at all. But to understand myself, I must try. I castigate myself, then in turn pity the girl I was, feel only tenderness and understanding. I want to shout myself down for a fool. But what would be the use of that? A fool or not, my story ended here in this vast, black emptiness, this geography of speed and arc. I long ago decided I was not to blame for that ending. I was only nineteen. This place has made me so much older than I was when I died.

So I pull back from calling myself a fool. I must try instead to understand. I took a path of least resistance, hoping that his way and mine would neatly, gently split, peel away as easily as a long leaf from a stem of meadow-grass. I was scared of the fight of parting; who would not be? You cannot be called a fool because you are scared to anger a dangerous person. That specific, special fear, that intimate, orchestrated fear, had gathered other fears into me. Letting the idea of love be present between us kept the most frightening danger at bay. He, sensing he might lose all, tried the strategy that wound me in so effectively the first time. Ryan's rediscovered care seemed to offer a return to what had helped me feel so secure just a few months before. But I knew as well how extremely things could veer, and I had learned too much about what horrors there were so nearby.

For many weeks, he did nothing to hurt or upset me. He took great effort to do the opposite. He claimed self-loathing for having been stupid enough to push me away, to let the extremity of his love for me push me away. He told me he was so sorry he had ever done anything to make me doubt him. Even in my fearful uncertainty, I felt such sweet relief at those words. It had not been my fault after all. I was grateful to him for coming to his senses, for no longer being consumed by doubt and jealousy. Grateful. I shudder at the recollection, furious; a frequency thunders out from me so shrieking that it must belong to sound.

It was a short time from my move to London until my death. Only a few weeks. There is no reason now for me to attempt a good account of myself, only to understand. But I do remember. It is part of me, the cautious joy of feeling that I was nearly free. Part of that joy came from his renewed care.

One day, a fatal day, he came to visit. We walked side by side across the gentle slopes and sweeps of a park. Dog barks flattened in the slight fog and cold of the day, the breath of runners misting as they passed, lost in the drive of their private music. I talked to him, openly, honestly, and told him how much he had frightened and hurt me. Because we both looked only at the ground before us, not at what such intimacy left bare on our faces, I was able to say what had always been shut off before I had formulated the words. My telling ended as we approached a group of broad and ancient trees. We stood in the dimmed light under the bare branches. I tried to see in his face the effect of my words. He wouldn't look at me. I saw that he was crying.

It was a mistake. I thought those tears marked something, meant something healing. If he was sorry after all, if he was even a little ashamed, then the harm was somehow lessened. How much easier to carry on as we were, believing once more in each other. I could stay with Paul and Marie as long as I wanted, they had told me. Ryan had no plans to move to London. We could just start again, in a new and better balance. Things, I thought, go wrong for people because of the circumstances they find themselves in, not because of the people they are. It was a mistake.

Chapter 15

Anna wakes early on her second-to-last day. After she has eaten and had coffee in the lounge of the hotel she goes for a walk. There is a headland with a rocky promontory, a small cone-shaped hill. Distance is as uncertain as size, but she aims towards it, a slow walk, time passing under her feet. Towards the edge of the town, she hears her name and turns to see Stefan wave at her from a building on the beachfront. He beckons her over. He is sitting in a wicker chair, at a small folding table in front of a building that looks like a boat shed of some kind. There is a large pot of coffee on the table. He invites her to join him. He pulls up a second, wooden, chair and gestures her to the more comfortable cushioned wicker one, then goes inside, coming back a moment later with a second cup and a carton of milk held against his body.

Stefan says if she doesn't mind he will walk with her; there is a small beach on the other side of the promontory they could visit. Anna is pleased to accept his company. He tells her the bay is less populated than this one, often completely empty. There, the wind buffets the shore in jumping eddies, not the long sweeps favoured by surfers. That and the tricky access ensures the bay remains usually unvisited. They finish their coffees and head off. The conversation is easy; they talk the main roads, the basic shapes, the broad strokes. She tells him she has no children. She doesn't tell him she had a daughter. She doesn't tell him her daughter is dead. She doesn't tell him her daughter was killed. She doesn't tell him that the man who killed her is called Ryan and he goes shopping in her home town.

They pull away from the shore and upwards, cutting across the landward side of the headland on a track that is not surfaced, two slim, dull snakes moving in parallel curves through stones and shrubs. There is a trail of bottles and cigarette packets at the edge of the track, enough to show that people do come here after all. Probably young people in cars, music hurtling from open windows, chasing down the promise of evening, the thrill of long night. At this time Anna and Stefan are the only people around.

The conversation stalls as their breath is saved for the walk. The track becomes narrower and steeper, fit for hikers only. Soon they are over the saddle of the promontory, and the path curves inland, around the edge of a small bay. The rocks between the track and shore are jagged and steep. She sees that further along there is a smaller path sneaking through the rocks down to the beach. The descent is steep but passable enough with care. Once on the sand there is a sense of enclosure, and, in spite of the increased volume of the sea as it bounces off the jagged rocks that surround the thin moon of sand, a sense of hush; though it is loud, the sound becomes soothing in its constancy, a blanket over all, a sonic lid keeping out the rest of the world. She walks to the water, kicks off her shoes and stands calf-deep in the sea.

Moments pass calmly in the rush of sound and wind that thicken the air, filling the curve of the bay, packing the spaces around them. A baffling wool of weather and noise. Stefan lies on the sand, propped up on one elbow, twirling a slim twig through the top layer of sand. His shirt flops around him as if spilled. He looks up occasionally, past her towards the open sea. She crosses slowly back and forth in the lowest reaches of water, looking at the sand by her feet, looking for treasure on the shore. Eventually she joins Stefan and sits too, knees up under her chin, held close in wrapped arms. It feels good to be in the empty space, away from even the sedate chug of vacation life at the hotel.

Stefan asks her when she is due to go back to England. The strings around her wrists, her waist and thighs pull threateningly tight. Not so gentle a reminder. She is silenced by everything that they mean, a gagging restriction in her throat. Ryan is trying to escape into her words. She swallows. And remembers with dismay that she is due to go back the day after tomorrow. So little has changed. After a pause, she tells Stefan she leaves in two days, apparently revealing something of the despair it causes her, for he looks at her closely and asks if she is all right. She tells him she has a number of problems, trailing off awkwardly. She tells him it is difficult for her to talk about. Stefan does not push her; her reluctance to talk is clear in the scratchy stringing of words she has managed to drag out. He says that if she wants to talk to him she can (and maybe talk with a relative stranger might help – everyone has told her so. Many, many times). She latches onto this gift, with gratitude that it has been offered, saddened that she won't accept it. So possessive are we about that which ruins us.

As they move back to more general conversation, Anna relaxes, and they talk, easy once more in each other's company. Stefan tells her of his divorce, the bitterness he experienced after losing his hand in a traffic accident. He had been a photographer for newspapers and journals, a successful man with a family and career he'd dreamed of. He tells her that after the accident, self-pity got the better of him, alcohol greased the wheels, and he became, he says, a horrible person. The relationship with his daughter here, and another daughter and son still in Germany, had to be painstakingly rebuilt over the last few years. But he and the children's mother parted for good. He then set up a business with a partner, sold out to the partner to come here. All these years told in a few moments, told with an ease formed in the softening wisdom of age. She knows this wisdom in others.

After some time, they pull themselves gingerly up from the sand, slowly and with care for creaking knees and ankles. Their joints are stiffened by sitting on damp sand that is cool in spite of the warm day. Stefan helps steady her as she slowly straightens up. They laugh as he has to jiggle a foot to get rid of pins and needles. The path back up to the track is a challenge for stiff legs, but the climb soon loosens and warms them.

She and Stefan part company at the same place they met. Anna heads back to the hotel alone. Back in her room, she sits on the balcony with her writing book. She feels grateful for Stefan's company, enjoyed being with him. For a moment she envies him, for the grandchildren, for the life he lives with his family. For the way he has let his misfortune drift away into the past like an untethered boat on calm water. She pulls away from envy and feels instead gratitude for small acts of friendship, looks forward to meeting Estela later that evening.

Before going out to meet her, she turns to the news.

3 January

Roadside bomb, eighteen killed.

So many people dying, I can't catch them all, it's impossible. Eighteen out of hundreds. And I don't even have the energy for all eighteen.

A reserved man, polite and ordered by an old-fashioned courtesy. Sometimes he and his wife will dance together in their front room, re-enacting the formal courtesies of courtship. A postcard sent from their youth. They are solemn but laugh gently at their creaking knees, wrinkled hands resting in imitation of uncertainty on thickened waists.

Two years old, sweet smile and fat feet. She is shy and curious. She holds out her little dress by the hem so she can look down at the pattern.

Athletic and agile, like his father. Under his T-shirt he wears a silver chain with a drop-shaped medal that he found in the street. He believes it will spill magic for him one day. He found it in a dusty corner at a precise moment of fervent hoping, a dull glint, a silver promise.

A languorous, moody girl of twelve. She hardly bothers to speak to her mother. Really, she loves her with a depth that would have lasted many times the short twelve years she has had. But she is moody with the early summer storm of her age. Prickly, tetchy, lazy with the unexpected heat.

A boy of nineteen who has the grace of a true athlete, an eye, an arc that understands speed and space. He throws, catches, runs, races and seems to glide, a fin that cuts through time and space, a bird's wing. He has the prowess of Achilles and the gentle grace of all his seven siblings,

raised in harmony and careful love by a widowed mother
and her two indefatigable sisters.

A girl who could do cartwheels the length of a football
pitch, bark-brown hair sweeping the sparse summer grass,
a steady arc of progress, four limbs turning turning
turning, as if to keep rolling away through the fields, into
the summer sky beyond. A girl with river eyes, an unsettled
green, or brown. A girl who felt the injustices of the world
as if they happened on her own skin.

She is there again, a ghost-glimmer on the page, a dusting of memory
amidst invention. No secret revelations, no subconscious rising; this is
not a leak of steam as pressure builds. This is a deliberate summoning.
She tries to look. But only in tiny increments. She tries to look.
And quickly the buffers are hit, the barriers lowered, the way halted.
Thank God. She turns away. Her own guard dogs turn against her,
snarl, quiet but menacing, eyes locked on her, a low growl as they
watch her leave.

But there she was, close enough to see details – a small mole on
her cheek, the flecks of green in her eyes. The one who sneaks aboard
and quietly insists she is seen, quietly says *look at me*. How she has
missed her girl, banished from thought for the trains of misery that
drift in behind her, quiet as her tread but choking and deadly. Woeful
veils blocking out happy memories. She is clothed in darkness too
impenetrable. So she is banished. Poor girl, she did not dress herself
this way; it is Anna who clothes her thus. Poor darling girl pushed
away once more. What kind of mother is she to banish the daughter
who has already lost so much? What kind of mother is she?

Chapter 16

I find myself in that room, looking at the carpet, the place where I died. Bland, utilitarian. An oatmeal backdrop for my cooling body, at once both heavier and less anchored than I ever was in life. Yes, it is where I fell. I can remember it, if I try, if I must. Oatmeal, magnolia, white gloss. The markers of a temporary home. A front door key and domestic utility made cheaply nice. I had spent the hour before my death bleakly mollifying, burdened by the necessity of such a routine. Burdened by the chemistry of panic under my skin. Burdened by the hollow expediency, by now, of my own words. I didn't quite know then that they weren't true, so gradually had they become untrue. So confusing and jarring had been the passage of those months that honest interrogation was a luxury. Of course I love you. No, I want to be with you. I'm sorry. And the true words too. I didn't mean to upset you. I'm not seeing anyone, I'm not interested in him, I hardly even know him. It doesn't need to be like this, Ryan.

A commonplace. An unnecessary argument between ordinary people. Nothing to gain in taking it so far. It wouldn't even be in the news. But violence, at least whilst it was happening, satisfied something in Ryan. Maybe just for the uncensored joy of giving in totally to anger, to an animal rage. But nothing to gain. Look at him now: dulled, quieted, less than he was. Those cruel moments of relish changed everything for him as well as for me. For Mum. For Dad. His parents too. So proper and discreet, so proud of their son. How their lives too changed when mine ended.

I can't be sure of everything that happened; there had been some snarling moments quickly covered over, buried by him, cast from view by me. I had made some new friends, I remember, on my course in London. I was excited about a project with Matthew and Ben. I liked them both. I think they were a cause of one of the black moods. But he mastered it. I thought it was a good sign. I was very busy anyway, for a number of weeks, and very excited about the new term. I went back home for the weekend to celebrate my twentieth birthday with the family and with Ryan. We were all going to go out for a meal. Ryan had asked that we first spend an evening just the two of us, as it had been so long since we'd spent any time together and he didn't want to see me only with everyone else there. I was late leaving for my train. I had had a birthday drink I think, with my new friends, and they decided to see me off. My good cheer was boosted by a bottle of cava that Ben had bought to drink on the way to the station. I regretted leaving the joyful time with my new friends for the flat and a tense little duet with Ryan.

Ryan had also been drinking, a bottle of good red wine that he'd opened without me as I was late. I was late by less than ninety minutes; it seemed unnecessary to take up solo drinking as a protest. But as usual, the pattern of trying to rebuild fell to me. I apologised, often. He was petulant to start with. He gestured to the table; a gift wrapped in stiff brown paper with a white ribbon sat next to the one clean, one used wine glasses. He said he wanted me to open it now. It was a necklace, curved silver sections with stars cut into it, delicate metal with a hammered finish. It was very pretty. I took off the necklace I wore all the time – a silver daisy on a silver chain, from Mum and Dad on my sixteenth birthday – to try it on.

I don't remember how things deteriorated so extremely. I know I had been trying to explain my enjoyment of my new project. I know that Ryan had become angry again, about me being late, about me talking too much about my course. I know that I felt a ghastly sinking of my whole insides that ended with a lurch into terrible fear as the first blow landed in my stomach. I was bewildered, panicked, I was trying to explain, trying to explain, trying to explain. No, you are mistaken. I love you. Those half-true, untrue words spent like a bribe, enriched by the lavish sales pitch of fear. I LOVE you. I pleaded as he punched me again, his face contorted, amplifying the violence with its dislike and contempt. No, Ryan, don't. Please don't. He called me a selfish bitch and punched me twice more, I think mainly on my arms, raised over my face. He grabbed the necklace he had just recently helped me fasten, pulled me towards his ugly face and punched round from his shoulder to the side of my head. The necklace broke, hung in his fist. I staggered and fell, hitting the other side of my head on the kitchen units. I fell to the carpet and felt the blackness swirl in like ink dropped into a glass of water.

There was a long time after that, feeling uncertain, confused, feeling things I don't know how to explain. I was glinting coal dust falling down a well, a satin cord that twisted in and out of knots in the grip of another's hands. I was a tiny area of grey plastic inside a mountainous block of grey plastic. I span, a crowd of me, we span through the dark. We clumped together and were pulled apart slowly. I was a slippery rope, an unwound gut sliding through a lightless slaughterhouse.

I first noticed the nothingness around me, then the buffeting of strange, unpredictable waves. I began to see the distant stars. Sometimes I came closer to them; they showed the size of a sun. Sometimes since then, I have got closer still. They burn, but how that heat beguiles me. How I want to burn up. But not yet.

My story is told; I am rid of the taint of my story. I have found myself again. Though other things are still lost or still broken. How I want to repair those breaks.

I have told what happened to me, but it happened to others too. There is more that I need to reel in. It has been terrible to see a side of my parents that I never expected to share. I wish Dad had been able to help Mum, to give her what he was able to painstakingly and courageously give himself. I wish he had been able to take her with him on those long, brave walks. I wish she could pull from within herself the taint of my death. I wish she could remove those million coiled miles of grief that mummify her, bind her.

Yes, I have my story, but there is something else I want. For her, from her – how can I tell the difference? She is my mother. I seek her out and, more often now, I find her. Recently I have seen her on a beach. And on a dusty road. I don't recognise where it is. It can be hard to tell if I am remembering or seeing sometimes. Because memories play out like films, placed before me, waiting patiently for me to understand that I have something to do with them. And what role in all of this for imagination? Perhaps I dream these sightings. But I have seen my mother, walking on a long dusty road, alone. I have seen her on a beach and swimming in the sea. I want to reach her. I want to take back the rope I put on her. The burden that she carries, it is too much, too awful to bear. My beautiful, loving, impatient, kind mother, her deep and generous heart is shrunk, a pond in cracked drought. How I wish I could undo that awful aridity.

But she doesn't see me. I can't reach into her as I do with Dad. No way to keep her company. I wish she could at least see me. Not perhaps as I see her, but somehow just to know I am there. Sometimes I get close, I know it, but she will look away. She always looks away.

Chapter 17

It is evening; night falls quickly. Dusk is a brief affair, a mauve curtain pulling swiftly across the interval of a two-act play. Anna has texted Estela and arranged to meet in the square so she can say goodbye. She wishes to thank Estela for her kindness, a care that has stayed with her.

In the square there are groups of teenagers, smoking. The girls sit in rows on the backs of the benches, orchestrating actions for the boys who push and move around each other, jostling one another, voices uneven and unnecessarily loud. They need to claim their presence with noise and movement; it is their right and their ritual. The warm wind pulls into town off the sea, drawn in, cavorting round them like a pack of playful dogs.

Anna waits on one of the tiled concrete benches around the edge of the square. She sees Estela coming towards her from the town. She is dressed in narrow jeans, slim turquoise-and-gold sandals and a patterned top that has copper and gold beads threaded on the thin straps over her brown shoulders. Around her neck is a jumble of necklaces, charms and chains, she has silver bracelets on her wrists, and her hair is pinned up loosely with turquoise flowers. She is wearing a small amount of makeup. She tells Anna she is going out with friends for a birthday later in the evening. She looks radiant and lovely. They sit side by side.

'Estela, I wanted to thank you again for being so kind the other night. It meant a lot to me.'

'It's not a problem at all, I do only a small help.'

'Well, it feels like a big help to me.' Anna pauses, searching for the next step, the beginning of the next path. 'It's been a strange time for me.'

Estela reacts eventually to Anna's silence, gently and briefly touching Anna's arm.

'If you want to tell me, is okay.'

A breath, a pause. She tells Estela that she has been thinking of her daughter. She tells her that she died. A few months after moving out. Hardly out of her home at all. Not properly gone, but gone forever.

Estela asks her when, and Anna thinks Estela is surprised when she tells her it was nearly ten years ago. Her awkwardness with these facts makes it seem a more recent loss, but she is used to this. People don't understand the constant raw breakage. They don't understand that not everyone heals. The outer layer has hardened; there is a semblance of repair. Her life is moulded in a thick layer, shaped by it. A mending clay, a cast, a substance of incomplete repair. Enough to get by. A conversation such as this requires a deliberate act of control lest the spoiled liquid underneath leak through and shock them all. There is gentle quiet for a few moments. Suddenly there is a cracking and an oozing, a rush of words. She tells Estela about seeing Ryan, barely managing to explain that he is the one who killed her daughter. She tells of the harrowing pain of knowing his life is ahead of him. She says she feels that what lies ahead for her makes no sense, there is no way for her to understand it. She talks hurriedly, in broken and unfinished sentences, knowing vaguely that it will test Estela's under-standing of English. The words come out, heedless, testing, with their jumble and their unexpected rush, even Anna's own understanding of what she is saying. Eventually she halts, repeats that her daughter's killer has come out of prison and she doesn't know how to be any more.

'I see why you say you didn't want to go home.' Anna is surprised by this. She doesn't know when she said that. She looks at Estela quizzically. 'When you were sitting on the beach, you said it then.'

'Sorry, I can't really remember, I… it is not like me to get so drunk, or to cry like that, it…'

'No, is fine, I am sorry that we maybe… come into your life without invitation.' She stretches to find the right way of expressing herself in English.

'It's just that it's nearly ten years since Caitlin died, and her father wants to have a big celebration. I can't stand the thought of that. There's nothing to celebrate. I understand his meaning, he wants to celebrate her life, but I can't, I don't know how. And now I've seen Ryan, I keep imagining him with a new life, with children, with everything. His debt has been paid, apparently, and the world is open for him again. There he is, in our home town. He's probably celebrating too, his freedom. I just can't bear it. I know it's wrong but I wish he, I wish I could… stop him existing.'

Anna is shocked by these words, which, at last, after so long getting stuck in her throat, catching on her teeth, making a gristle rope into her guts, have surprised her with their easy spilling. She feels an uncertain poise, a lightness, a bird in a town garden expecting a cat. But the cat is gone. She can see it behind an upstairs window. It watches her but cannot pounce.

She starts again slowly. 'I am stuck with the emptiness of the last ten years, all that has not happened during them. And now I've seen Ryan, of course he is free to do anything he wants with his life. He's out of prison and can have children, marry, prosper. He can play sodding golf if he wants to, or stay in bed all day watching telly. Caitlin had barely started her life – by now she could have done so much. I know she would have done.'

'This must be very painful. You have other family?'

'No, she was an only child. Like me.' Anna pauses, awkward and unsure. 'When she died, our marriage fell to pieces. So, I'm on my own. Though of course I have friends, lovely friends. I don't know what I would do without them sometimes, though there are occasions when they drive me mad.' She looks up, and they share a soft, brief smile.

'What was she like? Your daughter?' But Anna's reluctance returns, the brisk nurse of her upkeep appears, reapplying the binding. She smiles, and tells Estela, 'I would like to tell you. I hope I can tell you some time. I think you and she would have been friends. But do you mind if I don't just now? It would make me sad, and as it's my last night, shall we just go and get a beer?'

They walk together to the bar. Karl is sitting with a group of friends, other healthy sea-creatures, past the time of awkward display on the town square, into the sleek beauty of young adulthood. The sun seems stored in their beautiful faces and radiant smiles. A little bit of light captured on the waves and shared round with the other mere mortals later in the day. Karl waves at them cheerfully. Anna stays for one drink, then prepares to return to her room. She asks Estela to say goodbye to Stefan for her. As they chat awkwardly on the terrace, a goodbye for people who don't know yet what their connection is, Karl tells them both to stand with their backs to the sea and takes a couple of pictures of them.

Anna embraces Estela, sorry to say goodbye. As she is about to leave, Estela says, 'Perhaps, Anna, one day you can tell me about your daughter. I would like to hear about her, if you can, one day. It is sad for you to feel so alone.' Anna is touched by her words, understands the simple truth that Estela sees in them. But she is certain still that there is no answer to the misfortune that defines her; she feels regretfully that the weight of it pulls her from the reach of new friendships.

She wakes early on the last day of escape. She goes for a swim before the beach is cluttered, before it is patterned with bodies and their untidy skirts of paraphernalia. The sun is still low, hidden behind buildings but brightening the sky; the day has begun. The waves are small and steady, but the surfers' loss is her gain. She walks slowly into the water, each inch given with pleasant reluctance to its cool touch. This time she decides to swim out, past the hotel that rises with fauxmodernist poise from its rocky promontory. On the other side, at the back of the hotel, is a small patch of sand, a backyard, neglected by holiday makers. She swims round to it. She gets closer to the shore, intending to explore, but stays in the water. Small beaches on the edge of things, next to marinas, on the far side of harbour walls, often have a forbidding quality, unwelcoming, neglected. Like the undersides of some bridges, a little sinister and dark, with stagnant patches that collect the debris of bad thought. She remembers a walk in an unfamiliar town. Under a road bridge, an old mattress that suggested a grim resident. Peculiar rubbish trapped in concrete corners. The debris of furtive acts collected in the hidden recesses. She swims back a little hastily, out to the clear water before the hotel's sun deck and back round to the sunny sand of holiday life. She floats in the shallows, hands on the sand a gentle anchor as the waves lull over her, barely breaking as they meet the land. She stays for some time. She swims out again, under the water with her eyes open, seeing nothing but blurring of light and dark. Cool and restful under the water. A new breath and sink again, still, still, still, look at the blur of light and dark, try not to imagine shadows, sea-shadows that move slow and quiet, subtle silent threat. Death from below. The welcome sunlight breaks crisply across her eyes in shards as she resurfaces, short of breath; anxiety snags a first lungful of air. Floating in the deeper water, she looks back to the shore. She senses the water's cool weight below her. At least she imagines she does. On the beach, she sees the burnished boy, the Achilles of the dusty field, eyes burning into the sun. Lying on the sand, parallel to the surf, is the jeweller, black hair curling into the sand like washed-up seaweed. The old gentleman walks with his grandson, who darts back and forth like a sand-hopper, returning with shells and sea mysteries to show him. And there, way down the beach, a shimmer, the lightest hazel strokes, looking straight at her, is Caitlin.

Chapter 18

Anna sits in her coat at the kitchen table. Her case is on the floor beside her, her bag and purse on the table. What now? What now, she thinks. Leaving isn't difficult; it's the staying gone that is the problem. Out-running the elastic leash that holds her. She sits still, flat, dulled by the knowledge that nothing has, after all, changed. What now? All well and good that in other places in the world all manner of lives are happening, free of the dark weights that oppress her. Just as the news reminds her of the opposite, that in other places in the world people do not enjoy her comfortable certainties. Like her, though, they share the burden of loss. Children lost in rubble and war, or car crash, illness, violence. Parents the world over counting down, since the time of their child's death, to the moment of their own. Parents the world over not sinking into that malaise. Learning, like Michael, how to live beyond the terrible event.

Anna sighs, thinks instead about an evening meal – time once again to be on her own in this house. Time to pull it round her and discover whether it feels more like an embrace or a sarcophagus. She takes her case upstairs, finds warmer clothes: woollen socks, a jumper and heavy trousers. Then, picking up her bag from the kitchen table, she goes to her small car for a drive to the nearest supermarket to restock the fridge and the wine cupboard. She has temporarily lost the knack of seeing the day ahead as a series of chores that are a legitimate use of a life. She thinks instead, I must get some food, but what then? A dangerous question.

Anna sits at the kitchen table in her pyjamas. She twists the handle of a fork; the chink of metal on the plate makes small bounces of sound in the still room. The kitchen clock ticks. What now?

The evening is whittled down until finally it is time to go to bed. It is good to be in her own bed – she is glad to have found that small plea-sure in her return, but it does not soothe away the crinkles, the creases, the knowing. He is there, probably lying in his bed, still enjoying the pleasure of it after nearly ten years in a bed that belongs as much to Anna as it did to him. A bed of state. At least during that time she did not think of him living a life denied to Caitlin. His being in prison provided a useful, though she now knows temporary, stasis.

It is such torment. He must be there at his parents' home, his mother secure once more in her blind faith, ready to put this terrible unfairness behind them and welcome her precious son back as blameless as the day he was born. God, how Anna hated them, their willingness to believe it had all been a terrible accident. How she hates to believe they might be happy to have him back.

Maybe he is out with new friends, friends who, if he ever does tell them about Caitlin, will see it as his blind and foolish parents have chosen to, a terrible accident. Poor Ryan; he was reckless, but what bad luck. God forbid, but these things can happen. She could believe at least that they would have to be new friends. None of Caitlin's old friends would make room for him now.

Anna remembers the cards she got in the post over the years from Mel. Greetings, caring questions, her new address when she moved away from the village, a picture of her with a man and baby. They were kind, small connections, but even though Anna deplored it in herself, she resented them. Mel, such a good friend, someone Anna once cared about deeply. Almost as familiar, that straight, pale hair, bent over the kitchen table, as Caitlin's own. The two girls slamming doors between bursts of energetic pop music as they traded tops and hair decorations, combining and sharing their wardrobes to make perfect going-out ensembles. Before Ryan. Anna clenches her jaw, even less ready for happy memories than she is for sad ones.

She longs, suddenly, briefly, to see Mel, believing that Mel's clear certainties, her sense of injustice, would not try to tidy away Anna's anger. Mel never really liked Ryan, understood the flaw in him before he revealed it himself. But perhaps, like so many others, Mel too has moved on.

He was likeable enough, she supposes, Ryan. Likeable enough to easily make new friends. She liked him because Caitlin wanted her to. He had good manners, a nice face, though weak. The soft face of a pretty boy never becoming handsome as a grown man. He thought well of himself, but equally he seemed to think very well of Caitlin. He pursued her with a great zeal that, even then, Anna found uncomfortable in a way she could not place. He wanted so very much to impress Anna, and Anna had reached an age when that was no longer impressive. But she only thought him self-absorbed, too proud of himself, only needy. Not dangerous. She thought he wanted adoration so he could bathe further in the light of his own worth. She thought him a bit of a pillock. But her girl, she was moved by his ardour. She thought it was love. How wretched a love. How he made nothing of that love and all she willingly gave him, of her whole self. He made her nothing. And Anna looked blindly on, no harbour light to guide her daughter home, no fireman's lift, no rescue. No sixth sense or mother's intuition. No warning bells. She saw the bruises more than once, but she believed Caitlin's accounting for them. Her lies. She saw the bruises. They made not a sound, silent as mice behind the scenery flats of her tales. She didn't hear their truth, didn't heed the danger.

Perilous voice. Time for other, louder intrusions that will push away this hideous truth-telling. She switches on the television in the corner of the bedroom and dabs angrily through the options until she can find distraction.

She wakes in the smudgy grey of morning. Gets up, sits at the kitchen table with coffee, scrolls through news, anxious to install her familiar barriers and distractions. The violence of strangers gives her an explanation for her own dark hates. Thoughts of revenge, particular and violent, are muted, camouflaged as a universal anger at injustice.

So many crises and disasters. Lives changing in a glitter-flick across the surface of the planet. A disco ball of transformation. Where are the lives that change for the better? She does not, as habit, seek them out. What would those stories be? Light-entertainment platitudes. Random sparks amongst the sweeping dark patterns created by politics and war. A child returned home from war would make a star pattern, an immeasurable improvement in the lives of parents, siblings, lover and child. They might extend that star to favour the next linked to them. A pay rise for employees in the mother's business. An act of kindness from a sister to her neighbour. Little stars of luck, tender spokes of good fortune, trying to survive in all corners. But war and politics writes the surface with such bold designs. Blocks of misfortune and crisis visible from the moon. And there are subtler patterns too, subtle stars of misfortune, she thinks. When my girl died the world stopped, and no one even noticed.

The day arrives slowly, a flat stillness, a steady light. It is overcast and windless. Time for a walk. A visit later, a shop, another walk, TV. A lie down and sit up and stop thinking and turn away. Stomp and march and creep through the day with nothing to show and nothing to be seen, move along, there's nothing here. Be so interested, Anna, in the low level of coffee in the jar, in the sudden desire to eat – what? Lemon meringue pie, it might as well be – that your mind shrinks to the size of a shopping list and the minimal ability to drive a car and count the change. Be so absorbed by this unpaid bill or that unwritten email that you see no more than a few sheets of A4 paper and a screen that tells you what you need to know. Be bored, be still, be bloody quiet.

Let the trees smooth out these wrinkles whilst you walk among them. Let them shield and shelter, let them be beautiful enough to soothe. She walks in the woods; the echoing emptiness of a cold day is comforting. The glimmers of her ghosts still glide between the trunks – they too seem soothed and a part of this landscape. What a strange journey, to be killed there and made anciently at home here. Anna feels guilt at having wrought such imperious alchemy on those unknown lives but remembers that they are her ghosts only. She is no stealer of souls. There again is the boy, dressed now for winter warmth, looking upwards through the lattice of bare branches as if waiting for another plane to cross, even though there is no shadow on a day like this, and the plane would fly high above the Tupperware lid of the clouds. Anna and he think in quiet communion about the birds instead, their hush in winter, as if they wait it out for the spring they know to be coming. For now, they fly this angle, that direction.

Why? Where are they going? Why is that bird sitting there on that branch? It waits, it only waits.

Two days pass in boredom and uncomfortable uncertainty. She is not troubled by the question of the last few months: what shall I do with my life? It seems too absurd to examine such a grand question when she has lost the knack of knowing what she should do with the next few hours. She sinks into a hollow, absent kind of depression. Flat and bored and low. Pointless life. She ignores Sophie's subtle, worried frown, tells other friends that she had a good time, puts off meeting for the time being, anxious lest they reveal that the news of Ryan's return has reached them, hopeful it has not. She does not write in her book or add to her tribe of ghosts. But she sees them in corners, mourns their lost lives, as with each time she sees them she finds another part of the life they left behind. She buys teacakes on one of her shopping trips, for the little girl who likes to pick off the chocolate. They remain unopened on the kitchen counter. She thinks of the young man with the canvas bag, striding down the lane to discover her commonplace of woodland and muddy verge, her ordinary, flint-studded fields. He looks and sees it all as precious and new. She pulls on a coat and goes out into the lane, hoping to catch at his coat-tails a new sense of wonder, right now as good as purpose. But she walks a short way, turns into the field, and is halted by its emptiness and the cold. She goes home and sleeps on the sofa.

On waking, she looks at her email and sees she has a message from Estela. The message is short; she reads it as she waits for the accompanying image to appear. 'Anna, it was very nice to see you in Tenerife. I hope you maybe come back one day. Here is the picture I say I will send you. I hope it is not too hard for you now in England. I hope you find a way to make it better. Estela xx.' The photo is one of the ones Karl took as Anna was leaving, Anna and Estela in the square, lit up by flashlight against an aubergine-dark sky. They smile; Anna looks a little formal, Estela warm and cheerful. She smiles now, looking at the picture, glad that she has a copy. In the kitchen she opens a bottle of wine, pours a large glass and returns to the screen. The freedom of holidays, that absence of connection to the things that normally shape life, the undoing of ties. Why is it so hard, she thinks, for them to remain undone? We plug back into home like a socket shaped both to charge and restrain. She looks at Estela, her wide smile, tanned and freckled from hours outside. The silvers and stones of her jewellery shine in a jumble round her neck and the wrist, raised to pull a strand of hair back from her face. Anna notices amongst the necklaces a flower, a daisy. She zooms in to the picture. One of the chains has a daisy pendant. It is not, she thinks, exactly the same, but it is very like it. So hard to think of that sixteenth birthday. So hard to think of that precious time. Her heart starts to beat fiercely. She feels the danger of it. But she looks again at the photo and that little silver daisy. Where is it? Where is the one she gave to Caitlin all those years ago? Her heart beats; it warns her with its tattoo of beats, it warns her to be ready to run, but she doesn't run. She picks up her glass and goes to the top of the stairs. There, ahead of her, is her own bedroom door. There, to the left, is the door to Caitlin's room. Is the daisy necklace still in there? In one of the big cardboard boxes, or one of the small trinket boxes still sitting on the windowsill? Her heart warns her. It beats. It works as if she is running, but she is not. She walks slowly forwards, rests her unsteady hand on the door as if to feel its heartbeat. I am not steady enough for you, but are you steady enough for me?

Chapter 19

It isn't the first time she has stood in this room. It isn't the only time she has stood in the doorway, caught between retreat and advance. Caught in the evidence room of the past. Now and then over the years she has stood in the doorway, intent on finding something beyond the remaindering, the useless storage. At the beginning, she looked at surfaces that Caitlin had touched – a duvet cover, drawer handles, the tiny beads of a discarded necklace. She read diaries in despair, held scarves to her face. At the beginning, she sat on the bed and wept, she lay on the floor in catatonic grief, deaf to Michael's distraught pleading, not heeding the weary trudge of his feet back down the stairs as he departed to grieve on his own once more. When the time came, some months later, for him to leave, he asked if he could take some things. Anna had by then removed all the photos from the rest of the house, the albums, the framed photographs given as gifts, all the images of the daughter who was gone. The only way to carry on was for her to be gone altogether, she thought. Excised. No, not excised, but absent enough for a barrier to form. She sat in silence, staring at the wall of unruly shrubs outside the living room window, did not say goodbye as Michael left for the last time, with a pile of framed photographs and a pair of tan boots held in an embrace before him, a link from his old life to the new one ahead.

Barriers formed, slowly, slowly. Barriers that were only visible from certain, carefully choreographed angles, barriers that did not bear rubbing up against. Since those early days, Anna has created a conspiracy in which absence is played out by concealment. But the ruse is thinning; her greatest fear is being reminded of the artificiality of the refuge. The trick was as feeble as keeping a door shut, of setting guard dogs at the door of her own memory, setting them to nip at her own heels, to growl with tensed malice if ever she strayed too close. The door has remained shut. The boxes unemptied. The room is not a shrine; it is a guarded blank in her mind behind a shut door, a hiding place. The flat face of a shut door holding out for years and years against the dangerous intrusion of Anna's memories.

She stands with her hand on the door handle, reaching for the unfamiliar position of the light switch. Her heart still beats at a gallop, a reminder that should she need to run, it is ready. But she holds still, looks across to the window, the partially drawn curtains revealing a row of boxes and trinkets on the windowsill, backed by the glass-smooth darkness of night. What was left over when Caitlin partly moved from home. She half remembers other containers of jewellery and adornment in the larger boxes still on the bed. She can't remember if Caitlin wore the necklace, if it would have gone with her to the flat and to London. She has to hold herself rigid amidst the speculation, a force of will just to consider these slim details.

For courage, wine, she tells herself, going back downstairs in temporary retreat. The door stays open, the light on, a commitment to return shown in the unfamiliar shape of electric light spilled on the upstairs hall floor. Wine refills her glass. She takes the bottle up too. Do not blame her for the minutes spent sitting on the third stair, bottle in one hand, glass in the other, as if to weigh against each other. They both mean the same thing. She is a crossing point that links more or less of the same thing. Misery and misery, less or more. A sip from this, a slug from that. Get drunk on misery, risk being hungover for months. To look or not to look, this or that.

The bottle sits on the step beside her, the emptied glass turning gently, one hand cradling the oval top, two fingers of the other hand twisting the stem. She lets herself settle into knowing that she will look – she will open boxes and touch clothes, move books, search under photos and papers; she will be surrounded by what was left behind when her daughter died. Abruptly, she gets to her feet, picking up the bottle as she stands, and resolutely goes up the stairs and into Caitlin's bedroom. She puts the bottle and glass down on a chest of drawers that used to be a shelf for Caitlin's favourite books: *Middlemarch, Alice in Wonderland*, a dictionary that had belonged to Michael's father. She searches her memory for the other titles, knows that the books, after their short trip out of the room, have made their way back inside one of the boxes on the bed, where they have been for nearly ten years. There was a nature book, delicately illustrated with pictures of wild flowers and silhouettes to identify trees by their size and shape. Novels and stories, a few hardback classics; elegant editions suitable for birthday gifts. To the left of the chest of drawers, up on the wall, there are other shelves where the other books stayed, not taken to those temporary homes. On the end of the lower shelf are old study books and ring binders, the residue of study that was not ecstatically binned and burned in triumph the minute the exams were finished but kept, for future reference, or just as a reminder of a learning she cherished.

Anna stands before the chest of drawers, looking at the spine of a candy-striped folder that she can remember on the kitchen table, part of the evening ritual of homework. How earnestly she worked, her neat sloping handwriting covering line after line, consuming facts and ideas with a gentle, persistent hunger. Whilst Anna cooked in the other part of the kitchen she would look at Caitlin's bent head, the curtain of hair that fell to the tabletop, and marvel at her daughter's quiet application, certain that with it, she could achieve anything she chose. Anna feels the muscles in her face tighten, her elbows pull in protectively to her sides. Her heart reminds her it is still there, working on high alert. How she wants to flee. She clenches her hands tightly, pulls her fingers as hard into her palms as she can. The muscles of her abdomen and chest tighten too, a buttress, a corset. Holding her to the task that came with the photo from Estela, its kind intention somehow exhorting her to this unprecedented exploration.

There is no rush. She pours another glass of wine and sits on the edge of the bed. Drinking slowly. Scattered images of Caitlin chase across the screen of her recollection and spill with weak light across the surfaces of the room. The million different girls – the tall and slowly graceful girl, the tiny, fretful baby. Michael holding her hand in the cold shallows of a Dorset beach, the two chatting amiably when Caitlin was grown up, father and daughter watching tennis together. These pictures collide, slide past; Anna sips her wine, takes in the unfamiliar sights of the room around her as the projected memories skitter over the worn and lifeless surfaces, dampened with age so that one could not guess at the potency of the relics within.

She goes towards the windowsill, hoping she will find the necklace in the inlaid wooden box in the centre. But it holds some bangles, a small key, hairbands and hair clips. The one next to it is smaller, an old-fashioned jewellery case that belonged to Anna's mother. She caresses the surface, the black of the leather showing cracks of brown. She feels once more that she is a fulcrum, a link between these two women. Her mother, her daughter. A place-marker to show where they once belonged in the dreadful span of history. Her mother died before Caitlin. She is glad that her mother was spared the dreadful loss, but how much she would have loved to lean back into the past, to fold herself up in her mother's love and let go of the habits, the conventions that held her upright, made her adult. How, when her own structure collapsed, she longed to regress into the cave of dependency, the blueprint of self that comes in the shape of parental love.

Inside the jewellery box are earrings, cheerful little concoctions of beads and metal, pocket-money buys and a few gold and silver gifts. There is one pair made of a mix of green and turquoise feathers. She wore them with her hair loose, two thin plaits down each side of her face. Aged seventeen, poised between girl and woman, a little unnecessary foundation on her perfect skin, a little mascara and lip gloss. A rib twists inside and spears Anna's heart.

The next box is not jewellery sized; it is a tin, about the size of a shoe box. She takes off the lid. Inside are photos and letters, and Anna feels a stab as she recognises her own handwriting. She lifts the papers gently, afraid of what they might reveal, but there is no necklace at the bottom. She replaces the lid but lifts the closed tin from its place and puts it next to her as she sits on the bed. Her hand rests on the cover; the edge of her little finger feels the cold of the tin. She reaches across for her glass of wine, another smooth coldness. One for each hand. It is late, and though the beat of heart and heat of disturbed emotions have made her alert, she is very tired. She moves out, taking the tin with her. She goes to her room and puts on a long nightgown, a dressing gown, warm socks and slippers. Holding the tin, she goes not to her own bed but to the neutral space of the spare room. The red wine tastes ugly on her uncleaned teeth. She gets under the thin duvet, still wearing the dressing gown, and sleeps almost instantly, the tin sitting on the still, flat surface of the other side of the bed.

Chapter 20

She is woken into a new morning by her phone ringing. She stumbles back into her room to answer. It is Michael. Not too early, but not too welcome either.

'Anna, hi, I was wondering if we could have a chat. I'm going to be over your way later and wondered if we could meet up for a quick coffee or something. Happy New Year, by the way.'

Anna shields her eyes with her free hand, an involuntary attempt to evade even as she answers. 'I'm not sure, Michael. I'm busy.'

'Ah. Oh. I see. Well, when do you think you'll have time? Are you, well, what are you doing?'

'Things. Does it matter what I'm doing?'

Michael bristles at this, though he attempts to hide it, his voice conveys his habitual, underlying impatience. 'Do you want to plan for Caitlin's birthday? It really isn't that far off, and we've been talking about it for ages now.'

'You've been talking about it for ages now. Michael, I've told you, and you really should know by now, I do not want to have a celebration for the anniversary. I don't want to celebrate Caitlin's life, with anyone.' Anna frowns, takes a breath to collect herself. 'I have told you I will be there, but frankly I'm not sure if I will or not. I'm happy for you to do whatever you want. But you must please finally understand that I am not going to be a part of the committee, part of the team. I can't get involved. I don't want to.'

Unexpectedly, Michael loses his careful tone; his anger escapes, startling her. 'Anna, for God's sake, can't you just let things go? Can't you just make room for your daughter? Stop pretending she was never there. I mean, I know we've had this conversation a thousand times, but it's like you've erased her from your life.'

'I haven't, you know I haven't.' She is taken aback by the accusation and searches for a counter. 'I didn't even get rid of anything physical, at least anything that you didn't take with you. I just prefer not to talk about her. I wish there was no anniversary. I know you don't understand how I feel. But it's just the way it is. It's not something to understand, it's something to accept.'

'Christ, okay, I know, it's been going on long enough, after all. I wish you could see how sad it is. I would love to talk to you about Caitlin, our girl, to remember life when it was the three of us. I miss that so much, Anna. There's no one else to share it with. When she was little. I know I have photos, but all this time I would have loved to talk to you. I still miss her so much, you know. I miss sharing my family – okay, I know, my first family. But I miss that.'

Weariness cascades over her, leaden, bleak. 'Just do what you want, but do it without me, please, Michael. Just do what you want. I'm not trying to ruin your plans. I'm not trying to be awkward. I will come to the – what is it, a party? Or a celebration? I will come to whatever it is if I can. But you must just accept that I dread it. And before you interrupt, no, it won't do me any good, it isn't going to help me. I will come for everyone who loved Caitlin, I will come because one should. But not because it's what I want.' She resists, she resists. She resists Michael's tone, his need, his sadness. She resists her own. 'Every year we've had this. I know that how I am is disappointing for you. I know that—'

'I'm not disappointed. How can you say that?' Michael interrupts, unexpected sharpness in his voice. 'I'm unhappy, sick of this whole thing, this charade. I'm sick of the way you are now, how you've changed. Wearing your loss like a fucking… like a concrete invisibility cloak. It's poisonous, Anna. You never used to be so brittle, so distant. I know there's no reason for you and I to be close any more, God knows, but I still feel loss too. I just want to remember her, to think about her with love, as a family, or at least as a group of people who all loved her. I wish you'd lose this stiff reserve you've become so bloody good at.'

'I think there's no point in talking like this.' Anna's voice is leaden, stubborn. 'I'll speak to you soon. I can't rework myself to fit in. I'm not bloody plasticine. I am the way I am, and that is all there is to it.'

'Look, I'm sorry. I didn't mean to get angry. I just wish things could be different. I had hoped with time they would be. Call me when you want to.'

Michael hangs up abruptly. Anna is still tousled and uncertain from sleep. She hadn't wanted to have an argument with him, but her words came before she could hold them back. And this time, so too did Michael's. Usually, being cautious about upsetting Anna, he is diplomatic, even when trying to persuade. She is nonetheless irritatedly aware of when he disagrees with her, and though he is stubborn about his own wishes, he has developed the habit of mollifying, of treating Anna with caution. She goes down to the kitchen and makes tea, returning upstairs to the spare bedroom with a large cup. It feels safer to be in a neutral space, a guest in her own house. Less bound by the common rules of engagement. This is an uncommon time and makes new choreography of her presence in the house. Perhaps too, a small hope that in not acting entirely as herself, she need not be entirely herself. The blows that come may not fall on all of her. She opens the curtains and climbs back into the bed. The covers are thinner, cooler than on her bed, which has a thick and warm feather duvet. On the spare bed is a sheet, a cotton blanket like those in a hospital, a thin duvet. There is a spareness in the spare room. She is not sucked into the mud of herself on these flatter, smoother planes.

She lies in the flat bed. The room has a chill from being unused. She lies, feeling flat and cool, her hand resting on the yet cooler lid of the tin box. None of her things are in the room. A box of Caitlin's things rests potent beneath her hand. But she lies still, letting memories creep closer, trying out her resolve. She pulls away the blanket and sits up in bed as a corner of morning sun slides through the window, pushing a skewed plane of light slowly along the wall behind the bed. She dips her hand into the colour of sun, casting a too-wide shadow. The light on her skin refines, renders more delicately the web of subtle networks beneath the skin. Not so the shadow-hand, a fat burr, a knot of large bone.

She picks up the tin and places it on her lap. You could start here, now, Anna, open the box. But she can't just yet. An hour passes. And another. For the first half of the day, she lies in the cool calm of the room. As if in a hospital bed. As if in convalescence for an injury she has not yet sustained. She watches the sun move in the angles of light that enter the room. For some hours, she does not even think. She repairs herself in advance.

It is later afternoon; her drift is ended. She starts to think back to her phone conversation with Michael, realising clearly for the first time that he misses talking to her. She sees herself in a new way, as much a route to Michael's past as he is to hers. In avoiding him, she has curtailed his access, blanked out some of his map, leaving large areas of featureless, indeterminate green. Areas that she gladly skirts and that he terribly yearns for. He stands at the fence she built, unable to walk across on terrain he once roamed freely. She doesn't think that in all of the last ten years she has seen his need as anything other than an unwelcome obligation placed upon her. But this morning, she sees that she has taken something from him, that there is much selfishness in what she has made herself. Everything she does is ruthlessly orchestrated to mute. So successful has that muting been that she cannot be sure any more of what lies beneath.

She feels a prickling in her hands, a twitch of sorrow that starts in the heart and seeps down her arms, collects in corners, between bones, looping round tendons, little burning pools. A prickle in her palms. A shift of weights in her belly. If she cut herself, perhaps it would drain out of her. She would hang her cut hands into a galvanised bucket, sneak down to the lane after dark, in shame, and throw the poison into the ditch. It would take some time. Her arms feel leaden; she is burdened. She drags. She is a ghastly nurse, keeping a poisoned body just alive. A steady diet of callous harm and efficient patching-up ensuring that healing or death are both impossible. Now let it be the time for a new, ruthless approach. Let's at least see what the damage is, under these layered and layered concealing repairs.

She is scared, feels as though she should lay down dust sheets or wound pads. She pulls the hospital blanket over her head. She is scared, but she reaches for the littlest scissors she can find and starts to cut.

How to think? Where to start? The beginning is perhaps a reckless step too far. The middle, then. She had hoped the last time she would see Ryan was in court. She has thought as little as possible of that place and time; she never thought she would choose to look closely again. Yet here she is, nervous, reluctant, but with her hand on the door. There's a puck of noise as the tight seal is broken and the door swings open on a perfectly preserved scene. All is there, complete, intact. Nothing forgotten or hidden from immediate view. Ryan, his anxious face, his carefully smart demeanour, his pathetic, worried eyes looking up in beseeching hope at those who were deciding his fate. His reduced, frightened parents, folding into a small, coupled space, two magnets shrinking tightly into each other, she hoped in shame as well as fear. She looked for hours at her lap, at the ground. She remembers how the edge of her seat felt, the frame of dark shiny wood, the generous upholstery almost to the edge. Raw wood underneath the edge of the frame gripped by her clawed fingertips, rigid with the effort of keeping her silent and still. Though burning, she was too cold, too exposed to remove her coat. The second-to-last button of her beige mac rested on her knee, a swirl of chestnut brown and white, a cross of thread in the centre. What a lot of effort, that swirling, that carefully chosen detail, for a button. Next to that, Michael's left knee, a slight dullness of wear on his corduroy trousers, ridden up a little as he sat rigid on the bench next to her. He sat straight, indomitable, a series of right angles, only moving sometimes to bow his head. Solid, stone, centuries-old and silent. She, in contrast, curved this way and that, pulled with constant tension, the skewed twisting of a faulty bow longing to loose an arrow. A volley.

She had hoped that would be the last she saw of Ryan. She had hoped he would go away and never come back. She wished him somewhere blameless between dead and disappeared. Obliterated like the pain he caused. But the pain, it is not gone, it is buried beneath shifting sands, under peeling bandages, hidden behind convoluted evasions. How futile an attempt, like a child's unformed mind believing that eyes shut is the same as gone, that seeing is the same as knowing, that what you can't see isn't there. She is a grown woman. For nearly a decade she has been employing the futile strategies of a child. And how powerfully those strategies, in spite of their feebleness, have shaped her life. What a terrible waste, what a travesty, what complex destruction he caused. But less of me, she speaks in frustration against herself. So what if he uprooted me? So what? He killed Caitlin. They decided in that room that it was an accident. He meant only to hurt her, humiliate her, make her suffer. They decided he didn't mean to kill her. What was her death, then? An accident. He meant her to be alive for his begging, his needy bullying, alive to let him back in. He meant her to be alive for the next time he wanted to hurt her.

She flung spears silently. She hated him with all her being. Twisted into a machine for hating, with her beige mac and her husband, rigid and silent next to her. Those endless days of hate inside an elaborate box of dark, polished wood. She thinks it was there that she and Michael lost each other. She lost all her love. He lost his kindness. He could not keep a place for her, the loveless bitter twist of rage. Now she sees perhaps she was hurting him too. What began there ended inevitably, soon afterwards, in the quiet months that were supposed to be the time when life became normal again. He pushed her from him as an act of self-preservation. The momentum of that push didn't move immovable her, but sent him, like a man on ice, away. He waved sadly as he moved away, still reaching, beseeching, still hoping she might halt him. He pushed himself away, launched himself as of necessity into a new life. She thought it a betrayal of their daughter and for some time hated him too.

There was an afternoon near the beginning of this time in court, a sunny day with air that flirted with the optimists, the hoping hearts, the open souls, promised the full warmth of summer. Nothing promised to those such as her and Michael, sitting outside a cafe near the court with Michael's brother, Paul. It was late afternoon, and the sky was clear, almost completely, the sun behind a nearby office block. They had been there several times before in this, the new, inexplicable life. The day in the box had finished. It had been an undramatically awful day, a listless account of how her girl died, her million precious girls – the pigtailed, long-socked playground runner, the quietly studious young woman, the sleeping baby, the little girl bringing her a first cup of cold, weak tea, so proud. The future mother. The expert witness described the injuries that Caitlin received as if they existed on a blank canvas. The alchemy of transformation. She became a body, a subject, a victim, a site of injury. She became a passive recipient of harm. She went from a million facets of life to a blank page of death, written on in a new language. Contusion, bleed, haemorrhage, swelling. One could be forgiven for thinking it was these alchemies that killed her, not the violence of that well-behaved, beseeching man in front of them. After that hideous calm, the afternoon of dully intoned mysteries, numb and silent they headed for the outside, for air. Paul smoked and fidgeted, wretched with filial love. Michael moved chairs, got coffees, food they didn't eat. He held Anna's hand when he sat down. Her heart cracked open for a moment at the sight of his face, dark with shadows newly cast, pale with the awful strain. The new grey at the sides of his hair. His hand was holding hers, resting on her knee under the table. She squeezed and squeezed, screwed further down into herself against the horror of the loss of him too. She could not bear to see the man she had loved for so many years so bereft, so pained. She stopped looking. She rejected that further burden. Still she squeezed his hand. Such familiar, strong, well-turned hands. Perhaps she knew in the tightness of that squeezing that she was letting go of him. Banishing. So that when he pushed, he slid away, and she did not hold him. She held only herself.

These are the costs she holds against Ryan now. These are the costs that she, not he, has had to account for. The biggest to the smallest. He has accounted, apparently, for the biggest, has paid with a little under ten years of his freedom, and she presumes some discussion about his guilt, his sense of shame, his wish to make amends, never to them, but to the society he also somehow harmed. Scratched lightly, if at all. The biggest harm to society was the cost of making him pay. She holds it all against him still. She holds it against him for Caitlin, who does not, will never, demand recompense, will never measure the way that he must pay. But there is foolishness, for she holds it before herself, not against him. What is she to do with it? This incomplete accounting, a charge sheet of subtle wreckage. It is held so ferociously by her, woven tightly into the fibre of her body, carried secretly in her marrow. For all her blindness, she has always known it is there.

She thinks horribly about what Ryan might be doing now. She wonders if he is at home with his parents. A thirty-three-year-old man trying to get back on his feet. Even if it takes him several years, he has everything before him. Have they too, his parents, spent ten years banishing or avoiding thoughts, never telling people some things in case they ask others? Our son, he is in prison. He killed his girlfriend, very sad, lovely girl. But yes, we'd love to come for dinner. The state says my son is not a murderer, and it was a terrible accident. But still, you know, call me old-fashioned, it's a little embarrassing. We are ashamed of our son; we have never got over the shame of what he did. We have forgiven him. It's all in the past.

She thinks they must have forgiven him. She thinks he would only come back to the area where he used to live if they were part of the reason, the support offered to a man paroled. She believes, though, that he never felt himself guilty enough to need forgiveness. And if he has made his home a few miles from her own, what is she to do about that? She pulls the cotton blanket up, over her head. Pricks of light show through the soft weave. She can hear her breath in this small cocoon. What is she to do? She tries to picture his mother, Audrey, she remembers. Anna and Michael met them once or twice, were invited for a drink, the Christmas just before it happened. A shallow, well-meaning connection, like so many, designed to keep possibilities open. She remembers they thought the couple were nice enough the first time, though they laughed afterwards about a long and dull conversation about lawnmowers. We sent them a Christmas card, Anna recalls with wonder. Caitlin, she delivered it. But she is not going back to the beginning. What does it matter that there was a time when she didn't hate them but merely found them somewhat dull?

She has seen Audrey only once since then. Once across the car park at a swimming pool in Oxford. Anna, heart racing, got straight back in her car and went home. She has not been to that pool for seven years. Most of the time she thought Oxford was big enough to avoid seeing them. God forbid they ever get close enough to speak.

What could they say that would make any sense? Hello, how are you since my son killed your daughter? Hello, long time no see, have you worked out yet how you managed to bring up a son who is a murderer? What do you think of when you look at the interminable photo portraits you have of him on your living room walls? Or did you just leave up the ones of his non-murderer brother? The portraits were something she and Michael remarked on when they drove home from Christmas drinks; they were so numerous, and so charmless. Pity slashes through her. How do you deal with photographic portraits, a tangible manifestation of parental pride, when the pride has been, presumably, lost? Do you take them down? For the briefest of moments, she does pity them. She took the photos of Caitlin down. They are in the room next door, in one of the empty drawers where Caitlin kept clothes that returned in a box, sitting unopened on the bed.

Perhaps they did not lose pride. Perhaps they are as despicable as their son. Perhaps not one drop of Anna's fury, her hatred, was wasted. Perhaps they deserved it all.

She can resolve not to go into Oxford again. He is more likely to be there than his parents. He may not stay in the smaller town they lived in. She can resolve to shop online and get a supermarket delivery, buy clothing on occasional London trips, visit other towns. She can resolve not to see. She may live another twenty, or good God, even thirty years, in that same house. She can do her shopping elsewhere, meet friends in other places. Just don't go to Oxford. Or move to another place, as Michael has always suggested. Follow a modified version of his own medicine, one lacking the new family and new love that he found. The no-frills, generic version. Just a new front door, new Marks and Spencer, new hairdressers.

Moving house. Emptying, finally, that room. Finally looking at it all. What would she do with Caitlin's clothes, that beautiful red jacket hanging on the bedroom door, the dressing gown underneath it? The boxes, the framed photographs and diaries? From here, in this cotton cocoon, in this uncertain stretch, it seems impossible. In this untethered place, this hiding-den. She reaches over to the tin box beside her and puts a hand on it. Can she look at it all?

She feels hollow, weightless, ungrounded. She makes herself a toasted sandwich and tea with three sugars. But she only eats half, only drinks half. There is a brandy bottle on the side; she reaches for it, wanting the heat to generate inside her, wanting to bring a sense of being back to her insides, burn and heat that she can feel from within herself. She takes the brandy bottle and glass and goes once more to the spare bedroom. She climbs back into the spare-room bed. Sitting against the wall, she is aware of the empty-room coolness against her back as she lets the medicinal liquor warm her throat and belly. The taste of the brandy reminds her of the beach in Tenerife, watching boys play football in the evening light with a heavy hotel glass in her hand; she thinks it was on Christmas Eve. Boys playing football in spare spaces every evening, all over the world. How many mothers expecting boys home, to a parental timetable or to refuel a hungry, energetic body? Everywhere, groups of people relying on each other to come home. Someone providing food, someone cooking it. A well-worn argument to be endured, prosaic chats about schoolwork and social dramas. You'll never guess what she said. Shoes tripped over in doorways, fathers shouting for the millionth time. I thought I'd told you… You did, of course you did. Let me reassure you. Baffling, the expectation that once should be enough. Shoes kicked across the floor. Tiled floors, wooden floors, earth floors, underfloor heating. Families performing international choreography on endemic stages. She thinks about the house behind the woman in Baghdad; how does it look? She knows how it looks. To her it looks a certain way. It is emptier than houses she is used to, and she hopes that in seeing a grace and elegance in that emptiness, she saves herself from the charge of patronage. Her pathetic liberal hopes and meanings. Though she knows the truth is that nowhere in the world is life simpler. Life is always complicated.

Sliding away, slipping her mooring and drifting downstream, drifting across the surface at an indeterminate height. She sees the woman's garden from her usual high vantage point, but this time she swoops down, to her embarrassment landing like a martial artist in one of the more mystical Hong Kong movies. One leg bent, toes and fingers pointed downward, alighting on the ground with the light touch of a snowflake. Balletic kung fu. She supposes she should thank her imagination for not landing her with a thud on her left shoulder and hip, though she feels silly. The woman smiles at her. Anna walks towards her with an almost religious care. She can't escape slightly absurd spiritual stylings – she is even wearing some kind of gown. But after all, it is an escape, something able to exist outside of the tainted framework of real life, and, inexpert as she and her imagination are in such ventures, she accepts what comes. She is not yet in a position to dictate the terms. A novice director letting the cast improvise.

She walks cautiously towards the woman, and they regard each other with gentle curiosity. She sits on the corner of a low wall, hands clasped, elbows resting forwards onto her knees.

'You know there is nothing I can offer you,' the woman says as Anna sits, feeling the warmth of the air, feeling the freedom of real escape. Anna realises she is not disappointed.

Chapter 21

In the early grey light, Anna sits up in the spare-room bed. Another headache buzz-saws behind tired and scratchy eyes. Her shoulders are tight. Her mouth feels disgusting. She reaches for water, a beautiful big glass that she was self-preserving enough to carry upstairs the night before. It stands on the bedside table, next to an ancient radio alarm clock, either defunct or not plugged in. She reflects that this is the second night, the only two nights, she has slept in this room. Probably it is the longest time she has ever spent in here. Before, when she was not alone in the house and space was more pressed than now, she thought she might turn it into a workroom for herself. There is a smaller room that both she and Michael used and she now uses, opposite this one. But for a while she longed for her own space. Too much of what you want is killing, she thinks now. They used to have visitors who stayed for nights or weekends in this room, often Paul and Mar. They came before for fun, for family love. Then, when it was all difficult, they came to carry. In the beginning Paul and Marie made themselves available in the most generous way, offering to visit, to cook, to shop. Trying to be there for anything that would help. But after a while Anna resented their presence too, resented the stain of grief and loss she could read in their own faces. She resented the special fragile status their care bestowed on her. It was an effort she couldn't summon, after a while, to be grateful for their care, to reassure them in their anxiety for her.

She kept in touch with them sporadically, visited them in London a few times, but it has been a couple of years since she had spoken to them. As much contact as she kept with anyone beyond the handful of immediate friends. They did at least spare her any talk about Caitlin; they seemed to understand her in a way that Michael could not. She cares about them very much more than her contact with them suggested, loves them both with a sadness as if she were no longer allowed to love them.

Perhaps she should get in touch. Perhaps, once the more difficult chore of finding the necklace is out of the way. She steels herself.

She dresses, eats, takes aspirin. She chides herself for being hungover, for having drunk, again, too much the night before. She promises herself she will return Sophie's call, go to see her, get some fresh air, turn outwards. Away from the skewed beacon, the unfamiliar spill of light on the grey carpet of the hall. But for now, it pulls her in. For once, turning away, though it may be the familiar habit, is not the answer. She runs her hands through her hair, easing herself into fortitude. She turns off the light that has been on since she first opened the door and pulls back the curtains to their full extent. In the corner of the windowsill behind the curtain sits Tiggy, a battered toy dog too beloved to get rid of, a part of Caitlin's past, left for security in her old bedroom. In service of her augmenting briskness, her commitment to proceed, Anna offers it only slight acknowledgement. The room, having been closed off and empty, is not very dusty, though it looks flat and faded. She gives the sill a wipe with her sleeve pulled over her hand and straightens the two jewellery boxes in the middle. To the right are the bookshelves and a space where her desk had been. The chair is still there. On the floor are two cardboard boxes. Before looking in them, Anna goes to the kitchen and gets a duster. She wipes down the tops of the books and the shelves, then sits on the chair and bends over the boxes. Both contain folders, notebooks, papers. There is a pot with pens and pencils in it, several hairbands stretched around the outside. She puts it on the lower shelf, in front of the book spines, and leafs through the papers. The handwriting nearly halts her, but she persists, working her way through the boxes then stacking them neatly in the corner. The drawers in the chest are almost empty; there are a few T-shirts, odd items of clothing, none of which Anna remembers. The largest bottom drawer stays shut; it is where she put the photographs. The necklace won't be there, and she is not ready to look at them.

She wipes the top of the chest of drawers and returns once more to the kitchen for more cleaning materials, an ancient sticky mark in the corner of its surface having caught her attention. Cleaning as she goes helps bring an air of efficiency and necessity. She is working her way steadily through a job that belongs to the practical body, not the unreliable heart. On the bed are two large laundry bags, most of Caitlin's returned clothes. She puts them aside for now as being an unlikely place to find the silver daisy. They go on top of the boxes under the shelves. Two further boxes contain clothes and shoes, scarves and two coats. She wonders why Caitlin did not take the red jacket still hanging on the back of the door. She looked so lovely in it, Anna remembers. Next box. It is full of practical kitchenware, plates and cups, wooden spoons. Anna can't think why it is there. Then, with a painful rush, she remembers buying the things with Caitlin, working out together what she might need in a new life, outside of her mother's overstocked kitchen. She tightens her throat and jaw against the memory of carefree optimism, Caitlin's grateful hug and the pleasure gained at her carefully chosen purchases. For a minute, she is alone with a memory that has sweetness as well as sorrow. But she travels the well-worn path back to the same destination. These stupid kitchen items, dumb chunks of china and plastic, these cheap materials, these stupid, useful shapes – Anna bought them to make Caitlin's life with Ryan easier, to help make it possible. Why should she not have foreseen that she should do all she could to make it difficult or impossible? If you move in, I will steal your spoons and break your plates; if you move in, you will never be able to eat. I will erect barriers of carving knives and colanders before the door, I will shut you out with chopping boards and wooden spoons, tie your feet with this stupid, cheerful, striped apron. I will stop you. She clenches the thick cotton fabric in her hand. Steadies herself against her unreliable heart.

But why is this stuff here? Who thought it should be? She can't remember much of the time after they got the news. Can't piece together who did what and why. Who imagined, she thinks with anger, that I needed this stuff? Did I not already have enough to deal with? But a memory softens the ardour of her rage; she thinks she can remember Paul's apologetic and tentative voice saying that he would just go and get everything, there was no need for decisions to be made, he would just clear it all out, from their house and from the flat, and Anna and Michael could decide what they wanted to do at a later date. She thinks, with sudden astonishment, is this, then, finally the later date? Certainly, beyond Michael's retrieval of some photographs and those boots, she has prohibited any decision-making before now. She thinks once more of the map she has blanked out and her realisation that she made Michael a trespasser, shut him out of his familiar terrain. She has done more, wielded more, over these thin and unhappy years, than she ever thought possible. Not doing anything has, she sees, taken a great deal more than she accounted for.

She puts the box aside. It can go, she thinks. There is a second box, more household items. On top is a small china vessel with a lid, an old-fashioned mustard jar. She remembers it from the table in the flat, sat permanently next to a little vase and a pepper grinder. She remembers it because Caitlin bought it when walking with Anna and Michael through a flea market in town one afternoon when they had gone to visit her. She picks up the pot and removes the lid. There, nestled in small coils of silver chain, was the daisy pendant. She lifts it out, curious about how it ended up in the mustard jar. The flower is very like the one worn by Estela in the photograph; the only difference was in this one having slightly longer petals. She holds it draped across her hand and stares into the small silver flower settled in the middle of her palm. She slowly folds her fingers over it and walks across the hall to the computer in her office. Without putting the necklace down, she opens up the photograph and zooms in. They are indeed very alike. Though not identical. Anna sits in the office chair, leans back into its sculpted, manly car-seat form. She holds the daisy in her closed hand, resting on her lap, and gazes at a tilt. The line where wall meets ceiling becomes, at this angle and with this unfocused gaze, a horizon.

Memories, unsaturated, watered down, fractionally opaque, begin to form way off, at the edge of vision, distant and so thin. So weakly do they play, and so far off are they screened on that ceiling-sky, that she does not immediately shut down. She is watching a watery, distant screening, an undeveloped film barely held on clear acetate. Ghosts, though only one of them dead. Caitlin's sixteenth birthday, a regular day of school and work. They had pancakes for breakfast, Michael's tradition for both Caitlin's and Anna's birthdays. He took liberties with the fillings, allowing a second tradition of predicting invented and absurd concoctions that he was about to put before them. Plum duff and sprout pancakes, prawn mayonnaise with ice cubes. Worms and gravy. This day they had raspberry with lime cream. A memory of the taste came through, stronger than the distant filtered pictures, a disconcerting landing in the body, inside her mouth, as she remembered the beautiful sweet sharpness. Too close, too close. Skip flavours; keep to distant, cellophane views. The necklace was in a small wrapped box on Caitlin's plate. She seemed, Anna remembers, to be delighted with it. She put it on, wearing it beneath her school shirt. After that, she wore it often, or all the time? Anna can't remember. She thinks of memories of photographs where the necklace can be seen. There was one of her and Ryan, close up – was it on the wall in the flat? She was wearing a thin-strapped summer dress, and the picture was cropped just below the gleaming daisy. Anna looks back at the screen, comparing her memory of a photograph with the image before her. Still with the daisy in her hand, she clicks on Reply and writes:

> Dear Estela. Thank you so much for sending me the photograph, and for writing at all. It was so nice to hear from you, and to meet you. It made my time in Tenerife so lovely. I hope we can stay in touch. With thanks again, Anna.

She goes to the spare bedroom and collects the tin of letters and photographs, wanting to find further evidence of the little silver daisy. After all, to look for that, it is not the same as looking for Caitlin. But perhaps she does not really know what it is she hopes to find. It is a strategy, one that has already served to open that most closed of doors. She takes the tin back down to the kitchen table and carefully tips out the contents. She sorts two piles, letters and photographs. It is not that she has not seen a photograph of Caitlin for all these long years; she has not had, much as she would have liked it, the power of veto beyond these walls, in the homes of others who loved her. It is that she has not in that time actually looked at one. Most of the photos in the box are of others, but a few of them are of Caitlin too, with Michael, Ryan, herself, some other friends. There is one, taken in Paul and Marie's garden, of father and daughter sitting at the small garden table with a glass of wine each, both smiling towards the camera. Anna doesn't remember the occasion, perhaps a time when she was not there. It is a lovely photo. She falls in love with it, as if, having not been there, it represents a distant ideal. A man and his newly grown daughter, happy in each other's company, sharing a late-summer evening. How beautiful they both look, she thinks.

There is a picture of Caitlin and Anna standing together in the garden, hugging each other and smiling. They too look happy in each other's company. A black crow screams between her and the page. It lands, clawing on her chest, flapping ragged blackness before her eyes. She cannot look any more.

She puts the photos down, face down. A breath, a pause. She looks out of the window, watching bare branches move, the tips of trees reaching above the house up into the grey sky. She sees in the pile, just as she is ready to halt the dangerous experiment, what looks like the photo she remembers. It is a larger print than the others, and must be from the same time as the one that was on the wall. A close-up of Caitlin and Ryan standing next to each other in the sunshine. She is looking sideways at him and smiling. The silver necklace is bisected by the cropping of the picture. A half flower, a setting star. Ryan looks straight out of the photograph and into Anna's eyes. She tears him away, leaving Caitlin looking trustingly, smilingly, at a ragged cliff edge.

After a moment she gets up, feeling the need for a break, a splash of outdoor air, a walk in the woods. Refuge amongst the tree trunks. But she knows this is an intermission, not withdrawal. In the woods, her thoughts are mosaic-paved with broken fragments, too distracting, the wrong medium for ghost visits. She doesn't allow the fragments to become whole; small pieces are enough. She is thinking in tiny, intricate patterns. It is as if after years of thick beige carpeting, she has pulled it back to reveal a migraine-inducing interlock of tiny tiles. Each one a fragment of a picture, each one a potential for harm. They have to be small so as to remain harmless, and thus there has to be many, to fill the dangerous gaps. It is tiring, scratchy, unsatisfactory. But she finds that the beige carpet won't go back. The years have made it too stiff and heavy.

Chapter 22

Once back from her walk, it takes the rest of the day to read the letters. Not because there are many words, but because each of them bounces through her in a slow, reverberating arc. Each word dazes her. Each word takes its own time to land in her understanding. She is powerless in the irresistible iceberg-drift of their arrival. The careless cheer and love of her own words, a postcard from a holiday that she and Michael took when Caitlin was eighteen and staying at home. A letter sent to her at her new address – PS: here is some money for you and Ryan to buy something nice for the flat. Love you darling, good luck in your new home. xxx How easy those words were to write. There are a few letters from Ryan. She creaks on the edge of discarding them. But it is impossible; she is compelled to read them. Three are fawning with love, full of it. She sneers at his ardour, his praise. She feels her fury rising. One of the letters tells her how sorry he is. How much he regrets. He asks if he can come to London and be with her; he longs to put everything right again if she will only give him a chance.

The slow spell of the words is broken. Anna is almost drowned in her anger. The storm of it swirls around her. She moves in an ungainly trance around the house, unsure if she wants to break it or hurt herself or both. Finally, she sits down at the table with the remains of the bottle of brandy and a glass, agitated and unhappy. A scorch of liquor opens her throat, burns past the constricting emotions, fries away tears. She doesn't want to cry again. She hasn't cried for years. Or she hadn't, until a few days ago in Tenerife. It is not he that takes her so close to tears, but all that he is reminds her of Caitlin. She is getting closer to her. She is the fluttering in her throat, the choke. It is so unfair. Her poor darling girl never would cause such harm as has been done by her story. Poor Caitlin, her darling girl.

The telephone once more wakes Anna in the morning. Her friends are used to thinking of her as an early riser; they have not been close enough, since her return, to observe that she has drifted into new habits. She has kept them at a distance, as she does once more, almost revealing her irritation as she speaks. Tony notices the impatience in her voice, but it is not unduly unusual for Anna to be distant with her friends, and he knows that it is a time of year she finds difficult. He accepts too the explanation for her gruff and stuffy voice. She is run down. She doesn't explain that the cause is the hectic, lonely consumption of a large amount of brandy. She hurries him off the phone, promising to call soon. A shower, a pull-together, a strong coffee, a grip got of the situation. Not an immediate success. The hangover is worse than she has had for some time. The poison of Ryan is one of the ingredients. What is the antidote? How can she fight it? A square fight, a pummelling. Would that help? Oh, but it would feel good. She is in the shower, but feels so weakened that she sits on the floor of the cubicle, knees stiffly bent up in front of her, pulled away from the door so it is not pushed open. She feels a fool. She sees herself as an undignified, hungover woman, bent up uncomfortably in the bottom of her shower, fantasising about a fight. There must be more than this. She tips her head back into the corner, feels the water falling past her chin and onto her chest, the patter meeting the skip of her heartbeat. She is a drum skin between two weakling thunders.

She fills the coffee pot to the top with strong coffee. She forces herself to eat toast and boiled eggs. There is a grim determination in her actions; she has decided that action is required. The reasoning escapes her, but she knows she must see Ryan. Not to speak, but she must lay eyes on him. See what he is. She cannot bear to have him constantly in her mind, so perhaps if she sees him, places him, she can expel him too. Find him, that dandy ogre, that slender streak of monstrous trouble. She needs to look at him.

Upstairs, she dresses and dries her hair roughly with a towel. Taking her iPad to the dressing table, she tries to remember where they live, hoping for once that it is still the same house, in the same neat street, the same small town that she avoids on her route into Oxford. She hopes for the first time that they haven't moved away; she hopes that her prickly, uncomfortable sense of them all being too close, so rigorously ignored all these years, is a trustworthy sign. She knows the approximate location, near the bypass. There is a block of streets that looks right, a deliberate pattern of streets in the right area. She searches her memory from over ten years ago, remembers a quiet street with a town-planner's curve, a front lawn leading straight onto the pavement, a hedge between the grass and paved driveway. Which road it was she can't remember straight off, but she feels certain of finding it. She will find it.

The drive does not take long. But the whole of it is taken up with argument. Interrogation overridden by barked command. I am just doing it. That is all. No, I don't really know why, but I don't care either. She is alert, tense with negative excitement. There is no relish in her conviction, just grim purpose.

She turns left, following what she can of a ten-year-old memory. The same process takes her left again and finally into a cul-de-sac. All of the houses are similar, if not identical. She remembers the hedge between the lawn and the driveway, a flower border beneath it. Many of the houses could be the right one. The roads are quiet, children at school, people at work. She idles by at slow speed, eyes scanning the house fronts. She stops outside one that pricks at her memory in some way. It looks empty. She pulls up, sits watching the house. She fidgets; now and then her head wheels round to investigate any movement caught in the mirror. Nothing happens but her ticks and jerks of anxiety. She still feels ill with hangover. There is a man walking along the pavement towards her. She wonders about asking him if he knows the Edwards family. Audrey and Charles and Ryan. She hangs them before her mind's eye, paper targets. But she feels in the wrong for being here, so she does not become further implicated by asking. After all, what is she doing? What is she going to do?

The quiet harmony of the residential street lulls her. She waits but stops looking. She tries to remember what she can about them, Audrey and Charles. They can only have spent a few hours in each other's company. Charles was boring. Nice but boring. Audrey was self-effacing, small, soft, she thought. Anna had not been that interested in either of them, when they met socially. After that, she could not exclude them from some responsibility for their son, and thus she felt repulsion. The car heater warms the air, and the fug of headache drags her eventually into a sleep, her head balanced back on the headrest. She is woken later when a subtle movement nudges her head forwards and it falls towards her chest, pulling her back to confused wakefulness. Nothing has changed but the time. She has been there for a couple of hours. It could be many more before she finds whether this is the house or not. And if it is not, many hours again to watch the next. She knows she did not keep their address, but suddenly thinks that perhaps Caitlin might have done. She remembers an address book amongst the books and papers. Starting up the car, she heads hurriedly back for home, suddenly hungry again as the hangover begins to recede.

She shuts the door behind her; a haven, but a strange one, with its dangerous, uncharted territory, the open door upstairs. Both refuge and peril. Her eyes and head ache with the fat throb of residual booze. She goes to the kitchen for painkillers and turns on the kettle for more coffee.

Back in Caitlin's old room, she surveys it with something like revulsion, intent on making the search as clean as possible. She looks in the boxes that contain books and folders, the slim harvest of Caitlin's four months at university. Cautiously, she leafs through the notebooks and papers.

In the second box, she finds the address book. It is small and black, still freshly new. Newly copied-over addresses for student life, the promise of efficiency in the slim dark book with the word 'Addresses' in gold on the cover. On the inside cover is Paul and Marie's address and the nearest tube and bus numbers. The thought of her editing her important information, enjoying the fresh start of new stationery is painful to an almost unbearable degree.

The address she seeks is the second entry under 'R', after Ryan. She feels agitated, daring, uncertain. She asks herself again. What does she intend? Just to see him. To look at him. To know her enemy. She hesitates, looks at the number written beneath the address. Could she find out so easily that they are still there? Her heart beats; she takes the address book to the kitchen. Her arm rests at the midpoint of taking the receiver of the phone out from its place on the kitchen wall. Hurriedly, she taps in the number, knowing she won't speak, dreading what she might hear. There is no answer but a standard phone-company recorded message. She puts the receiver down hurriedly, horrified suddenly by the possibility of connection. Does she want connection? No no no. Keep me distant from those people. But let me see them. Let me master something. Let me understand my need.

Or just follow that need. Let it uncover itself, let it make its own sense. Weariness intervenes, and Anna lies on the sofa. She sleeps again, fretfully, shallow dreams in which images float like weeds below the surface of a moving river. Threads anchored somewhere, deep and secure, seen in murk as they ripple under the surface. A thread of pictures, a stream of images too partially seen to elicit understanding. Held fast in the ancient riverbed, the downward reach of the centuries-long water's journey. She is the walker on the grassy bank, not reading the subtle play on the moving surface. She is the dark and dredgy deep, the binding riverbed where disquieting weeds take hold.

Chapter 23

The next day she delays, fidgets, wheedles her way to and from the car. Now that she may have the address, she is not sure she has the courage. With the excuse that she must go out to buy food, she gets into the car and drives. Into the supermarket, then, as she knew she would, out heading north. She makes a couple of false turns, but soon she is in the road, three or four houses down. It is about three streets away from where she stopped yesterday. The house is very similar to her memory. The grass grows uninterrupted to the start of the pavement. There is the neat hedge, as she remembers, between the drive and the lawn, immaculately kept, with flowers planted at the base. Though it is the middle of winter, there are a few pansies and cyclamen with carefully weeded soil between them, a show of year-round care and effort. She wonders if it is from Charles or Audrey. Does Ryan help? He has that choice, to help maintain this prissy neatness, this immaculate façade.

Words from Ryan's letters rotate in her mind. *I'd do anything for you I love you why don't you listen to me?* She wonders what ten years in prison have done to him. What have these years done to him that has not been done to her a thousandfold? Can you beat me for the fucked-up way life has gone, Ryan? Can you match me for a shitty life? Can you tell me one single thing, one little story, one horror, that has made your ten years more of a prison than my own? Can you account for the absurdity of counting us equal now? The gasoline begins to roar inside her again. The crash and screech of it is a huge cost. She sees suddenly that repression was the only option, for to feel so much simply could not be tolerated. Perhaps she would not have minded wearing herself to death, but bodies have their own agenda. Feelings mean nothing to them, in the end. Her body would betray her soul, if threatened by it.

Sometimes she wished for death, but her body, through the passive, dead weight of its own life, fought her.

She is glad now that she has what feels like strength both to bear her anger and to augment it. She feels the power of it. But there is, after all, just a quiet street and a mid-range car, its engine running idly. There is no arena and no reckoning. No Ryan. She sits longer; she waits. After some time, the need to use a bathroom intervenes, and she heads home. She ignores two calls, paces the rooms of her house. She eats, she drinks some wine. The day passes. She sleeps.

She wakes, her anger idling like the car engine. Ready to spring back to life, waking her to a quick start. Mercifully free of her recent hangovers, she showers and puts on warm clothes. She makes, though she feels somewhat absurd, a thermos of coffee. She goes to the loo and gets into the car, noting on the drive the nearest shop that probably has toilets as she is intent on a long wait. This time she stops opposite the house, with a view into the large front room window. Nothing appears to move inside. She waits. She drinks the coffee. She waits.

After a long and patient stretch, she sees, in silhouette behind the glass, that there is someone moving, someone inside the house. She can't make them out – the soft light and shadow works with the reflection on the glass to smudge the interior with indistinct purple-greys. There is a shape, noticeable primarily because it moves. Anna sits up straight, trying to see as much as she can. But the movement stops. Shortly after that the door opens and a woman walks to the car on the driveway, unlocking it remotely on the way. She looks older than Anna; she looks like a soft, slightly plump grandmother. Anna strains to see but can't recognise her definitively. Audrey must be around ten years older than Anna, so it could be her. Before she can work it out, the woman has taken something from the passenger seat, a jacket perhaps, and gone back inside, shutting the door. Anna peers curiously around the whole scene, agitated, expectant. She watches the window for further movement, stares at the door, willing it to open and let her see whether she is in the right place. If she were to trust her chest and the beat of her heart she would say it could only be the right place. Time passes, and she returns to calm. She pours another little cup of coffee and settles down to wait. It is not a long wait. After some fifteen minutes, Anna turns from looking down the street behind her and there, standing in the open doorway as though framed, is Ryan. He holds his phone up to his ear, smiles as he talks, car keys in his other hand. Anna's mass is suddenly fluid. She feels giddy, nauseous.

She finds herself again in the clench of her fists; her weight forms behind those two points of condensed fury. There he stands, laughing now, relaxed, talking on his phone. Anna spills the last dregs of the thermos coffee on her lap as she casts it to the side and gets out of the car. Her strides across the street and lawn are long and rapid. Her whole body is straining now, like her clenched hands and the tight passage of her throat. Ryan notices her immediately. He turns back to the door but Anna halts him with a ferocious command that he wait. He is cowed, as he always has been, since the first day they met, by Anna, by her certainty – then by her indifference to him, now by the force of her will.

'You… you shouldn't be here,' he tries tentatively.

'Me? It's you that shouldn't be here! You think for a minute you've paid for what you did?'

'I have.' He tries to pull himself up, tries to look resolute and injured. 'I have paid, for a terrible accident, because that's what it was, and if you don't leave I'm going to call the police.'

'You pathetic little shit. You bullying, feeble little shit. You killed her, my beautiful girl. God knows how many times you hit her, frightened her. God knows how many times she should have called the police to stop you. You disgusting, pathetic man. I could do the same to you now and not give a damn. You haven't paid. We are the ones who've paid – my whole family has paid for you. Have you any idea how much you destroyed?'

Ryan looks at his phone and starts to dial. Anna knocks his hand and the phone flies out of it and into the bushes. 'I said, have you any idea how much you destroyed? You tricked her. You tricked her and then you killed her. And there you are, standing in front of me, wondering how you can get some protection?'

'Look, I'm really sorry that you—'

'That I what? What is it that you think you know about me? You're too stupid to know anything about me or anyone else. I saw you in that court room, you fucking pathetic man, with your simpering scared looks. The best thing that ever happened to you, the biggest gift any man could have dreamed of, was my beautiful, wonderful daughter loving you' – Anna's voice cracked with tears, but the hefty mortar of anger repaired the break – 'and you destroyed her life. And now you think you've paid? You have not. I hope you'll be cursed forever with knowing the terrible wrong you have done.'

Anna breaks the torrent of words; she notices that Audrey has come to the door, her face showing anxious distress. Anna turns on her. 'What, you don't like it? You don't want me to curse your son? Do you think he's paid his dues too? What a family. Did you forget to teach him that bullying is wrong? Did you forget to tell him he has no rights over the lives of others?'

Audrey reaches out towards Anna beseechingly, with a small raise of her left hand. Her face implores Anna to stop. Ryan is frozen between the car and the front door.

'Look at it, your nice little house with your nicely trimmed hedge, all those pretty flowers and the little fucking vases on the windowsill, as though everything is good, as though you belong with everyone else. But you don't.' Anna turns back to Ryan. 'You think nine paltry years and then a return to this lovely, safe little world, this respectable world, perhaps your own family, grandchildren for you' – she points at Audrey savagely – 'and nothing more said about it. You think that will work for you? I will keep reminding you, forever, of the harm you have done.'

Anna turns abruptly, deranged with fury. Her movement is spiky, verging on incoherent. She walks back to the car, drives away with her foot too heavy on the gas, swings the car round and, in a kind of holy blindness, revs hard and points it across the lawn where briefly it hurtles towards Ryan and Audrey. At the last minute, she turns the wheel and drives through the hedge, backing up on the front lawn and slamming the car a second time into another section of the hedge. As she negotiates the reverse, with the broken shrubbery caught on the underside of the car, she sees a look of frozen shock on Ryan's face as he watches her powerlessly, and behind him a kind of flickering sinking as Audrey falls downwards.

She gets the car half onto the pavement and half on the road, wrestles with the gears to find forwards and leave. As she tries to move in too high a gear, she turns and sees Ryan rush over to his mother, hears him call for help. She waits a second, desperate to leave, certain that a neighbour will respond, but no one does. She looks over and sees Audrey lying awkwardly across the steps, a trickle of blood on her forehead, Ryan bent over her and in a panic.

She breathes deeply, calms herself. Ryan is still calling for help She sees that he is torn between staying with Audrey and standing up to find his phone; he cranes his neck trying to see where it may have landed. For all the fury that Anna spat only moments earlier, for all the harm that she wished, she can't leave that horribly pale woman lying in that awkward way. She thinks suddenly of the two hunched figures, pulled like magnets into each other during the trial, the pity she recently felt for them. She gets her phone out of her bag and makes her way over, stepping over broken foliage and muddy tyre tracks on the once immaculate square of green.

She calls an ambulance. She sees that Ryan is too upset to be wary of her; he is anxious and frantic, concerned only with helping his mother. She looks at Audrey, quieted and confused by the sudden shift of mood. Audrey is breathing a little noisily and she seems to have a cut on her temple. Anna indicates the door and says, 'Shall I find something for the cut?' Ryan nods. He is trying to lift and hold Audrey in a more comfortable position so she is not angled down the steps. Anna goes to the kitchen, certain of finding a clean tea towel. There is a neat stack of them in the second drawer she tries. She gets a glass of water too. When she comes back out, Audrey's eyes are flickering open. Ryan is awkwardly cradling her head and shoulders, keeping her off the cement step. Audrey puts a tentative hand to the cut on her head, then gestures with a pointing finger and says, 'Up... up' in a quiet voice.

'Don't worry, Mum. Just lie still. The ambulance will be here soon.'

'No... up.' She starts to move, awkwardly at first, but her strength seems to gather. Anna notices with a feeling of shame that Audrey has a graze on her forearm, tiny spots of blood, where she must have caught it on the step when she fell.

'Sit me up, Ryan,' she says. He is uncertain. Anna presumes he is afraid of doing the wrong thing, but Audrey is trying to lift herself up to the level of the hall floor instead of being spilled down the cement steps. Anna puts down the water and goes to Audrey's side to help. Audrey sits awkwardly, her legs and feet splayed out, her back rounded as her head hangs down.

'Take me to the kitchen, please. I want to sit down,' Audrey says. Ryan wants to refuse – Anna can read the uncertainty in him – but he has little choice but to comply as Audrey seems set on getting there herself if he won't help. Anna feels a stab of shame that she has caused this harm. Perhaps she could have embraced the sight of a bloodied Ryan, or perhaps not; she is suddenly unclear. She goes once more to Audrey's side, helps Ryan to lift her up and supports her as she walks slowly along the hall to the kitchen. Holding Audrey under the armpit, feeling the heat of her soft body through the cowl-neck jumper she wears, looking at the spots of blood where the step pulled the skin off part of her delicate-looking forearm, Anna feels horrified.

'I'm... I'm so sorry, I—'

'Stop. Shh, please, let's just sit.' Audrey waves her hand, pointing at the kitchen table. Ryan pulls out a chair for her with his foot, and they help her to sit down.

'I should go, I didn't mean to—'

'Shh, stay. Ryan, kettle please.'

'I got you some water.' Anna looks with something like longing at the front door and the garden and the whole wide rest of the world.

'Tea, please. Better have some sugar. Sit. Please.'

Unable to do anything other than comply with the woman she has just caused bodily harm, Anna sits.

'Make us all a tea, Ryan.' Audrey's voice is quiet and a little breathy, but steady. Anna feels sweat prickling her palms. She cuts Ryan out of the picture, looks either at her hands fidgeting together on the table or quickly sideways at Audrey.

'Shall I stay until the ambulance arrives?' Anna is confused as to the purpose of her remaining.

She is grateful that Ryan puts sugar and milk on the table next to the tea; there is no awkward manoeuvre through the protocol, the 'how do you have it?' routine. It gives her a little time. No need to unravel what this strange situation requires. No need to work either with or against her instinct. No need to establish yet what her instinct is.

'I don't need an ambulance. I'm just a bit shaken.'

'Mum, you've fallen. You have a cut on your head; you might have banged it.'

'I'm fine, Ryan. I fell, and yes, I have a cut, but please don't fuss. There's no point in wasting their time. I don't want to go anywhere. I want a cup of tea and an aspirin later. There'll just be the odd bruise.' Audrey looks at the graze on her forearm. She rotates her hand and arm, as if to show that there is no impaired movement.

'I really didn't plan to, well, I didn't plan anything. I don't really know why I came here in the first place. I mean, I don't know what it is that I thought I was going to do.' Anna's words are quietly spoken. She looks at her hands on the table.

'I understand why you came. I think I kind of expected it.'

Anna turns to Audrey in surprise. She catches sight of Ryan, who is observing them both with a frown. She immediately looks back down at the table, her mouth compressing, her eyes shuttering off.

'Ryan, you were on your way into town, weren't you?' asks Audrey. Her voice is still quiet but she speaks firmly.

'Mum, I'm not going into town now. I'm staying to wait with you until the ambulance arrives.'

'No, I've said I don't want an ambulance. Please call them and tell them that, then perhaps go into town. I'm fine.'

'I should really go,' says Anna.

'Please, no.' Audrey puts a hand briefly on Anna's arm. 'Ryan, call, please, or pass me the phone.' Ryan sighs in exasperation, almost teenage in his resentful compliance with what his mother asks. He picks the house phone up from its base and makes the call. He hands the phone over to Audrey, who talks calmly and quietly, says she is fine, she doesn't need help. The conversation ends and she passes the phone back to Ryan.

'Ryan, please do go to town. I am fine.'

'No, Mum, I'm not leaving you here.' He briefly glowers at Anna over Audrey's head.

'Well in that case, go upstairs, please.'

He stands for a moment, hands on his hips, then turns abruptly and walks out of the room. Anna presumes he feels as much relief as she does. She sips her tea, wondering what she is doing there. But injury has conferred authority on Audrey and she feels obliged to respond to her commands just as Ryan does.

Audrey puts her hand up to her own shoulder, rubs it gently.

'Do you want me to find you some painkillers?'

'There's ibuprofen in that drawer, but I'll take some later.' Audrey pauses. She is cradling her shoulder but puts her hand down slowly. She sits neatly, her hands in her lap, looking straight ahead at the back door in front of her. There is a small trickle of blood still, on the side of her head, from under the soft white hairline. Anna longs to clean it, or apologise again, to be of service somehow. But Audrey is so calm and complete. She sits straight, still, aligned, in quiet command of the unusual circumstances. Anna simply waits. She feels herself calming too, borrowing from Audrey's Easter-Island composure. The drip of blood acts as a marker of her authority, as if part of an authenticating regalia. After a moment Audrey lifts her hands from her lap and interlaces her fingers before her on the tabletop. Though her actions are entirely natural, a ritual solemnity, a prescribed deliberation, imbues her movements. Anna is captivated, drawn along by Audrey, willing to concede all to this unexpected, gentle authority.

'I have hoped for years, even without knowing what I would say, that I'd have a chance to talk to you.'

There is another pause.

'It's not so much that I didn't know what I'd say, I know there's nothing worth saying, but still, I wanted to talk to you. Of course I couldn't contact you. But we are here now, and—' She stops, looks down at her hands for a moment, then, looking at Anna, says, 'I wanted you to know the terrible, terrible shame I have felt. I don't expect that to be any comfort or value to you. And I am sorry to be opportunistic, but here we both are. I hope you won't think that I expect my words to be important to you, I don't. But I think about you every day.'

Anna is stunned. Unable to speak, or to imagine what she might say, she looks back and forth, with furtive, sideways glances, between Audrey's profile and her blue earthenware mug, her eyes tracing up and down the bell-curve shape, interrupting it with her fingers, finding out its smoothness by touch as well as sight. Both women sit in silence for a few breaths.

'I don't for a minute expect I've been able to understand everything, the terrible way my son has changed your life. But I have tried to understand it. I have tried to understand the part I might have had in it. I love Ryan, of course, even when I hated him for how he changed everything, everything. Even when I hated him for that, I still loved him. His father couldn't get over it. He wanted to believe Ryan was innocent. When he stopped thinking of it as a terrible mistake, he sort of gave up. He died nine years ago.' She speaks plainly, simply. 'He couldn't bring himself to visit Ryan in prison. But I did. I had to. It became easy enough after a while. But this is not what I wanted to say to you. Why should you be interested in that? I think what I wanted to say was that when I saw you in court, I couldn't then believe what was happening to my son. I had never known anything of him that made me ready for it. I didn't believe he could have done those things, and as it became obvious that he had done, I believed it was a mix-up, an accident. Everything was so confusing then, and I didn't have the chance to think about it. Afterwards, I did understand. I could see what he had done. I do blame him for what he did, and I feel such shame that my son could be such a man. I think I just wanted to tell you that. When I saw you in court I wanted to shout at you: no, no, no, no! You are all mistaken, it can't be him, don't take your loss out on us. I know I didn't actually say those words to you, but I felt it. I didn't get even close to understanding your grief because I was dealing with my own, which, though it was much less, still overwhelmed me. But I wanted you to know that has changed. It seemed such an insult on top of everything you have suffered that anyone should try to take the responsibility away from him. I wanted to tell you that I did blame him for what happened to… for what happened.'

Audrey pauses for a moment, looking sideways at Anna as if to check on her desire to react, to allow space for her to speak, but Anna can say nothing. She waits, and soon Audrey resumes, her quiet voice steady.

'When I did understand what he had done, well, for a while I didn't really think much at all. It was around then that Charlie died. Things had become difficult between us because he would not admit what had happened, and he wouldn't visit either. He got very ill. His heart. Liam, our eldest, was living in Australia. He'd just got married, just before… just before Christmas. So I was looking after Charlie. He died two months after Ryan went to prison. Liam came back then, managed to stay for a few months, which was… well never mind all that, but after Charlie died and Liam had gone back, well, it was just me, and I had time for a lot of thinking. It took a long time to get past the horror of what had happened, of what my son had done to your daughter. I had a need, I think it was a mania really, to unpick every detail, everything I could remember from the moment he was born, trying to understand how I had brought up a boy, such a lovely boy, to be a man who did that. I was very lonely at that time.' She turns hurriedly to Anna and says, 'Please don't think I expect you to care about that, or that I expect anything from you at all. But, well, this may sound very wrong to you, but I thought of you a lot and of how we were connected by what he had done. I knew that however much I felt I had lost everything, it couldn't match what you were going through, though I knew it would make no difference to you at all, what I felt.'

Audrey stops again. She rubs her shoulder; she seems tired. She takes a few sips of her tea and carries on speaking.

'I see now how Ryan was the person who could do those things. I have learned a lot. There was something in him that made it possible. Though I do believe he has changed.'

'You aren't asking me to forgive him, are you?' Anna says abruptly, suddenly alert to the possibility of having been tricked into staying.

'No! No, not at all. Of course, I don't expect you to think anything about him, that is up to you. I've thought about it myself, whether I can forgive him. But it didn't ever make sense to me, forgiveness. I learned to accept what he had done and to accept the harm that could never be undone. Not because it was an acceptable thing, but because it was the only way for me to keep going. Please don't think I'm trying to persuade you about anything. You must hate him. And that is part of what I accept. Before it happened, I would have been very upset thinking that someone hated my son. So much can be changed.'

'How did things change for you, so that you could accept things?'

'I don't want to burden you with talk about me. I suppose I just wanted to say, perhaps for selfish reasons, but also because I felt so terribly sad for you, that I think of you, and that I wish there was a way I could have known Ryan in the way I came to know him. I would have done anything to protect her if my eyes had been as open then as they are now.'

'But I'd like to know. How did you get to a point where you can talk to me in this way? It seems from what you say that you've made peace with it all. How did you do that?'

'I'm not sure. I had a lot of time.'

'But I've had time too. So bloody much time. Time isn't enough.'

'I think I just kept picking over things. It wasn't very helpful at the time. In fact, I felt a little crazy for a while. I was too ashamed to go out much. I had dug out everything, all the things I'd kept, so proud of my son. Photos, school reports, school photos, little shoes, toys and Babygros. There weren't many letters but I had kept all of them, and every birthday or Christmas card. The first thing I thought was how disgusting my pride in him now seemed. I had kept everything. I wanted to burn it all, and to tell him next time I visited him that's what I'd done. But I felt so guilty that I couldn't allow that. For a few weeks, I even pushed back the furniture in the living room and laid all those things out on the floor. Like one of those films when someone is solving a crime, and they have a wall with strings connecting everything. I think that's what I thought I was doing. I kept making new arrangements of it all. It was a bit mad, but I was sane enough to know that I'd have no visitors so I could get away with it.'

Audrey stops briefly to sip her tea. She leans forwards with her elbows on the table, resting her forehead on her hands.

'Shall I pass you the ibuprofen now?'

'Please. Please make more tea if you would like. I feel a little wobbly otherwise I'd do it myself.'

'Do you think you should lie down?'

'No, I don't want that. I hope you can stay a bit? There's biscuits in that tin.'

Anna has a momentary bubble of laughter at the idea that she is being bribed with biscuits to continue with such an epochal encounter. If biscuits were the reason she would stay, they'd have to be pretty miraculous biscuits. But she does not want to leave, she wants to hear more of this strange, unexpected confession. She gets up, glad to have activity; perhaps such activity is in the end the chief therapeutic ingredient of a cup of tea.

'While I was going through that sorting and rearranging, looking at Ryan's past, thinking about him, I started to understand things about him. I started to understand things I had always found harmless in a new way. He is, always was, very vain. I was so proud of his good looks that I thought, used to think, it was natural. I mean, I thought if I looked like him I'd probably be the same. But I wouldn't. I wasn't like that, I've never been like that, even if I had been beautiful. There is a horrible side to it – he thinks he is better than other people at the same time as he's afraid of being nothing. Look, I don't want to keep on about him. It can't be nice for you to hear all this, but realising things about him was a start for me. I had to decide, almost, that I was still his mother. I had to be the mother of a man that I loved but didn't know how to be proud of. He didn't give me all the things I used to get, all that silly maternal pride in having a handsome young son who held doors open for people and impressed all my friends. He had done the worst thing possible. He had a mean, nasty side of his character that I'd known before but thought insignificant. I had to decide that because I still loved this selfish, terrible man, I was still his mother. And I had to look for another way to fill my life now the easy part of that was gone.'

Anna places two fresh cups of tea on the table and sits down once more. She feels strangely comforted to hear Audrey's words, told so simply and clearly. It was as though she were discovering a subtle but secret ally had been alongside her all this time. Her unexpected compassion for Audrey, the image of her alone in the living room a few yards away, the familiar yet transformed stage of a newly senseless world, turned her thoughts away from their well-worn paths. She was no longer the only centre of the devastated circle made by Caitlin's death.

'I started working, as soon as I was more in control again, at a domestic violence refuge. I was a volunteer first, and then I became a fundraiser. I don't work so much now, I'm retired really, but I still do lots of things to make money for them. Mostly buying cheap stuff and selling it on eBay for a bit more, as I can do that from home and a few little shopping trips to charity shops. It doesn't make that much, but it's important to me to keep it going. They struggle so much for money, there's never enough. It's not so much that I feel I'm making amends for what he did, because that will never happen, but it may be that someone else is helped, and that is worth doing.'

Audrey's hand shakes a little as she puts three sugars in her tea. She stirs the cup, then fidgets with the sleeve of her jumper, pulling gently at a fold at her elbow. Anna holds her mug with both hands, letting the warmth seep like comfort into her palms.

'It is such a sorrow to me that my son did what he did. I have tried and tried to see how I could have prevented it, how I could have made him into a different kind of man.' Audrey pauses again, and resumes uncertainly. 'I don't feel as if I have the right to talk to you about Caitlin.' Audrey looks at Anna with such a profound look of sadness that both women turn away from each other. 'But I think of her every day too. Every day. She was a beautiful, lovely girl. And I am so deeply sorry.'

Audrey stops speaking. In the small silence that follows, Anna is overwhelmed with the amount of what has passed, the volume of events. She is overwhelmed by Audrey's gentle act of trying to amend, overwhelmed by her presence in what for Anna is darkness. Audrey seems to be walking with slow purpose, holding a small, steady flashlight, walking through that darkness, showing Anna that maybe, after all, there are other paths.

For some minutes, they sit in silence. Anna leans her head forwards, her elbows on the table, her hands cradling and shielding her face. She weeps, quietly at first. There is a purity of sadness in the tears. No anger to rescue her from feeling it, no frustration to distract. Her shoulders shake, a small tremor; she sobs almost silently. Audrey reaches over, places her hand gently on Anna's arm. Two women sit for all of time in a tidy kitchen.

Chapter 24

Anna walks along the path at the field's edge. The day is brisk; wind scuds, flicking the sunlight on and off as small clouds buffet across the sky. She pulls her scarf up, squinting in the bright light. She walks a familiar path, on a longer loop than usual. Past the village and into fields beyond. She walks by the church tucked into the far end of the village, and on, passing the small graveyard. She thinks of her dead, wonders where they found their resting place, what customs and rituals accompanied them. Symbols of love and sadness, spoken in ritual, intentions embodied in solemn formalised acts of caring.

Though the dead in her notebooks are still companions in quiet moments, she has not written any new portraits since she got back from Tenerife. Since, she realises now, the moment when she looked from the sea to the beach and thought she saw Caitlin. She knew it was not her daughter, it was a summoning, a mirage, but in that moment, it was a sight she allowed herself. A shimmer of her child in the distance.

She recognises now that something changed in those seconds. The crowd she had gathered, the many to disguise the one, parted. The one face she had pushed aside, refused to see, was there before her, and she did not turn away.

She still feels a duty of care, a kind of love for the relentless, numberless strangers tucked inside the news stories and those familiar strangers written in her books. It is a love that flickers in her chest when she reads the papers or listens to the radio, for the souls she didn't know, for the loss to the world in their death. But she no longer needs their intervention in her own life, no longer needs the subtle barrier of the ghost chorus. Instead, she has chosen to offer herself to the living. She has applied to work as a volunteer in a refugee centre, teaching English and helping people complete their paperwork. Her training is due to start in a few days.

And still they sometimes keep her company, her invented ghosts. For a while, as she leaves the village behind, she feels companionship within herself, with some of them, letting her thoughts drift with the landscape before her and the stories she made for them.

She walks diagonally across a skewed field on the side of a hill. There are no paths, but the sweeps of the land, the directions of pull, suggest subtle ways across the empty expanse. As she walks, she remembers this place, tobogganing with Caitlin, with Michael. She remembers the exhausting fun, the simultaneous heat and cold of her cheeks, Caitlin's bright eyes. She lets the memory walk with her across the field, holding onto the picture of her child. She sees a child who is lost in time, not in death. At the top of the long slope, she pauses, a breather and a breath. She looks down the slope behind her, watching memories over again. Looking for the spot, a few yards to her left, from which the sleds were launched. Looking for the place further down where Caitlin and Michael had crashed into another sled, her moment of worry ending when the four well-bundled people stood up or fell about in joyful laughter, arms and legs stiff with layers of clothing. She looks down to the path at the bottom of the field, the route they would walk when bullocks were resident in the field, remembering a summer weekend walk with Paul and Mar, Caitlin coming along with reluctance. Down on that path, she and her daughter had trailed behind the others, talked about what she wanted to do in the future, her young mind beginning to formulate a desire to build, to make structures, to co-opt forces. Anna walks a little further and sits on the first step of the stile. The hillside lies before her, darkening and lightening with the play of cloud across the sun's face. She sees all of those memories, and others, in one go. She understands for the first time that if Caitlin were still here, these pictures would not be any different; they would still be echoes of something gone. Beautiful echoes.

Anna turns her face into the wind and the sunshine. She feels an uncoiling across her shoulders; the wind lifts ropes and the sun dissolves yarns. She climbs the stile and carries on with the two or so miles that will take her back home in time for meeting with Michael.

27 February

Dear Estela,

Thank you for sending me your address. I wanted to send you this. It is a necklace that belonged to my daughter, Caitlin. I noticed you had one like it. I hope that you may wear them both when you are surfing one day. I think you would have liked each other very much, and though I only met you for such a short time, your kindness was so important to me, partly because you made me, I see now, think of her, so I send you this as thanks and a mark of a connection that for me was very precious.

You asked me to tell you what she was like. I used to think she was like a young tree, strong and graceful. Her hair was light brown with a kind of crinkle in it that made me think of bark. She was tall like me, though she looked like her dad. She was very calm, she didn't rush into things, but when she had decided on something she could be very brave and determined. She seemed to be so complete in herself. She was studying to become an engineer and wanted to build bridges. She was also, like you, kind and caring. She didn't get around to kitesurfing, but I think she would have understood your passion. You can see the necklace in the photograph. She wore it all the time. I like to think of it being worn again, rather than sitting in a box somewhere, so I hope you might like it.

Last week, we had a celebration to mark her 30th birthday. I think I told you how much I was dreading it. But it was beautiful. I went in a group with five of my close friends. They were so lovely. And I saw people I had lost touch with, it was so good to see them. Michael, Caitlin's father, really did her proud, and though it was sad, I was so glad to be with those people. I wrote a little piece that one of Caitlin's oldest friends read out for me.

It has been a strange time. But things are much better now. I have some new plans and some things to look forward to. I hope that I might come back to Tenerife some time too, and hope that if you ever come to England you will come and stay with me?

I hope you are well and that life is good for you both. Will you pass on greetings from me to Stefan and Karl? I hope very much that I will meet you all again.

Anna x

Sometimes as I rush through the boundless stretches it feels as though I fly. I am learning. I am making wings, learning an ecstatic affinity with this realm of glittering dark. I can move through the blackness, making wide sweeps on its subtle cambers. I fly like a bird that swoops the curvature of the land on its updraughts. Bit by bit, I learn to read the blackness and command myself to move. I feel myself gaining a hold. It is beautiful, thrilling. I arc through the darkness towards a burning light.

Acknowledgements

Thank you to all the people who have supported me in writing and publishing this book. I have loved the sense of collaboration and feel privileged to have been given such wonderful backing, by each individual pledger and by Unbound, who made it all possible. Thank you Xander Cansell for patiently answering all of my questions. Thank you to the wonderful editors and designers at Unbound who pulled it all into shape.

To the other Unbound authors, at all stages, whose cheer and comments and advice has been such a tonic, thank you. All the friends who have encouraged me, read my work or given positive responses, thank you so much, it has been uplifting and inspiring. In particular Suzanne Harrington, you made me (quite insistently, it has to be said!) think of myself as a writer and your experienced, generous support has helped so much. And my very dear friend Sam Brown, as ever, your amazing support and friendship means so much. I am forever grateful.

MC, who didn't want to be specially thanked – I hope you can allow me this! Thank you.

I am, always, indebted to my wonderful family whose unfailing support and love makes so much possible. Mum Cally, step-dad Dave, Thea, Joe, and of course my Dad Phil, who sadly didn't live to see publication but whose enthusiasm for the project was, like so much else, a true blessing.

My beloved husband Pierre. Thank you for knowing I could do this and for making it a reality by taking care of the rest whilst I wrote. Your encouragement has meant everything to me.

Lilian and Phoebe, you make me proud and happy every day. Thank you for that, and for believing in me.

Patrons

Matilda Amos
Fizz Annand
Nathalie Bourgeois
Bernise Carolino
Sarah Chesworth
Lilian & Phoebe Deans Allison
Alex Dillon
Jessica Duchen
Jennie Ensor
Vanessa Gellard
Jacques Halé
Charles Harrison
Rachel Heaton
Paul Holbrook
Shona Kinsella
Stephen McGowan
Maxine Michaelides
Kate Millar
Joana Monjardino
Jo Nye
Frances Ratcliffe
Julie Rosenthal
Max Schaefer
Jo Shackleton
Kim Terrell